BRIDES OF THE STORM

To Shelly, Thanks for catching the bouquet + running my book.

Copyright © 2013 Amanda Albright Still

All Rights Reserved

Published by Gone Feral Publishing
1625 Market Street
Galveston, Texas 77550

www.GoneFeralPublishing.com

ISBN NUMBER 978-0-615-46690-3

BRIDES OF THE STORM

A Galveston Hurricane Mystery

Amanda Albright Still

Dedication

To everyone who dreams of writing a book, but doesn't do it because there's that little voice inside that says "You're not good enough." Well, you are, that little voice doesn't know anything, and you need to just write.

Acknowledgements

A novel starts with an idea, a daydream, or even a nightmare. Getting it from idea to page, to edited draft, and finally to book requires a few people. Some who love you, some who love your work, and some who hate your work so much, you're going to show them. On the loving side, I thank my daughters, my editor, my critique group, Facebook friends, and my husband.

To name some names:
Ann Haugen
Valerie O'Mahony
Mickey Platko
Cheryl Robbins
Pam Lewis Pecero

Ian Still
Katya Flynn
Ksoosha Flynn

Author's Note

A 1901 article in the New York Times spoke of a man who imagined himself to be a widower, and just a few days before his wedding, saw the wife he thought dead return. She had been visiting Galveston when the 1900 Hurricane hit, a hurricane that took what Galveston's Rosenberg Library estimates to have been 8,000 lives. The trauma was so great, that the woman was afflicted with amnesia and housed in a state institution until she recovered enough to know who she was. No follow up articles in the Times revealed how the incident was resolved. This became just another mystery in the aftermath of the Great Galveston Hurricane.

The exact number who died in the storm can only be estimated because whole families were washed away on the night of September 8, 1900. Survivors never forget the sight of bloated bodies washed ashore or the acrid smell of burning corpses. Many took advantage of the railroad's offer of free passage from the blighted city once communication had been established with the world outside of the island. Those who remained faced food shortages, martial law, and reports of men shot in the streets for looting bodies.

The islanders not only survived, but thrived by raising the island, building a seawall, and when industry went to the new harbor in Houston, becoming the Playground of the South.

Galveston, Texas: August, 1901

CHAPTER 1

I twisted the doorbell and listened for some activity, hoping to hear footsteps or voices within the great limestone house. After the ring, nothing. I stood with my two daughters on the wide veranda of one of the largest homes left in Galveston and waited for something to happen.

"Were you invited, Mama?" A skeptic frown tugged at one side of my ten-year-old daughter's plush lips, and she shot a glance toward the huge, carved door that remained closed to us. Theodora, better known as Teddie, was prone to distrust, so I shouldn't be alarmed.

Her eight-year-old sister, Eugenia, nicknamed Jinxie, asked from where she clung to my skirts, "Why aren't they letting us in?"

"Yes." I straightened the black crepe band on my arm. "We were invited." Yes, my daughters had been invited into the top end of society--the part that my friend, MJ, often wrote about in her society column.

I took a deep breath and pulled the beaded ends of my short jacket down a little farther over my blouse. "We were invited." I shifted the burden of a package bound with white ribbon to look at the invitation. "We've got the right time and day."

"Then why aren't they letting us in?" Jinxie asked again from my skirts.

I looked away from the impenetrable door to a window, one of the long windows all of us had in Galveston meant for raising the sash and walking through rather than just for ventilation. It might be unlocked, but I would wait for the butler.

"Maybe the butler needs to get the list or something." I looked through the window and saw nothing but lace curtains under portiere drapes. "He seemed a bit slow." *And old, very old.*

On the quiet street, I heard the clatter of well-shod footsteps. I turned to see a familiar slender redhead wearing a red dress covered with loops and squiggles of black ribbon march onto the street. She rounded the corner, where a man in a dirty pastor's shirt was passing out handbills claiming that the end was near and that the Great Galveston Hurricane and Flood a year ago was just a warning.

Eleven months ago, the hurricane of September 8, 1900, had torn the island apart. It killed more than 8,000 people, including my husband and the original parents of my adopted daughters.

I twisted the doorbell again and smoothed my hands over my ash-blonde pompadour to make sure I was presentable.

The redhead turned to the street minister with a glare that made him drop his pamphlets. "Find some rube to scare."

I'd known that glare since college when MJ Quackenbush--then, Mary Jane Smith--and I were roommates. She had married an older man whom we all thought had more money than vigor, but he left her a few months later with a son and debts at the finest saloons in Texas.

MJ's green eyes looked up, down, and up again to the onion tower of the carved-granite and stained-glass mansion.

I followed her gaze to a window where, through the glare of rippled glass, I saw a woman looking down at us. I raised my hand in a polite wave to the woman and saw she was gone. Perhaps the face had been nothing more than a play of the light.

"Mother-in-law hosting, I see." MJ stepped up onto the veranda, accepted my hug and kiss, and embraced the girls.

"Something funny's going on." Teddie gave her head of thick, dark hair a single nod.

"That old colored man answered the door." Jinxie's wide, gray eyes shifted toward the door since she had been told not to point. "Then unanswered it."

"Unanswered it?" MJ mouthed at me.

I nodded. "He said 'Welcome,' that he would just be a moment, and closed the door in our faces."

MJ gave a sage nod she must have practiced over tea as the society columnist for the *Galveston Daily News*.

"Have you ever heard of such a thing?"

Her head stopped mid-nod. "No, but the elite have their own ways of doing things, and rushing isn't part of it." She leaned against a pillar of the Ionic order. "A wedding is something planned to the slightest detail. Even a shower like this for a woman marrying a widower has its own rules. If they want us to wait, we--"

"I don't think we're getting cake," Teddie said.

I had told them there would be cake. I'd never been to a wedding shower that didn't have some form of cake. Even the one I went to a week after the Great Storm had a crumbled one that tasted of salt water.

I leaned into the door, turned the knob, and stumbled as though I had fallen into the entryway of high ceilings and stone floor by accident.

I saw two sets of closed doors beneath the staircase and a marble-topped table between them. I handed the gift to Jinxie and deposited my visiting card on the tray. On mine which stated, "Mrs. Gallagher, Legal Assistance," I'd written "Miss Theodora" and "Miss Eugenia" for the girls. At eight and ten years old, they were years away from getting their own cards.

I heard a door open behind us and turned to see the side door and front door both closed.

MJ brushed past me and set her card in the tray. She cocked a head with furrowed brow at me.

I nodded. I knew what she pointed out; only two other cards were already there, and one of those read, "Mrs. Abelard Wyngate."

Winifred was a shy librarian. She might not want many people at her wedding shower. Already using visiting cards with her married name indicated that Winnie was more practical than superstitious. Her future father-in-law might have the same name, but that would mean the mother of the groom set out a visiting card in her own house.

I set my parcel atop MJ's beside the visiting-card tray. Ours were the only gifts there.

"Hello?" I called.

MJ rolled her eyes beneath flickering lids.

"Oh, Dasha-Dash!" Winnie called down to me from a story above where I stood beside the balustrade carved with trefoils and gothic arches.

She knew me years, from when I was "Dasha" a diminutive of my Russian name, "Daria."

She ran down the marble steps so fast, I feared she would trip on the yellow ruffles at her hem. "I'm so glad you're here." She trained black-brown eyes at me through her spectacles, and wisps of black hair framed her face in mild disarray. She pressed her small mouth even smaller and slid the pince-nez higher on her long, upturned nose. In her soft, airy voice, she said, "Everything is just sodomized all to hell."

"Excuse me?" MJ stood with hands on the narrow hips of her red dress.

"Winnie, you remember MJ? The society columnist."

Winnie grabbed my hand and started to charge upstairs, but a silver-haired woman in a fashionable dress of brown taffeta puffed to a pigeon breast over her small waist trotted down.

"Mother of the groom, Miss Alice," MJ murmured behind us.

"Winnie, I've telephoned Abelard." Miss Alice had a low voice that reverberated with finishing-school poise and a slight, slow accent from somewhere deeper South than Texas.

Yes, this grand house on a major boulevard would have a working telephone line through the scarred city.

I gave myself a smug little reminder that this was not just the purview of the wealthy, since I now also owned a telephone.

"We'll figure something out." Miss Alice spun around and went back upstairs without acknowledging any guests.

I slid my hand over Winnie's arm to steer her toward me. "Why is she calling your fiancé?"

The face Winnie turned toward me sagged with pure misery. "Maybe she's telling him to write one hundred times, 'I will not have two wives at once.' " Winnie took my arm and steered me down the few stairs we had ascended. "Let's go to where we're not having a bridal tea after all. Maybe there's some punch. Maybe we'll get lucky and it will have rum."

MJ walked with us across the marble expanse. "If not, I'll find something that works. I'd prefer gin."

Winnie jabbed the air between her and MJ, "You seem good to have around."

MJ beamed as though she had been told she was the most popular debutante in all of Texas.

The colored servant in worn breeches and green tailcoat held open one of the sets of doors.

With the girls following, we entered a room as large as the first floor of my house. Inlayed wood covered the walls, and a shiny brocade of birds and flowers covered the settees. MJ looked at the crystal punch bowl on one end table and slipped through doors at the far end, which I imagined led to a dining room.

"Oh, you're in here." Winnie spoke to a woman on a one-armed empire-style sofa covered with maroon- and gold-striped silk. Winnie's voice betrayed no obvious emotion, but her pleasant, light sound scratched through the dark air of the room. Her hand gripped my arm tourniquet-tight.

The recipient of this comment had youthful features of round eyes, pug nose, and red cheeks. Her wiry brown hair curled around her face and was pulled back into a ribbon. A polka-dot tie surrounded the neck of her white shirtwaist. She looked like one of those actresses who specialized in playing Little Lord Fauntleroy. She smiled to show even teeth on the top and a chipped one on the bottom. "I'm not going anywhere, dearie."

Winnie put her hands on her hips and gave her head a little shake that released even more tendrils from her wavy topknot of hair. "You remember Abelard had a late wife, Lucinda? Well, here she is. Strangely, not late, not late at all. Early, as a matter of fact. As a matter of fact, the first one to arrive at my bridal tea."

Holy Christmas!

I linked my arm through Winnie's and pulled her back so far we almost bumped into my daughters. I craned down to whisper in her ear without taking my eye off this woman and her little smile. "Don't worry. Abandonment. Abelard can get a divorce based on that."

"Hardly abandonment."

Damn, she heard me.

Lucinda's finger entwined with a fat curl. "I've written to him every day since I've been staying with my poor, sick mother."

Winnie's nostrils flared, her mouth slid into a tight grimace, and her long neck grew a little longer. The last time I'd seen her look like that was in elementary school when she punched a bully for making the boy who stuttered cry.

I stepped a foot before hers in an attempt to keep her from lunging for the gamine brunette before her. "Remember the detective from whom I rent an office, Mr. Barker? He'll find out everything. He's the best there is. We'll talk to Barker."

MJ burst through the dining room doors. She held a cocktail glass of rosy liquid with a length of lemon peel. "Barker speaking to you again, Dash?"

I opened my hazel eyes extra wide at her in a wordless scold.

Miss Alice came around MJ with two cocktail glasses and gave one to Winnie. "Your friend from the newspaper found we had the makings for a martini." Miss Alice turned to me, but looked down at the girls with a smile. "Joseph will be out in a moment with your drinks."

"Thank you." Jinxie said it an instant before her sister could, and her face flushed with triumph.

"Go have a seat. Anywhere."

Teddie sat on the sofa right beside that interloping, supposed-to-be-dead wife. Jinxie sat beside her sister. Jinxie stared at the woman while her sister offered surreptitious glances.

MJ swallowed some of her drink. "You'd be Lucinda Wyngate." She looked as if she would extend one of those bony, freckled arms, but she spun the lemon peel in her drink instead. "We had our coming-out the same year. I'm MJ Quackenbush, but I was Smith then."

I accepted the cold cocktail glass from the frail black man and moved with care so as not to waste any of the intoxicating contents by spilling them on the Aubusson rug. I took a sip of the pink liquor to get the level down from the edge. The grenadine and vermouth gave a sweet taste that was a nice counter to the spicy gin and bitters. It tasted like Christmas.

I wandered over to where Winnie stood beside a writing desk with the fine legs and gilt edging of the eighteenth century.

Joe walked a wide path around Lucinda to offer the girls lemonade. They looked to me, I nodded, and they took the glasses of pink lemonade.

MJ spoke in the manner of a woman fighting the East Texas piney woods accent by holding her lip down tight. "I also saw you a couple of times giving out food baskets at the Civil War Soldiers' Home."

"Mmmm?" Lucinda made the sound with a question at the end, as though she waited for more information to follow.

Winnie polished her pince-nez on a ruffled sleeve. "Suppose it's better she came today than next week."

"Legally speaking, not by much." I remembered I was here as a friend, not as an attorney, and gave Winnie a gentle hug so neither of us would spill our martinis.

Winnie hooked a finger for me to lower my ear into whispering range. "I don't have any place to go. Abelard and I have been living in sin for the last week. It was just more efficient."

She could always stay with me, but I didn't want to say that while in the room with Lucinda, who seemed to have bat hearing. Sure, she hadn't heard Winnie, but as a librarian, Winnie was a better whisperer than most.

A rap at the door drew a sigh from Joe. He started toward the vestibule but did not even make his way out of the parlor before Professor Abelard Wyngate strode in.

He was a lanky fellow with the stooped shoulders, sallow skin, and hooded eyes of someone who spends most of his time turning pages of musty volumes in a library. He walked into the room and stopped. He took a pair of spectacles from his pocket, wrapped them around one ear, over the nose, and around the other ear, and stared at Lucinda.

A shorter, wider man with the same eyes and pointed nose moved around Abelard. He was probably a brother, but not the one whose picture I had seen in the newspaper or etched on the certificates of his family's railroad stock. The shorter fellow darted across the room. "Poor Winifred!"

No one ever called her by her full Christian name, not even her parents when she was in trouble as a child. Not even that bully she punched who cried and said he would tell on her.

The young man wrapped his arms around Winnie and blinked at her so hard, he looked as though he might damage his eyes. "Don't worry, old thing. You won't die a spinster."

Winnie held her drink away from the man as best she could with him pinning her arms to her side. "I can't breathe."

"Beau!" Miss Alice walked to her enthusiastic son and gave him a pat on the back. "Unhand that woman."

Beau pulled away from Winnie and gave his mother a look of downcast eyes, face turned from her.

"Yes, that's the youngest boy." MJ slipped over beside me and leaned up to whisper in my ear. "Youngest brother full of trouble. Quite the opposite of Professor Baggy-Seat over there."

Lucinda shot a glance toward MJ and me but then trained her attention back on her husband.

I glanced at Winnie to see whether she had heard this description of her bridegroom, but she was busy glaring at Lucinda, who stretched her arms toward the baggy-seat in question.

Abelard blinked and pulled his gaze from her to look around the room. He strode toward the door.

I wondered whether he had been calculating the room measurements in his silence and found the spot to be equidistant from Winnie and Lucinda.

Winnie's gaze, honed by her glasses, was more penetrating than Lucinda's smile, and Abelard faced her. "She says she's been visiting her mother for the last year. Wrote you every day."

"Her . . ." Abelard turned to Lucinda. "Your mother died in the flood."

Lucinda's smile fell to a frown and her eyes to her lap.

Both of my girls now stared with unblinking eyes at the woman beside them.

I watched Lucinda to try to determine whether she was sad at the loss of her mother, at getting caught, or at not being believed. I could not tell since she did not even seem to breathe as she glanced at her hands. She drew her head up and toward Abelard. "I didn't want to say, it's so embarrassing, but I've been in a mental institution. I was so distraught by the storm, I just, well, I didn't know who I was."

Abelard opened his mouth, but the words died somewhere inside him.

Another man came into the room. This was the taller brother, about the same size as Abelard, but with a well-fed shape and close-trimmed whiskers. He looked older than he had in the papers.

"Head of the family store," MJ whispered from behind her cocktail glass. "Dad left the bank and railroad for him to run since work interfered with his golf game." She held the glass aloft until she caught Joe's eye and signaled for more with a finger tracing around the room.

"Sextus!" Lucinda's smile returned. She stretched a limp arm toward him. "I'm so glad to see you again."

Sextus gave her the barest of bows and turned to his mother. "Where's my wife?"

Winnie emitted a cranky sigh. "You think he's afraid he's going to find a second one lurking around, too?"

"Sextus?" A short, thin blonde with large blue eyes walked in from the vestibule with such a light, fast step, she might have been borne by fairies. She put a hand on his arm. That said "wife" to me. She must have been upstairs. "What are we going to do?"

Sextus patted her hand then turned toward the settee. "What are you going to do, Abelard?"

CHAPTER 2

I hopped on one foot through my dark front parlor to finish buttoning up my boots without stopping my progress toward the front door.

A pair of green eyes in the morning darkness of the shaded front parlor caught my eye, and a creature made a lunge for me over the petit point stool.

"And you can stop that now," I said to Dewey the cat. I looked at the scratch on my hand where blood made red beads.

For a cat missing a front leg, the piebald terror managed to claw with the best of them. He jumped from the sofa and ran out of the parlor and up the stairs with a flounce of black and white tail.

I steadied the marble bust of some long-dead in-law who had had herself sculpted as Aphrodite. I had changed nothing in what had been my mother-in-law's house when I inherited everything after the storm. I even inherited the housekeeper, whose every relative had been washed away. I pulled my handkerchief from the sleeve of my lace suit covered with beads. I'd been fortunate to find this out-of-style dress several sizes too large, so I could re-cut it in a modern, pigeon-breasted shape. When I had finished sewing it, I wrapped a black serge mourning band around my left sleeve.

I blotted the beads of blood with my handkerchief. The handkerchief once belonged to someone who also happened to have a "D" in her name.

My clothes, my house, and even my job, which I had learned apprenticing in my husband's law firm, were all secondhand.

I jumped at the sound of Teddie scuffing down the stairs. She leaned towards the wood spindles to give Dewey's leaping ascent a wide berth, and she trotted down to me. Light filtering through the lace shade dappled across her face.

Even my daughters were secondhand. I spoke fast to dispel this rotten thought from my mind. "You moved your things into Jinxie's room?"

She nodded.

I smiled at her, and she frowned back. I reached forward to hug her, but she stepped from my grasp into the shadows of the dawn. I left my now-stained handkerchief on the marble-topped end table.

"Are you really going to help that woman?" Teddie stood in the large, tasseled archway to the entryway, her hands on the hips of her white cotton dress.

"No," I said with a little laugh. I sat on the satin and wood settee and patted the seat beside me. "I'm helping the other woman, the nice one, Winnie."

Teddie walked toward me, but did not sit. "No, she's the one trying to steal that other woman's husband."

"Hardly steal," I said. "Even if she weren't my friend, well, that first wife pretty much put her husband out with the trash. What right does she have to come back two days before his wedding?"

"That wife didn't realize she'd survived the storm. " Teddie played with the top ruffle of her skirt. "She didn't know who she was."

Jinxie slipped down the stairs, slid past her sister, and walked to where I sat.

"Maybe other people survived it without realizing." Teddie watched her long fingers wend through the fabric of the ruffle.

Oh dear, her original parents. I stood beside Teddie, careful not to get close enough to make her move away. "Darling, I don't think that's possible."

Teddie looked up at me. Her slanting brown eyes shone through the dark with tears. I put my arm out to her, but she ran away and up the stairs before I could touch her.

I had to find out what Lucinda had been doing for the past several months, so my daughters would know that their family's story was not the same as hers.

I felt my own eyes cloud with tears and looked down at Jinxie beside me.

Her large eyes looked up at me, and she threw those slender arms around me. She caught me about the thighs in a tight embrace.

I rubbed her hair, which had now grown past her shoulders from when it had all been cut off to cool a fever she had in the orphanage. "I love you." Figuring word got around upstairs, I said, "I love your sister, too."

"Come on." The housekeeper we called Aunt Cornelia stood at the stair landing and gestured to Jinxie. "We're all up. We might as well have breakfast."

"I love you," Jinxie said to the damp air somewhere between Aunt Cornelia and me. She gave me another hug before walking the slow walk of a prisoner headed toward the gallows.

I heaved open the carved wooden door that looked as though it had been stolen from a European cathedral and marched up the walnut and marble staircase before I lost my nerve. I licked my finger and slicked back some of the ash-blonde tresses the humidity had freed from my pompadour. I charged forward.

Why was I so scared? I had no answer, no answer other than an image of that muscular, charming, and sometimes ill-tempered Scotsman, Barker.

I raised the skirt of my pink chiffon dress with jet beaded stripes and stepped onto the paneled landing where my office was separated from that of my landlord. I snapped my parasol closed and pivoted away from the white wood and rose wallpaper sanctuary of my office and toward the closed door with a glass insert etched, "L. Barker, Consulting Detective."

I raised my hand to knock on the mahogany door, but shaky-handed apprehension overcame me. I hadn't seen the man for weeks. I hadn't seen him since, well, since he did something rash that tingled me to my toes. He might have been avoiding me. He might ignore the knock as I do when my girls peek out the front window and see a seed drummer with his grip of begonias and corn plants.

I adjusted my manhole-cover-sized hat and put it at the right rakish angle. I wanted to make a good impression, a professional impression. My gloved hand reached down and wrenched the brass door knob.

Locked.

"May I help you, Mrs. Gallagher?" a voice said behind me. The voice of rolling Rs and words that clipped off before the ends sounded of heather and haggis.

I spun around so fast, the beads on the hem of my skirt slapped against the door.

The tall, athletic form of Barker stood before me and his office door. With ramrod posture and square jaw, he didn't so much stand as impose, bending the wood and steel of the office around him. He stood so close, I could catch his smell, a combination of Florida Water and a musky scent, which I liked to think of as barely civilized masculinity. "Mrs. Gallagher?"

"Um, yes . . ." I said, and hurried to think of something clever. Nothing came within the half-second I had allotted, and so I said, ". . . I wanted to talk to you." With a flash of thoughts that felt too big to fit into my brain, I realized why I feared talking to him. I suspected he wouldn't help me find out what Lucinda had been doing and I had no idea how to discover this on my own. Yes, I feared he would reject my request and reject me now that I needed him.

He leaned even closer. His blue eyes beneath their thick black lashes bored into mine, and his full lower lip neared mine. His arm slid past my hip.

I closed my eyes and drew in a quiet breath.

His key turned the lock, and when the door opened I stumbled back in a pirouette that gave me a quick view of Barker's office, from the roll-top desk below the back window, to the door to his small laboratory, to the plush green settee beneath the carved walnut around the window.

In his vast office, I was surrounded by moss-green wallpaper depicting ferns, columns, and books. The wainscot was carved to look like acorns and oak leaves. Two plush green chairs sat on either side of a small settee, and a door went off to what looked like a large closet or small laboratory. The picture with elaborate frame and crude photograph were the only personal items decorating the room.

The big-eyed woman cut from the page of a newspaper was no lover of Barker's. She was a woman who had used her wiles on him, and he failed to stop her before she poisoned seven people. She was a reminder of his failure and the duplicitous nature of women.

Several times, I'd thrown this away, finding the memento horrific. Somehow, it always made its way back onto the desk.

"Must be something important you want to talk about." He turned back to me with a smile that twinkled in his eyes. "Can you now tell me what's happened to your friend?"

I gasped. I tried to think how he had reasoned that out, but I only came up with a single clue that got me a small part of the way. "You saw I still have my street gloves on and hadn't stopped in at my own office, so you knew I had something urgent."

"What you would consider urgent?" He looked out the great window framed by art nouveau curves of carved wood, his hands shoved in his pockets.

I ran over what he had seen of me, what he could know, and what he had induced. "I imagine you assumed this was about a friend because my urgency showed this was important to me." I knew how feeble this would sound to the great detective, but I plowed on, since "always forward" was my way. "That would be either family or friends."

He turned his head toward me to arch an eyebrow in disdain. Why did I put up with this man? Because he knew more about finding information than I did. And, well, he just did something to my insides that wasn't proper, but certainly wasn't bad.

"No, do you have another guess?" "Guess" hissed from his mouth like the worst sort of swearword.

I thought hard, considered making something up, but nothing came, so I shook my head until I had to grab my hat by the bows and feathers to reset the angle.

He stepped toward me and gave a little sigh out of the corner of his mouth that made the tall, athletic man look surprisingly like my diminutive third-grade Sunday school teacher with her silver ringlets. "The way you look, lass." His broad hand gestured toward my dress and circled before my face. "And the way you act. Aye, that told me what I needed to know."

I forced my muscles stiff so I couldn't squirm. I hadn't done anything wrong and would be blowed if I'd act as if I had.

He folded his arms and leaned back against the window. With his straight posture, this move looked borrowed from a marionette. "If your daughters had you worried, you would have run over here without concern for your appearance."

I nodded, even if I didn't feel as though I wanted to tell him he was right.

"A client, and you would have just come by my office when you spotted me in the hallway."

"If I saw you," I said. I feared he knew I watched for him to come in and even hoped he would talk to me.

"The way you keep fussing with that hat and wearing all those buttons, beads, and serge. You want to look professional or make me think you're professional because this is about something personal, a friend."

You could be wrong, Mr. Smarty Britches. "It could be a . . ." I realized I had been jerking my head around and looked straight at him. ". . . A lover I wished to help." What a stupid thing to say. I sounded as though I were trying to make him jealous. Maybe I was, but I knew he did not have that capability; he was immune not only to me, but to the charms of any woman. He believed passion interfered with his intellectual abilities. He was one of those new scientific types of men.

He gave a deep, throaty laugh. "Now, tell me what I can do for you."

Tell me why you kissed me and then just walked away. Tell me why you haven't spoken to me for the last four months since you did it. Tell me you didn't feel a spark of something for me, so I can go on with my life. "Tell me what you know about Lucinda Wyngate."

"Ach," Barker said. He raised an index finger in a silent bid to pause me as he strode to the newspaper on the roll-top desk and flapped it open to a page, after all the news of how much money Houston would budget to rebuild our city and before the stock market numbers.

"I didn't read the morning paper. I was too busy trying to get my hat at just the right angle." I said this as though trying for sarcasm, and I hoped he didn't realize I lacked the gift for that.

He looked up from the pages to give me a quick wink of blue eyes through that long fringe of lashes. "Ah, here it is."

I let out a hot sigh from deep within me. "No surprise, MJ was there."

"At what was supposed to be a wedding shower?"

I nodded. I figured his near-clairvoyant ability would allow him to see my movement although his back was turned to me.

"Maybe you shouldn't escort members of the press if you don't want them writing up things about a woman coming to reclaim her husband from a friend of yours."

"How did you know . . ."

"That the bride--not the wife--was your friend?" He smirked from his perch on the desk. "I dedu--"

"Indu--"

"Deduced that from the fact you wanted to know about Lucinda. That presupposes you knew about Winifred."

"And presupposing something is inferring what you cannot see from what you can." How did I end up standing less than a foot away from him and even shaking my finger at him? "That is inducing, not dedu--"

"With your contacts within the press and undoubtedly with the corporations you represent, I'm sure you can find out all manner of things about the poor woman."

"Poor woman?" I sank down onto the settee. My parasol clattered to the floor so loudly that the noise drew dark-haired Evangeline, my secretary and typewriter, out onto the landing between my office and Barker's.

"You know she's lying," I hissed.

"I do?"

Evangeline walked up to the doorway, looked at me, looked at Barker. Barker leaned back and laughed at what I said. She turned around and headed back across the floorboards to my office.

She probably just wanted to tell me she'd finished the table of contents for contract amendments she had worked on until well after dark on Friday. I'd left her to work and went home to my daughters. I felt guilty about that, but she seemed happy for the extra pay. Yes, the table of contents had to be what she wanted to tell me. We needed to get it out to the large law firm that had commissioned us right away.

I turned back to Barker. "I know she's lying."

He set both of his large hands on the desk and leaned forward to glare at me. "How? You could only have met the woman yesterday, and not for long then. Did she hold her tea in an especially duplicitous way? Or perhaps kick a passing dog?"

I felt part of my lip curl in a sneer, but I pressed it down.

On the landing between our offices, the telephone on the wall trilled. Three-one-two: that was Barker's ring. Evangeline grabbed the telephone and said, "Mr. Barker's office, may I ask who is calling?" She turned to Barker with a smile that faded as her eyes grew wide and her mouth gaped.

I stood, fearing some malady had turned her apoplectic, but she turned away to say into the long, black transmitter of the telephone, "Oh, yes, well then, I'll see if he's in, I suppose." She hung up without even another look at Barker and gave a sigh so flustered, it blew out in a series of short breaths.

Well, that was curious. She usually sported an "I'm a professional stenographer and have the correspondence course diploma to prove it" comportment.

Barker stood as Evangeline walked into the office. He gave her a kind smile that sparkled to his blue eyes. He was good with women, perhaps because he didn't care. He found us a threat to his objectivity and amazing intellect, and about as attractive as a case of German measles. He said, "Someone wishes to talk to me. They want me to come, right away, and found the information to impart too delicate to say where those on a party line might hear."

Evangeline gave him that same look of slight fear almost everyone gave when he did this wizardry. "Yes," she said with a gulp. "I guess so." She scowled at me and turned back to him to whisper, "Molly Perkins. She wants you to come over right away." She shot a glance at me. "I suspect you don't know who Molly Perkins is, being a proper lady and all."

"I have no idea who this Molly person is. I assume she is a criminal, and as such, her acquaintance with Mr. Barker is hardly surprising. I mean, he is the foremost--"

"Not a criminal," Barker said. He took a straw hat from the rack by the door. "What she does is legal, at least here in Galveston."

I now had an idea of what Molly Perkins did. "I suspect she sets up shop down Post Office Street."

Evangeline nodded, and Barker smiled at me as though I were a beagle who had caught a particularly large rat.

"Now, Mrs. Gallagher, will you accompany me?"

I stood. "Why would . . .?"

"You couldn't possibly, Miss Dash," Evangeline said. Hands on her hips, dark-haired, olive-skinned Evangeline looked surprisingly like my freckled, blue-rinsed mother. It must have been the frown. "Not there, especially since you have to return the calls you've received. There's that friend of yours, Miss Winnie, and your daughter's Sunday school teacher has called several times already today."

"Oh dear," I said. My mind flittered through a few scenarios, and I couldn't come up with one that was good. A chill came over me, and I blinked and breathed in as deeply as my corset would allow to cast away the goose bumps now covering my arms.

I raised an eyebrow at Barker. "Why on earth would you want to escort me to a house of ill repute?"

His posture went even straighter than I thought possible without a brace. "Because this involves women."

"Unfortunate women."

"Women nonetheless. I suspect this is something serious for her to call this early in the morning and not to take the time for her man to come around, but who knows with a woman? She may have lost a pair of hair tongs and may be inconsolable. One of her gender--no matter how different the social standing--would be helpful."

    I looked from Barker's pleasant smile to Evangeline's widened eyes and creased forehead in shock.

CHAPTER 3

I stood behind Barker on the corner of Post Office and respectability, that was on the twenty-five-hundred block between Post Office and Fat Alley.

Fat Alley was not an address someone would write on a letter, but comprised the rear buildings of Post Office and Market Streets. It was a narrow lane of carriage houses, trash bins, and shacks where gambling and prostitution spilled over into the wide boulevard of fashionable houses. To the east, Post Office held family homes and shops. I only suspected what it held here, since no proper lady ever went down here, and no true gentleman would ever tell. I expected to hear a din of laughter, singing, and even the tinkle of roulette wheels. Instead, the street was quiet, except for the clucking of some chickens and the clip-clop of distant horse hooves.

Barker rounded the corner onto Post Office, and I dashed to keep up with his long stride. We walked past a girl next to a picket fence who looked up at us. She stood not much taller than my oldest daughter but would not have been mistaken for a child, with those eyes, sunk into her head as though weighed down by anyone who had ever touched her.

A chance, that's what I could offer my girls, a chance to have choices--the sort of choices this girl may have had once, but no longer.

We passed an iron railing that surrounded a raised cottage, more like a cabin, with a shingled roof overhanging the porch. The door hung open, and through it came the smell of stale beer. I thought I saw the back of a man whose wool pants were cuffed high enough to show bony ankles.

I struggled to keep pace with Barker's broad strides and ended up almost throwing myself into a hop at every step. I said, "I'm not doing this to get away from work."

"I didn't think you were." Barker raised his hat to a pair of women staring at him from an open window. One turned to the other with a giggle.

I raised my arched brows high to affect the urbane look of the girls in Charles Dana Gibson's drawings. "Although I certainly do have plenty of work right now."

"I imagine you do." Barker eyed a man entering a saloon across the street but said nothing.

"You were right, of course, when you told me that publicity would be good for business." I wondered if he even remembered saying that, it was so long ago. "I thank you for eventually getting the press to run a nice story about me."

He looked at me, confused. No, not confused, but disinterested.

"About helping the Russian Embassy and how grateful they were."

"Yes, I know."

A woman in a faded red crepe dress and creeping skin started toward Barker. I took his arm, and she slunk back through the drape that served as the door to a small saloon.

I released his arm. "And I've gotten so much work since then! I wish I had more time to spend with the girls. I even bring things home now that they're out of school. I mean, I might as well read a contract there as in the office."

Across the street, a banjo plinked out a collection of notes that failed to form a tune.

"Mrs. Gallagher, you have no need to tell me all this."

Oh, yes, I do. When I'm nervous I babble, and you, sir, make me as nervous as a cat near a bathtub.

"Yes," I said. "I just thought you might wonder why I have agreed to come with you here."

"And so you told me what the reasons for your coming are not," Barker said with the barest hint of smile.

I sped up so I would not look like a puppy tagging behind him.

We passed a gigantic wreck of a house that may have once been an elegant home for a family, but now weathered yellow paint had turned to beige and peeled from gray boards. Many buildings had not been rebuilt after the great storm, but this one looked as though it had sustained years of damage through neglect. The two galleries, one set far away from the street, had fretwork falling from the columns and even a fallen column. The tin roof of the cupola was rusted until holes would allow anyone who might be in that tower to know exactly what the weather was like outside. The grass was overgrown, except where the iron gate had fallen to smash it flat.

"Well, that place is no den of ill repute," I said. "I mean, no one would dare enter it."

"Oh, that's the very worst place along here," Barker said. "Work of Chinese tongs, it is. Grabbing nice young ladies off the street. Making them serve in the place."

I stopped and stared at the place. I wondered if there were something I could do to help the girls within. "Surely, we could contact the police. I mean, forcing girls, well, that's illegal."

"Not much they can do," Barker said. His hand at my elbow urged me farther along. " 'Tis legal, after all."

"But by force!"

"The police say they aren't going to get involved with some girls making a little extra money washing shirts."

I stopped where I could see inside the tower, thanks to the fallen hurricane shutters. The rooms were empty, and plaster had crumbled away to show the planks of wood beneath. "Shirts? What? Shirts?"

"Yes, the most disreputable white slavery laundry ring."

I cocked my head at him in confusion, and then I saw a smile widen to a grin. "I see." I flushed, but raised an elegant eyebrow with almost-closed eyes again. "Making fun of the lady who is shocked by all this. That's probably some place where the poor owners died in the storm and can't repair it." The city held many of those.

Barker fixed the blue spectacles over an ear, across his nose, and then around the other ear. " 'Tis my house." "House" sounded like "hoos," but I'd become used to his accent.

I looked at the house, and then shot a glance at Barker and saw he was serious. I said nothing more for the next two blocks until we got to a house of multiple turrets, jutting windows, and verandas, all covered in neo-gothic fripperies. The tin roof was shaped like embossed fish scales, and every inch was covered in new paint of creams, reds, greens, and grays.

We started toward the carved wooden doors, but a clenching in my gut stopped me. I grabbed Barker's arm and whispered, "I came with you because I'm curious, plain old curious. I figure women like this know how to handle all sorts of trouble. What would they find--what problem would they have--that they need to get help from you?"

Barker frowned at me. "Something very bad, I fear. That's why I could use your help."

"Are you joking?" I asked.

He gave the sort of flinch backwards and narrowed eyes that my cat gives when he smells something unpleasant. No, he wasn't joking.

I shrugged. "I never know these things. I'm not good with irony."

He patted my hand where it rested on his arm.

"Yes." I almost spit the word at him. "Because I'm a woman and you think we all think alike, the unfortunates here and those of us from decent homes." I tried to keep my voice light, but a bit of acid slipped in. If he was as disinterested in women as he claimed, then why had he taken me in his arms and kissed me so many months ago? And why had he followed it up with months of silence?

Although the clock had yet to chime 9:00 a.m., a woman stood framed in the front window wearing a sumptuous evening gown.

He opened the short gate and gestured for me to walk in.

I took a deep breath and plunged forward.

Having the police meet me in this area would not help my reputation. Still, I walked with him around the wraparound porch of the polychrome house and glimpsed in the side window, where I saw a colored woman with a white kerchief on her head that matched her apron carrying a bundle of towels downstairs.

I looked away. I didn't want to see what that laundry had on it.

Normal business. Would what I was about to see be much worse? I forced myself to breathe deeply and gulped in the air. I'd sooner die than faint in a place like this.

Behind the back of the house lay a garden that held flowering plants, a healthy, deep green in this season when most of us lost all but the heartiest plants to the heat. A kitchen garden like the one in my yard held prickly okra plants, about the only thing that would grow during the sweltering, sweating months of summer in the South, but this one also held tomatoes, herbs, and sunflowers.

Barker took my arm again. He hopped up on the side porch where stood a door almost as ornate in wood carving as the double front door. This would lead to a gentlemen's parlor, where the men could step out on the porch and smoke without danger of setting the house on fire. At least, that is what it would have been in a normal house.

He opened the door. No knock, no tentative hello--he just marched into a service porch where another colored woman, this one older and heavier than the first, sorted white towels and sheets. The sharp smell of bleach and the soft smell of soap filled the area.

I gave her a nod, but she did not look up from her work.

Barker steered me into a charming, small office of coffered wood paneling, with wallpaper, curtains, and plush furniture in shades of apricot and blue. Behind the desk, stood a curtained archway. Barker took off his straw hat and smoothed back hair cropped too short to need smoothing on the top and almost shaved off at the sides.

Behind a desk that looked to be a French antique of delicate carving and gilt inlay, a woman stood. She wore a black dress with jet beads and a mourning brooch at her throat with a swirl of gray hair beneath the tiny glass dome. The sharp edges and gothic lines of the brooch had an old-fashioned style that looked as though she were the widow of a Civil War veteran.

"Mr. Barker, glad to see you again." Her voice held a slight twang, but was cultured and low. She flicked a black lace-covered hand toward the pair of heavily carved Renaissance revival chairs before the desk. "Have a seat." She nodded to someone in the hall behind us, and the door closed with a soft click.

"Yes." Barker held his arm out to me. "You needed my assistance, Molly." It was a statement, not a question. He moved one of those big hands toward me for an instant. "It was urgent."

She smiled, her lips trembling over her teeth. "We'll just stay here for a minute. Might just be a client around and I'd prefer he not see a detective."

I tried not to listen, but heard a rhythmic creak of either bed or flooring from somewhere overhead.

Barker looked at me and gestured to a chair before he sat. "I've asked Mrs. Gallagher along since, well, women are involved, and she kens the ways of your sex better than I."

Molly gave a nod to someone in the kitchen I did not see. "Gallagher, huh?"

"Yes," I sat up even more primly than my corset demanded. "You may have seen me in the rotogravure section of the paper."

"You're the attorney lady. Your husband was an attorney, too, as I remember."

I held my breath to stifle a flinch. I could not stop myself from blurting, "Did you know my husband?"

She leaned forward with her lacy elbows on the desk. "If I did, I wouldn't tell you about it. All the men I know, for whatever reason, are strictly confidential." She leaned back to laugh, with her mouth open wide enough to show wax outside her gums to keep a youthful plumpness to her cheeks.

I pointed through the thick air toward her locket. "You had a chance to say goodbye to your loved one. After the storm, my husband was never found."

Her eyes drifted down to the black ribbon wrapped around my sleeve.

"Molly," Barker said in a soft voice and with a glint in those blue eyes. "You had something you wanted to say."

The woman shook her head slowly at Barker and sighed. She didn't seem in a great hurry to get to the point, even though the way her hands clenched into fists and then splayed stiffly looked apprehensive. Her hair waved back into a chignon that ignored the current fashion for the pompadour. She may have worn powder, but no more cosmetics than that. If I had seen her walking down Market Street--and I could have without noticing her--I would have thought she was the wife of a banker before procuress.

My initial response was to glare at her, but then I remembered the whole thing about Jesus being nice to her kind, and I smiled.

She let out a low growl, but then straightened up and fixed a smile on Barker. "Coffee?"

I craned forward to see through the archway behind Molly, which I imagined to be the kitchen.

Above, a groan sounded.

"For me, yes," Barker said. "I believe Mrs. Gallagher would prefer tea."

"How . . ." How did he know that? How did he know that I couldn't stand coffee, not when that was all we had for the first couple of days after the storm? The water had been tainted with saltwater, so we tried to overcome the taste by making coffee with it. I never could blot the salty taste from it now.

"You looked to the kitchen, obviously to see if another beverage was on offer," he said.

A young black woman with a flouncy apron carried in a tray with cups of flowered china so thin, the sun shone through them and made the gold rim look as if it glowed.

The girl silently held up a cup and pointed at the cream and sugar.

"Milk," I said. I pulled my veil up and tucked it into my hat.

She handed Barker a cup of black coffee and took the tray to leave.

Molly watched her walk out the curtained archway. She let out a slow leak of air and then turned to Barker. "One of my girls--she's dead."

A breeze moved the curtains, but did not cool the room.

"Oh dear." My fingers tightened on the thin saucer. I knew this kind of woman could fall prey to death from many sources: drug overdose, alcoholism, abortion.

"More than you know, Mrs. Gallagher." Her hands wandered over the items on her desk: pen, inkwell, reading glasses, pages of what looked like accounts. "Mr. Barker, this may be the worst thing you've ever seen." She frowned hard enough to show wrinkles puckering her face in a look that told me she knew what the worst might be.

A loud thump and another groan sounded upstairs.

"How so?" Barker asked. He drank his coffee, despite the steam I could see rising from it.

Molly gave a shudder and buried her face in her hands for an instant. She took a breath and then pulled her hands to her lap beneath the desk. "You'll see. I just want to tell you what I can about the girl. You see, I don't know much. She was new, and had only been here about three months."

Barker nodded.

Footsteps sounded down the stairs, followed by a loud man's laugh close outside the door.

"I didn't know much about her. Know she came from New Orleans and worked in a place that wasn't exactly . . ." She frowned at Barker. "Madame Chartier's place, but she checked out clean."

I tried not to blush, but could not help it. I knew she referred to the regular medical screening unfortunate women go through for one of those Gentlemen's Diseases.

"She's new, so I didn't know her that well, but she lived in a dream world, that one. I caught her at least twice kissing clients yesterday."

"Kissing?" I took a sip of tea. "That's an extra charge, perhaps?"

Molly rolled her eyes and gave a little shake of her head. "A client isn't a beau. No kissing, leastways, not on the lips."

I felt foolish, as I always did when wrong, but then I realized this was a type of work in which I did not strive to be an expert.

A large door closed at the front of the house.

Molly pushed back her chair and stood. "This might be more than she can handle, Mr. Barker." Her look glanced over me. "It's grim."

I straightened to my full height a few inches above hers. "My father was a country doctor, and you've no idea the things with which I used to have to help."

She tipped her head at Barker.

"The lass has some pluck. If she says she can stand it, I'll not deny her."

Molly pulled back a velvet portiere and strode into the front parlor. Barker gestured for me to go ahead. I ignored the twisting of my stomach and followed her into a dimly lit room that appeared to be in a perpetual twilight with thick curtains, dark velvet-covered couches, and electric lamps with dangling beads. A woman in her underwear and corset sat and spoke with another in a tea gown, while another in a paisley dressing gown picked at a thumb until the skin was red and raw.

I pulled Barker down to whisper in his ear. "I can't say that I don't think it would be a mercy for someone to be relieved of this misery."

Barker's heavy brow furrowed into a shadowed frown.

We walked under a curtain of beads dangling from an arch in the wide center hall to a back room opposite the kitchen.

"Come back and see me when you're done," Molly said, backing down the hallway toward her office. "I'll call the police then, but nothing's been touched since I found her just before my man called you."

He opened the door to a bedroom that was even darker than the rest of the house, with heavy brocade curtains pulled closed and black wallpaper with dark green vines and maroon flowers. An earthy scent lingered in the room. In the dark, the loud pattern of the wallpaper seemed to come toward me. Oh no, that wasn't all the pattern of the wallpaper. Something was wrong.

Instinct blocked out thought, and I flailed to push the scene away and get out of the room. Barker caught me, and I struggled against him to back out of the room.

"I need your help, Daria." His voice was soft, but his accent was even stronger than normal. His sound was the only way I would have known that the sight got to him. "But only if you can stand it."

I took in a deep, calming breath. He had never said that before. I covered my nose to keep out as much of the stench of death as I could in this room that had begun to smell of rotting meat. The smell was no worse than what I would find in a neglected icebox, but it reminded me of the reek of death that had hung over the island for weeks. Sometimes even now, the wind smelled of rot. I looked around and let my eyes adjust to the darkness of the room. Told myself about how strong I was, and turned back to Barker.

A woman lay on the bed. Coagulated blood that had stopped running at her death now pooled over what had been white sheets. Her face was intact, showing a small mouth of pouting lips now hanging open, round cheeks, and pale blue eyes. The skin of her throat grew white and gaped around an incision across her neck that was straight on the left side and jagged on the right. Her hands were red and raw, with blood chipped and dried on her left palm. The undersides of her arm held slashes that had bled before she died. She wore a corset, chemise, lace pants, and stockings over a body of small breasts and plump hips. Her pale arm held a crude tattoo of what looked like a box--no, a treasure chest--with the letter G above it. In a tidy sort of horror, a slice on the lace pants below the corset revealed where her abdomen had been hollowed of some of the angry, red offal.

Swagged cords around the drapery of the single window weren't cords, but instead were the woman's intestines looped over the curtain rods. Thick splashes of blood covered the edge of the curtain and, in a wide splatter, altered the pattern of the red roses on the wallpaper.

I breathed in to get enough air to croak out words. "What is loose in the city?"

Barker's shoulders hunched up in a shrug, and his head shook. He stepped to the window, examined the curtains with their horrible trim, and gently opened the drapes--without touching anything other than fabric--to let in the sun. A lace shade was caught in the corner of the window, but no blood had leaked from the thick curtain above.

"Murderer left through this window." He shoved open the tall window. "They closed the window, probably to keep people from noticing something amiss, and that's when the curtain got caught." Careful not to get close to the parts of a human being strung over the curtain rod, I looked past Barker to see a walkway bordered by plants and a low fence between this house and the next. The walkway led behind this house, through the vegetable garden, and to the house of whitewashed boards behind. Even at this hour, a black woman and a white woman leaned over the balcony to talk to a man in the alley, who was the right age to be in college and wore the rumpled muslin smock of one of the many local medical students.

"Walking along here unseen wouldn't be tough," I said. "Not in the dark." Even with the window open, the smell filled my nostrils and made me gag. It reminded me of the smell of death stalking the streets after the storm. I reached up into my sleeve to get my handkerchief, but it wasn't there. I'd left it at home. I wished I had never seen this room, that the extent of my knowledge of injury had been that blood drawn by a playful cat. I put my hand over my mouth to block the smell.

But I had seen it and could not pretend it away any more than I could pretend away seeing my neighbors search through the rubble that had been their house to find a lost child or seeing the burning of bodies in the street. I coughed. "This isn't any worse than what I've seen after the storm, but this . . . a person did something this horrible."

Barker backed up, and I had to shuffle out of his way rather than risk falling on this floor stained with the end of a human life. "Now." He looked around the room. "What happened in here before the murderer walked down the pavement?" His long, wide finger traced the air over the pattern on the wall of the poor woman's blood. "Her throat was sliced. That's what killed her. She stood here, by the window." He leaned out the open walk-out window and looked into the mud below. Without turning back to me, he pulled a handkerchief from his pocket and passed it back to me.

I covered my nose and breathed hard to get the air through the cloth.

"Footprints out here," he said. "Heels pressed facing the window, almost obliterated by ones exiting on top." His blue eyes covered me from head to toe and must have figured I could handle this since he gave a little nod and said, "Probability is that the murderer came in the window rather than the door. No other entrance." He looked at the streak of blood along the wall. He glided his hand over the trajectory. "She died standing beside the window. One blow from someone who knew how to kill."

He pulled a small, leather-bound notebook from his coat pocket. He licked the tip of a small pencil and scribbled a few notes. He looked at the body on the bed. "Death wound goes down her neck." He turned to me to explain, drawing his pencil across his own throat. "Starts higher and goes down. He looked at the dead girl's arms again. He used his pencil to move her leg and look at the back. A series of deep scratches on her calf. "Behind her. Her wounds are all on the back of her arms and legs. So she fought, but with her back to the killer."

I stepped before him, assuming the girl's last position as I thought of the scene around me.

Barker's body closed to mine and his hand slid over the lace at my throat. "Killer was right handed, taller than the girl." Barker made a few calculations with an invisible person before him. "Shorter than I, but taller than you."

I'm a tall woman, over medium height, but not the tallest woman I know and shorter than many men.

Barker backed away from me and scribbled some more. He looked at her hand and arm, walked around the footboard of the bed, and used his graphite pencil to tip the girl's arm out for examination. "She was killed as soon as the person came in the room, probably before she had time to shout, but she defended herself."

I stepped toward him and he pointed out a gash and bruise on her forearm. He looked at me and then back at the body. "You can see where she fought for her life, even if it was only for the last few moments of it." He looked at the window and then at the girl. "She died at the window. She heard a noise, walked to the window, and the killer slipped behind her. She fought as soon as she felt something."

He used his pencil to push her arm over so he could look at the underside. "She has needle marks, so her reactions might not have been fast. We'll need to search her room."

I looked around the room heavy with the slight smell of offal and groaned. My knees weakened, but I urged myself to buck up rather than grab the doorjamb of this foul place. "Why does that matter? Haven't we seen enough?"

"This isn't her room." Barker spoke while looking at the woman's unshod feet. "This was just where she entertained her last client. She'll have a much smaller place upstairs with a roommate or two."

"Just like college," I said through gritted teeth. Although when MJ and I shared a room at the Baylor Women's Annex, college girls raised chickens and grew corn to make money.

"She had no shoes on when she died. There's been enough time for the blood . . .Ah, you see, it has settled on the bottom side of the body." He walked to the window and used his pencil to open the thick curtains. He leaned back to make sure the disgusting decoration did not come in contact with him.

I looked at the wall, willing myself to see more than the offal from the curtain rod. "She didn't know her assailant."

Barker gave me a nod to encourage me to keep talking.

"She went to the window, but she didn't cry out. She was waiting for someone--I'd guess . . ."

Barker gave me a harsh look that furrowed his brow over aquiline nose.

I drew up tall. "I induce from the evidence--her lack of clothes, for one thing--that she waited for a, um, a beau." I silenced the question on Barker's lips with a finger held aloft. "A client would have come through the door." I looked around the room. "But he came and killed . . . no, a beau--a lover--probably wouldn't have killed her before there could even have been an argument. Someone else came in. She fought."

Barker gave me a smile and nod that--in another man--I would consider to be a compliment to my logical talent. From him, it could have just been unexpected glee at my ability to string words together without lapsing into talk of pixies in the garden. Perhaps this observation was the sort of feminine skill that got him to ask me to come along here, but I doubted that.

"And that someone placed her on the bed and then hollowed out her belly." Barker started toward the door but then turned around to face the body.

"What is it?" I asked. "I figure we've noticed everything about her." I'm sure the panic sounded in my voice, and I should have just shut up, but I blurted,

"Thinking about the poor, dead girl is bad enough. Knowing a madman is on the loose to knife people--I assume she was knifed--is worse. What is to stop them at the fallen women." I thought of myself and my daughters in our house not far away. "Any woman on the island might--"

He held aloft a hand so insistently that it jittered. He stood that way for a silent moment. "Look at the slice below her corset. It's through her under-things." His eyes moved along the trail of blood to the intestines hanging from the curtain rod. "The killer did not bother taking off her clothes, not even her corset, to get to more of her guts. None of the rest of her body is savaged."

"Perhaps he was interrupted?" The breeze through the curtains picked up even more of the smell, taking it beyond what I could stand, and I pressed the handkerchief back to my nose.

Barker shook his head. "He or she--they for expediency--took the time to hang the--excuse me--bloody intestines like sausages in a butcher shop and close the window when they left."

I wished he'd used an American swearword. "Bloody" was too evocative of the truth. "Perhaps we aren't seeing everything. Beneath the . . ." A woozy feeling buckled my knees and spread up to my stomach. "She may have been violated. Even a prostitute--especially a prostitute--can be the target of . . . the most evil desires of the most evil men."

Barker pocketed his notebook and caught my shoulders before I sank to the polluted floor. "I cannot tell you why they defiled the body like this after death." He led me to the door.

"How could you understand? Who understands the actions of someone so obviously crazy?"

"Even the mad act with logic." He led me out into the hall and closed the door behind us. "They do things with a perfect logic, according to what they believe."

"Barker, I don't believe you make sense." I leaned against the bronze wallpaper with red swirls and pink Chinese vases. A woman with her dark hair in a loose topknot peered out a door at us but then went back into her room.

"An old woman who eats flies, that doesn't make sense," Barker said. "But if she believes she is a frog, it makes perfect sense." Barker's hand on my arm urged me down the hall.

"Maybe he believed he was a butcher," I whispered. "Of people."

Barker nodded.

I staggered under the heat, the smell, and the emotion. I leaned my hand against the wall. "What will I tell my daughters?"

"Must you tell them anything?" Barker urged me on with a hand on my back.

"Not if they aren't at risk." I stopped outside Molly's office. "Can you tell me that this madman will not prey on the ladies or the girls of the rest of the town?"

His face could have been carved from stone. It said nothing, and one of the many things it did not say was that my girls and I would be safe in our section of town.

"There are many things I don't know about being a mother," my voice croaked from my dry throat. "But I know I am to protect them from harm."

Barker patted my arm and said something in an accent so strong, all I could make out was "capture" and "killer." He strode into Molly's office.

Molly stood behind her desk and over an open drawer of a filing cabinet. I wondered what those files held, but since I saw no lock, I imagined it was about towel vendors and grocers rather than clients.

Barker leaned down and whispered in my ear. "We need information from her, so you need to be nice."

I shot him a glare and hissed, "When am I ever rude?"

His blue eyes might have been twinkling at me below those black lashes, or they might have been laughing at me. I couldn't tell, so I turned away to face Molly with a spreading of my lips that was as close to a smile as I could get after what we had just seen.

Barker bobbed his head in a polite little bow. "You need to call the police, Molly."

"Yes." She slammed the drawer closed. "I . . ." She frowned. "I wanted you to see her first. My girls know I take care of them. I wanted them to know you were on the case."

"I'm honored by your trust in me."

Molly's brown eyes showed crows' feet and creased in a smile at him. Her eyes narrowed when she looked toward me. "Mr. Barker isn't a client. He lives down the street, and the girls know they can trust him."

Barker held the chair for me and then took his own seat. "You did not need to explain."

"Someone had to." Molly gave a grin that went down into a frown as much as it went up in a smile. "She was itching to know." She gestured for someone in the hall to come in.

I prayed they would come in and interrupt this conversation.

The dark-skinned maid with hair in a wiry pompadour walked through the curtained doorway. She brought in a pair of rolled towels, steam rising from them, and a glass of amber liquor. Barker took the glass from her and offered a charming grin before she left.

I pulled off my gloves, put the wet towel to my cheek, and did not meet Molly's or Barker's eyes, although I knew both sets were on me. Molly filled a small crystal glass from a decanter with a badge stating that it was sherry.

Barker let out a shrug with a sigh. "She fancies me. I thought she might be over it, but a few months ago . . ." He looked at me and must have seen the blush I could not keep from turning my cheeks boiling-lobster red. "Well, my research indicated she was still afflicted."

I scowled at him. *Research? That's what his kiss was?* I heard myself mutter, "You could have just asked." And my dignity wouldn't have had to suffer in such a place. "I've been a widow for less than a year. I hardly have it in me to . . ." I finished the sentence with a shrug.

Barker rubbed the towel over his hands. "As I've said, women are something I don't understand."

"What man does?" Molly laughed. She handed me the glass of sherry.

I thanked her in a voice softer than any I thought I owned.

Barker smiled at her again. I didn't think I'd ever seen him smile this much.

I sat and then felt my chair rock as Barker's muscular frame took a small chair beside me.

Barker took out a notebook and his fountain pen. "Did she have any customers last night?"

"Yes." Molly brushed the back of her skirt to the side to sit in her office chair.

"Who was the last to make use of her trade?"

Molly looked at me.

"She is an attorney." Barker's pen scratched across the paper of his notebook. "Hire her for some nominal task, and she will keep your privacy."

"I'm a corporate counsel. I draw up contracts, review trusts, things like that. Not a defense attorney. Certainly not a trial lawyer."

"I know who you are. I saw you in the newspaper a few months ago."

"I--" I started to explain that maybe a lady could appear in the paper for more than just marrying and dying as my mother had insisted, but I realized this wasn't the right audience for that. "I got a nice note from the Russian consul general after my publicity."

"Now, Molly," Barker said. He whirled the glass in his hand, took a drink, and held it in his mouth for a moment before swallowing to say, "Tell me, Molly, tell me about the police chief."

Molly looked at the sherry decanter, handled a glass, but then turned back to us. "How did you know?"

"Why wouldn't you call the police before me? And you hesitated when you mentioned the police. You had something to say, but you didn't want to tell."

"My clients are private." Molly's eyes bounced between Barker and me. "I don't give that information."

I felt a flinch within me, and the scene I had just witnessed filled my brain so quickly and so completely, I feared my head might explode. "Not even to solve a murder of that girl?"

Molly looked me in the eye and shook her head.

"When did he leave?" Barker savored the whiskey again.

"Around eight-thirty."

I remembered Barker moving the girl's arm. No, rigor mortis was just starting. She was dead only a few hours, killed sometime in the early morning.

"He's a regular client." Molly dawdled the little gold stirring spoon within her cup. "I can't imagine he would . . ."

"Seems unlikely." Barker spoke with a gentleness in his husky, deep voice. "If you could let me know who her other clients were, I would appreciate that."

"She just arrived three days ago from Louisiana. She hadn't had time to develop a client list."

Barker nodded and turned a smile toward her that caused a friendly dimple.

"I just got her results back from the doctor yesterday." She shot me a glance. "I run a clean, legal place here."

So I sat as still as I could and thought about great expanses of nothing to keep away any horrified expression, but I could not stop the words from my mouth as a thought occurred to me: "That's the same time Lucinda Wyngate came to town."

"Not so unusual," Barker said without looking up from what he wrote in his notebook. "Trains and ships run on schedules."

I looked at Molly. "Have you heard about Lucinda Wyn--"

"What can you tell me about the girl?" Barker asked Molly.

"Not much. Fresh off the boat, she came to see me. She seemed to have potential. She'd been working for a few years and didn't seem to like it too much or hate it." She set down her sherry glass. "I can always tell which ones are, you know, desperate, and which ones have let those ladies from the church make them think that they're awful." She looked at me with murderous intent.

Now was not the time to tell her I had marched with the Assistance League women to try to make her occupation against the law. I opened my mouth to defend all the ladies from the church who were only trying to protect those who couldn't protect themselves, but I remembered how no one--not the police, not the church--had protected this young woman. "She didn't deserve to die that way." I heard my voice come out breathless and even deeper than my normal sound. My eyes even had an embarrassing runniness.

Barker gave Molly another smile.

She shrugged back at him. "She was new here, and even if they're experienced, I like to break them in easy. That's why I set her first appointment with the police chief. He's a friendly guy. Always good to the girls, not too choosy. Nice way to see how they do with the general public."

"Do you know his opinion of her?"

I resisted an urge to roll my eyes at how Barker and Molly spoke of the girl as if she were a waitress.

She shook her head. "He wouldn't tell what--"

"What do you think his opinion was of her?" Barker's smile slid all the way up to his big, blue eyes. She beamed back. I'd bet I wasn't the only female sweet on him.

"He had a smile." She trained a hard look at me. "And the towel sure needed to be laundered after that."

I furrowed my brow at Barker.

He whispered, "How they keep count on what to pay for the girls. Each customer gets a towel." He sat quiet and frowned. "Why was she back in that room, then?"

"No telling." Molly scratched the side of her face and showed her short nails, trimmed but bitten down to the quick. "It was a slow night and so no one else was using it, but she didn't have any clients. She didn't have any reason to be there."

Barker stood. "I'd like to see where she stayed."

"My maid will show you up." Molly took a pen from a holder and opened a file. "Don't be a stranger, Mr. Barker. We can always find something you would like." She looked up at the file to stare at me. "Maybe something blondish, tall, brown eyes."

"My eyes are hazel." I realized I had my hands on my hips.

She turned to Barker with a smile. "She does have it bad for you."

"Thank you for the sherry." I strode after Barker through the curtain behind Molly's desk. He turned back and I saw Barker before me with a huge smile plastered across his face between high cheekbones and a square jaw I wouldn't have minded punching, except that I had seen him in a fight before and he was no slouch. "You needn't grin like a maniac." Instantly, I regretted my words and felt my stomach churn at them. "Oh my! There is a maniac loose. I didn't mean to imply it might be you."

"You didn't." Barker stopped in the hallway. "Until just then."

The maid scooped her hand for us to follow her. She walked through a kitchen with a couple of cabinets and a table in the middle of the room. The table had the knife marks of cooking, but also planks tilted up and a footblock in place.

I muffled a shudder.

When not used for slicing up stewing meat, that table would have been used for some sort of surgery. I walked on behind Barker and the maid.

"You know which one she was," Barker said.

"I know them all." The maid said walked up a narrow back staircase.

"I'll bet you know everything about this place," Barker said.

She turned to look down the stairs to him with a smile.

"Like I'll bet you know when she slipped into that room."

"Yessir," she said. "She's been there every night since she arrived. If she hadn't stopped, the girls were going to have a word with Miss Molly."

Could one of the other prostitutes have killed her? No, not because such evil couldn't fester in their heart, but because that wouldn't fit the evidence of the murder; they wouldn't have come from the street without someone in the house noticing.

"This way." The maid gestured down a narrow, clapboard hall without adornment. She gestured her hand toward the first room. "Hers was the bed near the door."

A woman in a dressing gown walked toward us, but turned toward one of the other rooms instead. She leaned back out and gave her dressing gown sash a tug to reveal a naked figure with large breasts and ample hips below.

Barker walked on as though he had seen nothing.

The maid raised her skirt above her ankles and trotted away to the stairs.

We followed the maid into a room with white walls, an oak wardrobe, and two iron beds. A single nightstand stood between the two beds.

The maid walked out and Barker followed her. They spoke in the hallway for a moment in voices too soft for me to hear before he came back into the whitewashed room. He pulled open the drawer and dropped the contents on the dead girl's bed: stockings, powder, and a pen case. He opened the pen case and found a small vial wrapped in gauze.

He unwrapped it to reveal a few ounces of heroin.

I peered around Barker's shoulder. "Why hide something that's legal?"

"So Molly wouldn't find it. She does run a clean place and takes care of her girls."

I rolled my eyes, but Barker didn't see, so I said, "And letting women sleep with men is your idea of taking care of them?"

Barker turned back to look at me. "Some women don't have the same opportunities in life as you."

"Yes," I sneered. "My life was always easy." My adoptive father had been a doctor, but my original parents in Russia, before the missionaries rescued me and brought me to America on the orphan train, had been of angry drunks. My earliest memory was a kitchen full of blood. I thought my mother was dead, but she survived the beating, only to face more before people from a church found me on the street.

"I've seen you consider others with so much charity," Barker said to me. "Why can't you do so toward these women?"

"Why can't I?" I wondered aloud. "Because I have seen husbands lose interest in their wives and their families to take after women such as this. Yes, the men are as much to blame--more to blame--but cleaning everything up and pretending this place is respectable just isn't!" I wished I hadn't been so loud.

Barker turned away from me and opened the wardrobe across from the bed to reveal a dressing gown, an evening dress, a corset hung by its strings, and a pile of clean white drawers, chemises, and combination garments. "You want to protect these girls, and you can't. They live a dangerous life."

I wanted to protect my girls, too, but I couldn't. They were hounded by fears and might-be-trues.

"Find anything?"

He frowned at the stack of chemises. "Maybe." He lifted them, and at the bottom of the wardrobe was a book. Barker set the under-things aside and picked up the book. He opened the blue hardcover and thumbed back the first several pages. The rest of the book had been hollowed out. A folded piece of paper sat within.

Barker dropped the book on the bed and unfolded the letter.

He read, " 'Dearie, come to Galveston. I know where it is. We will have the treasure. We will be together, my dearest love.' It's signed 'Guy.' "

"Why would she keep that?"

"Why do women keep any letter from a man? I wonder why she hid it." He looked at the planks of the ceiling to run through possibilities. "Molly might not approve of Guy. Guy's wife might not approve of him consorting with prostitutes. Any number of reasons."

"Treasure? That was her tattoo."

"Aye, Guy was her treasure," Barker said. "Could mean anything." He tucked the letter into his breast pocket and gestured toward the door. "But Guy probably came with her from Louisiana."

I tried to put thoughts of the murder scene from my mind, but they would not leave. I focused on the tattoo: just the tattoo and not the death and terror around it. "I've never seen a woman with a tattoo."

Barker gave me a gentle smile. "I doubt you've seen many prostitutes' arms." He let out a sigh. "We're done here."

I hurried down the stairs. I wanted to be out of this place and away from its horror.

Barker grabbed my elbow when I rushed past Molly's office door to head to the back door. The door to the room where the murder occurred was closed, and sounds within of men's voices and heavy footsteps sounded as if the crime scene was altering. "We'll be going, Molly."

She looked over a lorgnette at the files and receipts on her desk. "You take care, Mr. Barker."

A tall, narrow man in a suit with a flowered vest held the door open. He gave me a wink. I sped outside. At the gate through the picket fence, I waited for Barker.

He took a second on the walkway to look around while he smoothed his hair under his straw hat. While inside, he had somehow acquired a brown paper parcel.

I didn't know if I dared ask him what he had.

CHAPTER 4

Barker peered down the wide, open boulevard. Once, trees lined the streets and obscured gambling houses amidst the saloons and whorehouses.

I looked down the street: colorful houses of high Victorian trim, bright clamshells topping the road, and the occasional gray tree stump. After the storm, almost every tree on the island had died, and none remained on this street. I saw nothing that could have captured his attention so thoroughly that he stood straight enough to have been strapped to a board without appearing to breathe. "You had no business telling a madam--telling anyone--that I have a pash on you."

"Made her realize you are a woman with feelings." He said "with feelings" in the grim tone most of us would use to say "with typhoid fever." "And not the pinched *besom* you appeared."

Someday, I'd ask him what a '*besom*' was.

My mind flashed through the images of the dead prostitute. Remembering the smell made me want to run away and whimper, but I would not let Barker see that. I gave him a smile as coy as I could manage after what I had just seen. "I think you like the thought that I might be attracted to you. A conquest to brag about, and yet you know you are quite safe with a woman widowed less than a year."

Barker stepped forward and passed the package to me with the deftness of the hero of a cover illustration for an action magazine. He was the square-jawed Frank Merriwell taking the field for Yale.

The package was soft and spineless.

Barker stepped to the sidewalk in silent strides of those long legs. I kept pace, but he stepped before me and threw his arm out to keep me from going past.

He peered forward.

I saw it: what Barker watched. Between the house with a mansard roof and one with a turret, a figure slipped toward the alley.

Barker hotfooted his way across the street.

I tucked the big package beneath my arm, pulled my skirts above my ankles, and tore after him. My pace made the package bounce and slide as though it were filled with kittens trying to get out of a bag.

I started to turn toward where we had seen the figure, but Barker caught my sleeve. He nodded toward the next gap between the buildings. I bent my knees to keep my steps as silent as his. We walked past a house of broken windows with the sour smell of spilled beer leaking into the narrow space between houses.

In a window on the other side, I saw the back of a woman wearing a loose kimono. Her hands behind her, she jerked the velvet curtains closed.

Houses here were as close together as anywhere in Galveston, where double-gallery homes stood only about four feet apart. This was supposed to provide a wind break during storms, but the effect now was claustrophobic, with tall clapboard buildings on either side blocking my view of anything except Barker's broad-shouldered back before me.

He bent down, and I used the opportunity to look between the buildings to see a man in a dark suit--our quarry--stroll down the alley. His stride told me that he had not noticed that we were following him, but he did give his head a quick turn to examine either side of the alley before he passed.

In this neighborhood, people probably always looked for what might be coming down an alley, but he did not look far enough to see us.

Barker did his silent cat run to the alley, but stopped beside a building with a slanting roof that showed that it must have once been a stable. Now black and white men sat together around a table with cards and poker chips on the surface.

The man in the black suit ambled to the other side of the alley. He was white, but only in the sense of race. Dark smears of dirt settled over his cheeks and neck. His beard was short but uneven. The suit hung over his narrow frame, and the arms were rolled up to show cuffs beneath soiled with red mud.

I had no idea why we followed an obvious hobo, but I knew Barker had his methods.

Barker leaned against the wall of the poker stable, and I stepped into the mud and shrubs to press behind him.

I tapped his arm. He ignored it and continued to watch the man with bare ankles walk through the alley, so I tapped again.

Barker glared at me.

I pointed at the man, pointed at Barker, pointed at myself, and made a loop with my hand to convey making my way to the end of the block to follow him from a different angle.

Barker frowned. I figured the greatest detective in the country had a good idea what I intended, so his hesitation was at leaving me alone in this neighborhood. In daytime, when people had seen me with him and I only intended to go a couple of house-lengths down, I figured I could take the chance.

The hobo reached the corner.

I gave Barker a shrug and darted off toward the front of the houses and to the corner.

There he was; the hobo came my way.

I leaned against an iron fence, opened my change purse, and rummaged through the silver dollar, several coins, trolley token, and a silver powder holder as though something important might lurk within. This effort shifted the package, and I dropped it.

I looked to the hobo to see whether he had noticed, and with a thrill of nerves realized bobbing around so much was not the way to keep him off his guard. I looked down at the package.

I could still see his feet and ankles splattered with more of the red Texas mud.

A man stepped up behind me. As I stood, I held the package before me as though it were a weapon and turned to give the sideways glare I hadn't used since I was a child on the streets of Russia. Some things come back when you need them, and the man crossed to the other side of the street.

I'd lost sight of the hobo for an instant. There he was, in front of me on the sidewalk.

What is he doing? Why did he dart into the alley for half a block and then back out on the same street?

I spotted Barker--at least his hat--peering from the alley a block away.

I waited a few moments to follow the hobo, since I didn't want to try to match his aimless amble. A woman walking that way in this place would look like a prostitute on the prowl.

The hobo reached into a garbage bin, left on the street for the re-established trash pick-up service. This must have been part of his normal circuit, which was why he had gone from street to alley to street.

I stepped toward him in my normal, determined walk.

He pulled a broken umbrella from the can.

I could not see Barker, but he was good at this sort of thing, while I was walking down the street in a section of town where I didn't belong and doing so in a rustling, green silk suit.

Where was Barker?

I had expected the hobo to be finished in the trash can by now, but he still rummaged, so I still walked, not knowing what else to do. I'd already dropped my package. If I did it again so soon, people might assume I was not only a prostitute, but also a drunken one and an easy mark.

I did not see Barker anywhere.

I kept walking.

Then I saw. I saw that it wasn't mud on the hobo's cuffs and ankles, even on the back of his neck. It was blood. I drew in a deep breath to keep from panicking. I kept walking. The best thing I could do was keep walking as though nothing had changed.

I had no idea if Barker was still out there.

I was past the hobo. I was fine. He did not know I had seen.

Wind batted at my hat and billowed my skirt. I did not even dare attempt the modesty of holding it down because I feared he would see my shaking hand. I gripped the package tight.

He turned to walk in the same direction as I. I resisted the urge to grab him and start screaming. Even as rheumy and rawboned as he was, he was tall and could overpower me. I needed to get to Barker or the police to catch this man before he made his way to my neighborhood.

His eye caught mine. His expression started as vacant, but as his gaze wandered over my shoulder, it turned to fear.

I glanced back.

The man I had glared at earlier staggered behind me. He pushed his hat back to show greasy hair stuck to his head. "You with him?" he said to me. He pointed to the hobo and as his hand drew back, he reached for my skirt.

I turned and, holding tight with both hands, smacked him with the package and ran.

He grabbed my skirt. He might be staggering with booze, but his grip was tight, and I hit the pavement hard. Knowing he would make a move for me, I whirled around and drew my feet back to put a kick in a particularly soft spot, but he turned back. Actually, he was turned back by a blow from one of those big fists of Barker's. I had no idea how he got behind me, but his hat was gone and his seersucker jacket dirty and crumpled.

    The drunk struck a blow at Barker's face. It was faster and straighter than I imagined someone so lost to alcohol could make, but Barker ducked, made a feint to the right, and then smashed his fist to his chin so hard, the drunk fell back to knock a few pickets from a fence.

    I scrambled to my feet and saw the hobo eye Barker with fear.

    The hobo ran.

CHAPTER 5

Slipping on the seashells of the road, I took off after the hobo. I had never been a good runner and certainly was not while wearing a corset.

Barker's high-stepping, straight-backed sprint passed me.

The hobo lacked endurance, especially since he spent as much time looking behind as forward. His pace became erratic, and his loose brogues scrambled to catch hold on the slick seashells.

He started to fall, but Barker caught him by the shoulder of his suit before he hit the ground.

Barker pulled him to his feet and looked around the street. He headed for an alley.

I stopped for a few moments to breathe as deeply as my corset would allow, picked up the package from where I had dropped it, and followed them down the alley to a carriage house with the door missing and windows shattered, probably from the storm.

Within the backyard, a chestnut horse watched us and gave a head-tossing whinny before going back to chewing grass.

Barker pushed the hobo against the wall and then brushed the man's lapels flat. The lapels and the jacket showed darker areas splattered across them. Barker stepped back to stare at him.

I panted too hard to speak, so I could not take the tough role while Barker patronized the man. I didn't know why Barker was going easy on the man. He made the better antagonist, especially when dealing with someone who could commit such a brutal murder.

Unless he didn't think this man was the murderer.

"Tell us about your trip to Molly's," I said between raspy wheezes that I hoped implied the threat of facing a desperate woman.

"Yes," Barker said. "We need to know."

The hobo's eyes grew wide, the whites spreading over the edges of the brown irises. He gasped for air, and his rasps were even louder than mine; they grew until they outpaced the horse's whinnies.

"He's hysterical," I said.

"Ta," Barker said, thanking me in the terms of his land and with a good load of what I expected was sarcasm.

The hobo's whines were almost as loud as a scream. The carriage house shook with the noise. The only sound above it was the panicked whinnies of the horse.

"Don't slap him," I said. "That just makes them get louder." We had to get him calmed down before someone came to get us away from him. We needed to know what he knew.

"*Ta*," he said. This one I knew was spat out with sarcasm. Barker had been with me when I'd seen someone lapse into hysterics.

I stepped forward and lifted my hand to pat his shoulder, but stopped before my hand could make contact with the blood-soaked suit. Instead, I offered a smile and slid my hand back down to my side. I used the low, husky voice that I always used to get the attention of a boardroom full of arguing men. "Tell us. You can trust us. We'll help you." *If you are the murderer, we will help you get hanged.* "Come on, you need help. Talk to us."

Barker pulled his silver flask from his coat pocket, unscrewed the lid, and held it under the nose of the hobo.

It worked like a sort of gentleman's smelling salts and slowed the hyperventilating man.

The hobo grabbed for it, hands blackened with dirt. "Thank you," he said between gulps of booze and then of air. "Thank you . . . thank you."

"Molly's," I ventured with a smile.

He looked at Barker and ran his hand over his nose so fast and hard that I thought he might have caused damage.

Barker took a quarter from his pocket and handed it to the man. The hobo looked at the silver coin for a moment, then at Barker, and gave him a smile with almost a full set of teeth on the bottom and an expanse of gums above.

I stepped back. I didn't know if it was my imagination or his exertion having warmed the cloth, but I could smell the blood on the suit. "Tell us about Molly's."

The hobo still looked at Barker. He slid his dirty hand over his face and head, knotting up his beard on one side and getting his uneven hair to stand up. "Molly's? I never been there. That fellow who works for her runs me off every time. He's a mean one. That guy, the one at the front door." He took another sip and shook his head.

Now that we'd gotten him talking, Barker must have figured as I did that we were better off not interrupting his wave of sentient thought.

The hobo continued, "Not Molly. She ain't mean. She's a good lady."

I nodded while Barker walked around to look at the hobo from different angles.

"Some of her girls are nice, but that guy at the front door. He's got a mean streak." He nodded at his own memory. "Reminds me of a couple of the sergeants during the war. Sade--Sadie--Sadis--you know. I was in the war. Really. Texas Infantry. Hoods." He pointed out the broken window of the carriage house toward the horse. "Not cavalry." He laughed.

I smiled, but I felt my eyes knit in a frown. The First Texas Infantry had seen the hardest action in the War Between the States at places like Sharpsburg, Fredericksburg, and Gettysburg. Had he seen so much killing that it turned his mind to a dark enough place to kill that girl? Or was he just lying because he coasted through life, getting around people?

"Why aren't you at the Confederate Soldiers' Home?" I asked.

He put his hand on his hip and gave a little wiggle, like Teddie when she was about to tattle on someone. "I don't like those people. Nope, don't like them." His head shook and looked as though it might not stop.

"I never saw you there," I said.

Barker gave me a curious frown.

"Well, I never saw you there." His head jingled back and forth in a taunt. It showed more of his shirt and the pink stains on it. "Those people, I didn't like those people. They kept talking about Confederate gold."

"I've heard those legends," I said.

"We'd be rich, we'd be rich, we'd all be rich!" He swung his hands around with such a flourish that, if the flask had had any liquid left in it, he would have baptized the three of us. "That's what they said."

"The suit," Barker said, his arms folded across his chest. "Where did you get the suit?"

The hobo looked down as though in a moment of discovery at the black serge covering his body. He looked up at Barker, appeared to see something he didn't like, and looked at me.

"Where did the suit come from?" I asked.

"I didn't steal it."

You'd be in less trouble if you had.

"Where did you get it?" Barker's brogue became even stronger as his patience weakened.

The guy jittered through a few nods and said, "I found it. I found it in the alley, near that restaurant on Post Office." He ended with a shrug and some teeth sucking that indicated a search for any remaining whiskey.

"Tell us about it," I said.

"I didn't steal it," he said.

I started to assure him that, "We know you--"

"Tell us about how you found it," Barker said. "Or we'll assume you did steal it and tell the police."

He gaped for a moment and said, "It was just in the alley, rolled up there next to the . . . the rain barrel.

They've got one, there at the restaurant. I don't know the name. The one with the good chicken. They give it to me free, sometimes."

"Did you notice it's soaked in blood?" I said.

He grabbed his rolled-up cuff. "That what it is? Figures, a restaurant and all would have blood." He raised a quavering finger. "And the cook the . . . um, the . . . person from the kitchen, he got blood on his suit and left it in the alley."

Barker frowned for a moment. "We've got all we can from you. You can go."

The hobo lunged toward the door, while Barker's deft hand grabbed the silver flask before the man dashed outside.

I watched the hobo run down the alley. "Do you believe him?" I leaned against the wall. I knew I couldn't expect a direct answer from Barker, schoolmaster detective.

"And why would I?" He took the package from me.

I wanted to ask him what was in there, but he'd probably just make me guess. I had to think hard about any clues the hobo might have given. "His hands." I fought to make this sound like a statement rather than a question.

My decisiveness must have passed muster since Barker nodded with a little smile.

"Dirty," I said as memory swelled in my mind. "They were dirty with old, dirty dirt."

"Dirty dirt?"

"Yes, brown and even black, but no blood."

"Aye, there were no scratches or bruises."

I hadn't noticed that, but I wouldn't tell Barker. "So, the murderer went to the alley, doffed the suit a couple buildings away, and walked away in their union suit."

"Or some clothes that fit beneath the suit. The thing was big and probably too long for our murderer." He furrowed his brow at me. "I cannot think why the killer wore something too long." He took my arm. "Come." He led me down the alley to his house, just a block beyond.

Barker's grip on my elbow attempted to lead me toward the back of his house where once-whitewashed boards fell to the ground around the cistern.

I pulled away. "I have to get back to the office. I've lots of things to finish up before dinner." I looked at the watch pinned to my shirt. Ten o'clock. I had mountains of work to get done before taking a noontime dinner break, and Aunt Cornelia could get fussy about that.

Barker didn't let go. His grip was not hard, but those strong fingers weren't soft, either. "Sorry, lass, you don't want to go back looking like that."

Barker led me past a small house on the back of the lot. It was at the rear of his rambling house, where fresh timber showed repairs on the back porch and on the balcony that wrapped around from the front.

I slipped on the loose boards of the steps and clutched Barker's arm before I could fall, then released my grip. I needed to stop grabbing at the man if I wanted to dispel ideas of having a crush on him. Heck, I didn't think I should be alone with him for that reason. "I need your help, Barker. Not just with walking without injury through this haunted house of yours, but with finding out where Lucinda has been for the last year."

He looked at me without a word and closed the tall, narrow door behind me.

Inside, a hallway ran from the back door to a large room, dominated by a great crystal chandelier in the center of a ceiling of chipping plaster. The only other furniture in the front room were four Louis XIV chairs, each with a different pattern of carving and tapestry fabric in russet tones. The floor was probably of the same boards as in the hallway, but it was covered with a painters' tarp stretched flat.

I walked forward through a short hallway until I found the kitchen. I stepped around the empty bucket in the corner, which sat below a dark spot on the ceiling where water must traverse its way down from the roof, through the walls, and then here. The sink was new and clean. Behind it, plaster patches showed dark against the paint of the wall, and overhead the plaster and canvas had been removed and new, pale boards stretched the length of the room. I turned on the cold water and then lit the gaslight. I did not try the hot water to see if the boiler was lit and working because even cold water was lukewarm this time of year. I sure wasn't going to try the electric light switch at the corner of the room; the fixture dangled empty with patch marks around it.

As the deep porcelain sink filled, I went into the modern, clean, tiled bathroom to look in the mirror. Blood smeared the back of my glove. I must have rubbed it on my face because the hollow beneath my cheekbone was a rusty red.

Despite the sweltering weather, I shivered.

I threw my gloves into the bathroom sink and scrubbed my face with the amber bar of soap. Water dripped from my cheekbones, chin, and nose, but I scrubbed more where I still imagined red on my cheek.

It was just the mark of where I had rubbed it. Calm down, Lady Macbeth.

On the way back to the kitchen, I looked over my dress. Bodice and cuffs were clean, but now saturated to the point that I dripped. The hem had a little road dirt on the bottom, but that was normal when walking through the wet, uneven streets of Galveston. I spotted the side of my dress.

Oh no, no, no!

Blood darkened my green skirt in wide swatches. The dark wallpaper and maroon flowers had hidden how far the blood had sprayed.

I slid off my silk jacket and struggled with the tiny buttons on the back of my blouse that the housekeeper had fastened earlier this morning. I pulled and even tore at the loops and buttons binding me into the garments. I didn't care about decency: I wanted to be free of it, free of all the blood, and miles from a murder that made no sense. I doffed my gauzy cotton petticoats with the edge of blood on them. I didn't know where Barker was and didn't care. I grabbed up the bundle and, wearing only my corset, lightweight summer combination garment, and stockings, searched the kitchen for a large sink or even a washing tub.

The kitchen was antiseptic in its level of cleanliness. No dishes out, no crumbs on the oak table, and none of the tin cans on the counter or overflowing trash I expected of a bachelor's quarters.

I shoved my garments under the water, comforted by the sight of blood rising from the cloth and swirling into nonexistence in the water. I thought of clothes and the person who committed the murder, how they had thrown away the dirty suit in the alley.

"You'll be wanting this," Barker said behind me.

CHAPTER 6

I turned to see Barker holding out that now-battered package wrapped in brown paper, and I remembered that I wore only the barest of underclothes, thin enough to show my naked body beneath. Worse than that, I remembered that I had removed my clothing in the home of a man who knew I was attracted to him.

My face burned with shame. What must he think? My mind went through a series of possibilities in an instant, most circling the notion that I was attempting to seduce him and doing a particularly bad job of it. I swallowed hard to put these thoughts from my mind, but what filled my head was the sight of the death-clouded eyes of the prostitute.

I stepped close to him. I had to do something. I had to get those thoughts of the dead woman out of my mind before I lost my mind. I thought about him thinking I had a case of it for him. Maybe I did, I couldn't be sure. I liked when he kissed me, but my life had been so full of changes since the Great Storm that I didn't know how I felt about much of anything other than my daughters.

Barker pulled the strings from the brown paper and opened the package to reveal a white lace dress with a gossamer lavender sash and underskirt.

As he set the paper and string on the smooth waxed surface of the kitchen table, I moved in toward him. Instead of taking the gown he held, I pulled his shoulder down to press my mouth next to his freckled ear. "Whether I have a mash on you or not, you don't have to fear me." I breathed slowly and allowed my chest and corset to heave with the deep draughts of warm air. I caught my arms across my corset to increase the soft white swelling of my cleavage. "I'm a widow who misses the presence of a man, not some maiden who wants to fall in love."

He backed up to look at me with those unblinking deep blue eyes. His hand slid over my hair, and his face neared mine. "You've had a shock." He slid his hand over my jaw and, before I could lean into his touch, stepped back from me. "You should get dressed."

I nodded. A migraine-bolt of images brought the dead woman back into my head. "The evil of doing that. I can't imagine how . . ." My hands felt numb, my jaw clenched, and my body began to tremble. I thought of my daughters and feared this insane killer would not be content killing the ladies of the line. "I keep seeing the room, the intestines, such vile filth, and how the person cast aside their own dirty clothes. I don't know why the dirty clothes bother me."

Barker wrapped his arms around me and held me to his firm chest. He did not speak, but he pressed his head against the top of mine.

I took a deep breath and felt the trembling subside. With a weak hand on his chest, I pushed Barker away and turned to the kitchen table. "Thanks, um, and thank Molly for me." I took the dress and held it aloft. It would be tight in the shoulders, but most everything I wore was, since I had broad shoulders. My mother used to say I had the shoulders to support many cares. The rest would fit well, with it narrowing below the hips and ending in a short, lace train. "If she pays me--"

"She will pay you."

"Well, when she does, I will give the money to my church. Good manners--almost as important as being a Baptist here in the South--dictate that I should talk to that woman, but I couldn't take money that was made that way."

Barker didn't look at me, but he pulled a high-back wooden chair up to the kitchen table and sat beside me. He stared past me--either out the long windows to the second-story veranda or just into that space where thinking came easier. "Leaving the dirty clothes bothers you, and me as well."

I listened to him while I stepped into the dress.

"The killer dropped the clothes in the alley," he said in a slow voice I imagined was conjuring memories.

I shoved my arms into the narrow three-quarter sleeves with lavender ribbons threaded through the eyelets. "Yes, probably the only neighborhood where a man can wander down the alley in his underwear unnoticed." I swallowed down a shudder.

"Not even there," Barker said. "The murderer would have to have worn something beneath the suit, and that was why it was wide."

I gave him a grimace over the high collar that I smoothed into place. "The murderer left with intent. They left home--or hotel, or flophouse--ready."

He smiled at me. "Clever lass. Aye, the murderer left the house with a purpose."

"I need help lacing this up."

I wondered if he would balk. Barker had an aversion to women that began with his days in Britain when he was tricked by a sweet-faced murderess.

I slid the corset cover and petticoats on. They were a close fit, tight in the shoulders, but a little loose in the bust. I wondered whether Barker or Molly had been the one to figure out my size. Whoever it was knew that I needed petticoats as well and had provided a set in lavender satin.

"I need you to lace up the dress. Don't skip any of the--"

"Yes, I understand the principle."

But is any of your knowledge practical? I thought about how practical it might be, about his hands on the small of my back while he steadied me against the tugs of the lacing. I resisted the urge to lean into his touch and became desperate to remove those lonely, lusty thoughts from my head before he noticed them. I had to think of something else, something other than sex or murder.

"Will you help me figure out where Lucinda has been? My client needs to know."

"Your client?" Barker's efforts at the laces jostled me back, and his hand on my shoulder steadied me and moved me forward. "And is Miss Winifred paying you?"

"What does . . . ?"

I could feel his glare on my back.

I let out a puff of air more from emotion than from the pressure he put on the eyelets down my back. "No, no, no. She's a friend. I haven't asked her for--"

"You haven't had the nerve to ask her for money. Do not call her a client until . . ." His words trailed off, and his fingers no longer jabbed at the laces at my back.

I turned around to see him and saw he looked up. Although he stared at a spot in the ceiling where a hole in the plaster revealed the shiplap of the ceiling boards, I knew his mind was back at Molly's. He didn't see corset strings on the ceiling. He saw the poor girl's intestines draped over the curtain rod.

He said, "The dead lass still wore her clothes."

"Her underwear."

"Aye, but all the clothing she had in that room."

I leaned against the sink and stared at him, trying to figure out what he was thinking. All I could conjure to my mind was, "Madman's logic."

He nodded. "Wanted her dead, wanted her defiled, but did not want to see her naked?" He spun me back around to keep at the laces. My housekeeper was much faster at this, but she just grunted and told me to keep still.

"You don't think the body was, um, defiled?"

"Molly's doctor will check for that, but no, I do not think she was defiled." Barker's firm fingers laced up my back. "I've seen other cases like this. There was that one in Vienna and the Ripper in London. Those . . ."

"Played around with the body. So what does it mean that this one didn't?"

"Could mean the killer wasn't crazy at all." He gave me a pat on the back that either meant he was finished lacing me up or that it was my turn to run around a track with the baton.

I spun around to face him. "How could someone kill a woman, kill her like that without being a thorough lunatic?"

His broad hand in the air patted down my objections. "No crazier than any other murderer. They did the dismembering and all that for us."

"It was someone who wanted her dead, just wanted to make it look Ripperish--"

"Ripperish?"

I nodded so hard, I dislodged a tress that was lank from the heat and humidity. I spun it around my finger and tucked it back in my once-elegant waves of hair, pulled and ratted into a pompadour that now hung loose around my head. "Why would they do that?"

" 'Tis what I am hired to find out," Barker said.

"And I've been of some assistance," I said with an embarrassing whine that sounded more like desperation and childish petulance than I wished. "You could help me find out what I need to know about Lucinda."

Barker pushed his suit jacket back to put his hands on his hips, and I forced myself not to back away from his controlled, straight posture. "You can pursue this without remuneration, lass, but I'm too busy to take on a hobby."

I balled my hands and put them behind my back so Barker would not see that I stood in his kitchen, making fists at him. After a breath, I said, "Maybe this will help your investigation."

He gave me a sardonic smirk. He was right; I was grasping at straws formed of fairy dust.

"Oh, oh, that coincidence! The one about them coming here at the same time." I bobbed on the balls of my feet and flapped my hands, just short of applauding myself. "Maybe it wasn't a coincidence."

His brow shaded his eyes in a frown.

"Maybe it wasn't a coincidence," I said in the singsong of a child forced to apologize to his little brother. "Maybe there aren't coincidences."

I got a little smile for that.

"You think Lucinda and this prostitute were working together?"

The frown came back even stronger.

I slapped my arms down at my sides. "I don't know what to do. I negotiate contracts, I write trusts, but I don't know how to investigate."

He walked over toward me and lifted his hand as though to caress my shoulder, but then flicked a dust mote in the air and put his hand in his pants pocket. "You already started the investigation. You found out Lucinda arrived at the same time as the prostitute, probably on the same boat. Where did it come from?"

"New Orleans," I said as though I expected to get a star for the right answer.

"Aye," he said slowly. "If she came from there, perhaps that was where she went."

"She had to have left the day after the storm. Someone would have noticed her otherwise." I twisted my finger in the air. "Lucinda was well known in society and she would have been recognized if she hung around town any longer." I nodded. "I need to check the shipping manifests. I can do that. You see, I work with the shipping companies, and they keep this sort of record. Yes, I can do this."

Barker stared at me in silence. I started to look away; I didn't like eye contact. But I felt as though I would lose something if I looked away, so I met his gaze.

He gave me a smile and a wink.

I looked down at the heavy lace clinging to my figure. "Thank you for the dress," I said, giving a little tug to the lace at my bodice. It did fit just fine, better than any of the secondhand clothes I usually wore. Whoever had figured out my size did even better than I usually do. I turned to the door, but whirled around just before I got there. Did Barker know me that well? "Who figured out this would fit me? You or Molly?"

"Neither." Barker leaned against the table and crossed his arms. " 'Twas the maid. Someone most folks never notice."

I leaned against the door. The dark shellac felt cool against my cheek. "And she notices everything." I stood up straight. "That's who you were talking to after I left the house."

"Aye, and thank you for leaving so noisily and giving me a distraction."

I gave him a nod. He knew I hadn't done that on purpose. I knew Barker would clam up if I asked him directly what she had told him, so my words came at him sideways. "So, did she know anything?"

"She had an idea." His blue eyes sparkled with an inner glow that also gave him a dimple deep in the hollow of his cheek.

"About . . . ?"

"Why Molly recognized Lucinda's name when you said it."

"Damn!" I flinched at my own crudeness. "I hadn't noticed that." I gave a quick huff. I detested getting things wrong. "So, what was her idea?"

"Blackmail." He pulled his watch from his vest pocket. "Ach, we must be getting back." With a gentle hand on my arm, he slid me away from the doorframe so he could open the door. His hand vibrated to urge me down the steps.

I dawdled across the yard for a couple steps and saw Barker rush past me without waiting. I hitched my skirts up to the top of my boots, and in a couple blocks, trotted up to him. I spoke fast to keep from panting between my words. "Blackmail?"

Barker slowed his steps so I could catch up with him.

"Blackmail?" I repeated. We were only a couple blocks from the office by now, so I had to get the information out of him right away.

"Aye," he scuffed down the alley and kicked a stone toward a carriage house. "Nothing certain. The maid saw Molly ask one of the girls once after she came back from the post office, if they often send love letters to their clients."

"Lust letters," I huffed.

"Molly saw Lucinda talk to the girl at the post office."

"You saw that I spoke to Molly, but that does seem unusual."

Barker kicked another piece of brick that the storm had loosened from a house out of the way of alley traffic. "The girl then had enough money to buy a ticket to the theater."

Beside us, a woman frying chicken looked up, and I felt hunger pangs. I knew I shouldn't. I should never be hungry again with what I had seen, but I also had left the house without breakfast.

"And she thought Lucinda might have been responsible for that?"

"Aye, and there were other, similar stories."

He sure had garnered an amazing amount of information in the few minutes he took to get a dress for me.

I gave a sigh and looked at Barker. "You--we--have to find the murderer. I don't want my daughters in a city this dangerous." I walked beside Barker but did not look at him. "I'm not sure I can make them love me, but I can keep them safe."

"I'm not sure you can do that," Barker said. "You can love them, you can be yourself, but my investigative abilities have shown me that no one can give another safety throughout his or her whole life."

I wanted to ask him what he meant, but I lacked the courage to do so, and we walked in silence to the office. When we got to the door, Evangeline stood with the telephone to her ear and gestured me to come upstairs and take over.

"Sunday school teacher," she mouthed as I took the receiver.

CHAPTER 7

"Mrs. Brickley," I said into the telephone in a voice as soft as a prayer, with which I hoped to soothe the Sunday school teacher whom I could hear huffing through the static on the line. "Haints and spooks, well, that's long been part of our literature. They can be explained through logic and science, and we needn't be afraid."

I believe the sweet old lady on the other end of the line sputtered. I think I heard her count to ten before she said, "You have to find out where in blue blazes your daughter got that book and forbid her--forbid her--from ever reading such things again."

"No," I said. I closed my eyes, but opened them again when my mind filled with images of the prostitute's mutilated body.

"What did you say?" Mrs. Brickley said in a terse voice that reminded me that the sweet old thing did have a way with a ruler that smarted on the knuckles.

I didn't care about this. I leaned against the wall and closed my eyes for a moment. I saw that woman's body, torn up to the point that the murderer had almost taken away her humanity. What did I care about my daughter telling the other kids a ghost story?

Evangeline looked at me from the office doorway and then ran back inside to stare out the window.

I said into the receiver, "I'm glad my daughter has decided that reading is fun. That will help her in school. Goodness, if I didn't enjoy reading, I would never have made it through law school."

I stood up, but still leaned my elbow against the wall telephone.

"Miss Dash, we aren't talking about you."

Barker walked past me to his office. He tipped his straw hat, and I could see a grin creasing his whole face. He must have heard my entire conversation.

I screwed up my mouth in a scowl that must have lacked beauty and maturity before I turned back to the telephone. "In a way, Mrs. Brickley, it is about me." *And my inference that you think I'm a lousy mother.* "Why, when I was a child, my friend and I asked the librarian for a book on hexes."

"Hexes?"

"Yes," I laughed at a memory that I hadn't recalled for twenty years. "We wanted to cast a spell on our English teacher because we thought she was giving us too much homework."

"Did you? Did you do such a thing?"

"Well, no." I looked in my office and saw the back end of Evangeline as she peered through the window to the street below. "We found it had a lot of mumbo jumbo about getting a hair of the person and finding herbs in the shadow of midnight. It was all a lot of bother, and we figured studying was easier."

"I never knew you believed in such things. This makes everything a very different case."

"No, it doesn't." I knew I was loud enough for Barker to hear, but the conversation wasn't going well for me, and I might as well make it worse by being bold. "And I wouldn't say I believe in them. I'm saying that reading just one little book, a book of ghost stories, hardly makes one a familiar of the demons."

"You're from Russia, aren't you?" The phrase tripped from her mouth in the careful, forced-lightness one would use to ask, "You're an escaped prisoner, aren't you?"

I sighed. I seldom told people that, but ever since the picture of me in the paper helping the Imperial Russian delegation, people just seemed to know. "Yes, I was adopted from Russia as a child. I fail to see how that is relevant to my daughters." Although I was the one to make the conversation about me rather than let her pick on my girls.

"Well, Russians are Catholics. And Catholics believe all sorts of unholy--begging your pardon as a Catholic--but unholy things."

"I'm not Russian Orthodox; I'm as Baptist as anyone." Before she could say anything about Baptists not casting spells on their English teacher, I said, "Good day, Mrs. Brickley." I think I heard her reply before I hung up.

I stomped into my office. I might have no clue whether or not I was a good mother, but I certainly didn't need some wizened-up old thing to insinuate that I was a bad one.

Evangeline turned toward me from the large windows at the front of the office, her mouth gaping. "Lucinda Wyngate wearing a lavender satin day dress."

"Is this some sort of game? Do I now say, 'Ethel Barrymore in a green housecoat'?"

Evangeline flicked her hand toward the window. Her normally olive complexion had a strange rose tint. "Downstairs."

The great arched door to the building creaked open.

Evangeline gasped. "She's coming up here."

On the stairs, I heard a cheerful laugh and whispering--more than one person whispering.

Lucinda stepped up to the landing and craned around to see in my office. Two girls burst past her: the sun-bonneted forms of my own daughters. What were my daughters doing with her?

"The nice lady brought us up," Teddie said. She picked up her curls to let the dark hair spill loose over her shoulders. She gave an expansive gesture of hand arcing toward Lucinda and then shoved the hand in the pocket of her yellow-checked pinafore. Teddie swiveled a bit and looked up at Lucinda as if she were a porcelain doll come to life. "Said we weren't to play in the alley."

I shouted, "Don't you know . . ." That there's a lunatic out in those alleys who murdered a woman for no reason? I bit my lips closed. No, they didn't know, and I had no reason to worry them about someone targeting a very different part of society than our own.

I stepped around my desk and turned toward the girls with my side to Lucinda, who stood in the doorway. "You were playing in the alley? What? Where's Aunt Cornelia?"

"She sent us here on account of we were driving her . . ." Jinxie looked down to think for a moment. To remember. She was dressed as her sister was, but in blue gingham. She smiled her toothless grin. "Driving her up the insane tree."

"And you didn't come in? You played in the alley until . . ." I looked at Lucinda, who watched my interaction from the doorway.

Her eyes held a wide-open look of surprise, but her face of smooth cheek and small, plump mouth held no other expression.

I smiled at her. "Hello, Mrs. Wyngate." I extended my hand to shake. "I'm afraid I'll have to recuse myself, as I will be representing Winnie, Winnie Bain. I'm sure I can refer you to an excellent substitute." When she did not take my hand, I lifted it in the air in a lopsided shrug and dropped it to my side.

"I have no idea what you mean." Her voice was low and pleasant, her accent more country-Texas than my own broad Southern sound. "I'm here to see a Mr. Barker. Figured I'd come to call to make an appointment." She looked over my office; from the wallpaper of sage-green stripes blossoming into pink and white hydrangeas; over the pictures of Clara Barton, Susan B. Anthony, and my daughters; and on to the pale woodwork and rag rug. A frown creased her white skin. "Is he in, Dash, dearie?"

I smiled at the image of Barker's ramrod posture standing amid the floral fripperies of my office. "No, his office is across the hall, Lucinda, darling."

My daughters smiled at my customary term of endearment even though it wasn't focused on them.

Lucinda stood in silence for a moment but then spun around to leave, her skirts swishing into my daughters, making them giggle.

"Oh," she whispered and backed up into my office so fast, the girls had to hurry from her path.

I put my hands on my hips, cleared my throat, and said, "Excuse me, but we have work to do. So, if you'll . . ."

She turned toward me and raised a finger to her lips. "Shhh!"

She shushed me. In my own office, she shushed me. In front of my daughters.

Calling on the strong, steady voice of command I'd learned from the man who sold me the horse and trap I had before the storm, I said, "I think it's time you leave."

She pasted herself against the wall just inside the door. The girls did the same on the other side, only their faces held joy while Lucinda's wrinkled forehead and bit lip showed agitation, if not fear.

"Do you want I should call the police?" Evangeline said from just behind me.

"No," I said. Such an act could lose customers once word got out, and it would. Still, I didn't want my daughters to see me allow this woman to take over my office for her childish games.

"Miss Dash?" Evangeline stood beside me with a crease to her brow and set to her lips that told me she was determined to get this woman out of our office. She looked as though she would take a broom to Lucinda if I wished.

I thought for an instant. "Call the library. Winnie might like to have a talk with this person."

Lucinda had to have heard me, but she gave no sign. She continued to lean against my wall. She stood so still, I believed she held her breath.

Footsteps pounded--those of several feet--outside the door.

Evangeline stomped out the door and to the telephone on the landing between Barker's office and mine.

The girls, overcome with their own ability to hide against the wall undetected, giggled at each other.

"Shhh," Lucinda told them.

"That's enough out of you," I said. I saw my finger flap at her in a scold, and it reminded me of the Sunday school teacher. I needed to talk to Teddie about that, but wondered what to say.

I saw who walked past: Abelard Wyngate, his father, and his mother, trailed by that brother, the only one of the crowd who had hugged Winnie, whose name I couldn't remember, even if he was in the newspaper more often than the rest.

They knocked on Barker's door and were ushered in by Clark. Clark's name may have been "Clark," or it could be his job and Barker's pronunciation of "Clerk."

Clark smiled at Evangeline, who held the telephone.

Without a look at me or at the girls, Lucinda slipped from the office and must have gone down the stairs since Evangeline looked in that direction, but I could not hear her steps on the marble stairs.

The Wyngates entered Barker's office without looking back to see her.

Why did they need a detective?

Evangeline held her lips toward the brass transmitter on the wooden wall telephone, but dangled the receiver toward me.

I shook my head.

"Thanks anyway, operator." She hung up and came back into the office.

"Now girls, I have room for you to play here in my office," I said. I gestured to the two small desks I had set up near the window that looked over the harbor and ocean beyond. With chalk, books, and paper, it looked woefully schoolish and sapped of all fun. "I'm sure we can find something for you to enjoy here, without disturbing the hobos in the alley."

Teddie shoved her lower lip up in a look that spoke defiance, even if she said nothing. Jinxie gave a sigh and said, "I'm bo. . ." She stopped herself. She knew the words forbidden in my house just as they had been in my mother's: "bored," "hate," and "stupid."

"Aunt Cornelia said we needed to get some fresh air and sunshine," Teddie said.

I refrained from arguing with her that there wasn't much of either to be found in a city alley. That seemed a very adult perspective that would make no sense to a child. I still walked along the alleys to find old nails and interesting bits of brass that might remain from the storm. "I have some time right now, and we can think of something fun to do. How about ice cream?"

"Aunt Cornelia wants us back soon," Teddie said. She turned to leave.

"Yes, Dash dearie," Jinxie said.

Before she could exit the door, I grabbed her arm and whirled her around so fast I think she was airborne for a few seconds. I growled at her, "I am 'Mama' to you. If you choose not to say that, then I am Mrs. Gallagher, but I am never 'Dash dearie' to you. Is that clear?"

Those luminous green eyes filled with tears.

I leaned down and gave the top of her head a kiss. "I take it that's clear, then."

Teddie stared at me without moving, as though my snake-headed moment of rage had turned her to stone.

I bit my lip and let my hands whirl around for an instant while I thought of what to say. I didn't have any idea, but I figured I would start with something pleasant. "Your Sunday School teacher is very fond of you." I shot Jinxie a glance, but I could not see the head beneath the sunbonnet, the one that flinched with obvious sobs. "Fond of both of you."

"She's nice," Teddie said. She looked at me and waited for me to get to a point.

Yes, but she can be a right Tartar when you confess things. I wondered for a moment if that was the type of person who had killed the prostitute, only crazy: someone outraged by the vice so rampant in a successful city like Galveston.

From within Barker's office, Miss Alice let out a shriek. Rapid words from several men followed the sound. I did not make out Barker's voice among them.

"She and I had a little conversation this morning. I liked hearing how you get along with the other girls and talk to them."

"I get in trouble for talking too much," Jinxie said to her toes.

"Thanks for that confession, Jinxie." I clapped her to my side in a hug. "I don't know about talking too much. She told me, though, that you had read a book about ghosts. I wondered if it might have, um, scared you."

"It was a good book," Teddie said. "That library lady you know gave it to me." She pursed her lips in what I assumed to be disapproval of my friend, Winnie. "It's all about those sisters who have séances and some of their stories."

"You know, I enjoy a ghost story," I said. "I don't believe them, though. When someone dies, they go to a better place. They don't hang around here. The stories are fun, though."

"But sometimes the memory is so strong," Teddie said so fast, she took an audible breath. Her sister made a snide mimic of the sound, but Teddie pressed on without noticing. "Some people have such a strong . . . a strong. . ."

"Presence?" I supplied.

She pointed at me as though I'd won the carnival cigar. "That while their soul might have moved on, their spirit remains. Sometimes, they, you know, stick around. Some can invade the thoughts of others, sensitive folk, and change them into what they was."

"Change them into what they were?"

"Yes, so they act like the ghost. Well, when the ghost was alive. They've got all sorts of stories of people who never liked lemon pie, but then eat nothing but lemon pie after their lovey died, someone who had great

. . . great . . . uh-huh, 'spirit energy.' Well, when that person died who was crazy about the stuff."

I smiled. All she said was full of hokum, hogwash, and lemon pie. Mrs. Brickley would find this book one big mile-marker on the road to hell, but this was the most Teddie had said to me in a month. I knelt and opened my arms and flapped my hands to encourage the girls into a hug. They pressed against me, and I kissed their heads. "You have fun reading that book or anything else you like."

From her desk, Evangeline made a "humph."

I turned to see if she held a look of disproval for what I said to the girls. I doubted she would, since she considered the girls to be one smile short of sprouting angel wings.

Evangeline wasn't looking at me, but instead toward the door.

A man stood just outside our door. He was a little beefy, but had a symmetry to his features and a winning grin that made me think he was more appealing than handsome.

I stood and smiled at him.

"I don't mean to bother you," he said in the cultured tones from the dusty halls of an East Coast university. "I thought I'd seen Lucinda here." He blinked. He had a hard blink, a sort of nervous tic that wasn't rapid or repetitive, but his eyelids came down hard when they did come down.

I remembered him, the young Wyngate. I knew he had sent letters to actresses and that he once had a woman's lover shoot at him, but his name was vague to me. I'd only heard it once, I didn't remember when. Ah yes, as his mother scolded him for clinging to Winnie.

He opened his mouth, probably to ask whether Lucinda had been here. "You're Beau Wyngate, aren't you?"

"And I thank the lovely lady for remembering me. Most people find me forgettable."

"Oh, surely not," I said with a smile that brought out the dimple. I might be able to find out why his family was seeing Barker. I wanted to know since that would help my friend. I just didn't know how to do it. Asking him, "So, why is your family seeing a private detective?" just wouldn't sound professional and, well, lawyerly.

The girls dawdled past me to their desks.

School desks. I realized no kid wants to be trapped in a school desk in the summer, but I hadn't thought of that when I bought them. I just thought they would be something all their own in their mother's office.

Teddie frowned at me-- not so much at me as at my dress. She said nothing. Jinxie gave me a smile and a big wave, as though I were across a train station and not less than the entire distance of the rag rug from her.

As soon as they occupied themselves with pulling paper and wax crayons from the cubbyhole beside their desk, I took a deep breath to dispel images of the unfortunate woman's murder from my mind. Just as my parents had delivered me from a life of begging for coins on Nevski Prospekt, my job was to make sure my girls had everything a family could offer.

"Of course." He leaned against the doorway and shot a glance back toward Barker's closed door. "I'm the one everyone forgets. The one most likely to mess up the accounts and then smack my thumb in the ledger books." He held up a gloved thumb and wiggled it to illustrate.

I laughed.

"Yes indeed, I'm the boll weevil on the family cotton bush." He set his hand on his satin cravat. "It must be a cotton reference with my family, my mother having grown up on the old plantation."

"Yes," I said. "I remember reading about your mother's family still retaining the plantation. So many families lost theirs after the war." I turned to the girls with a little bit of history, although they did not look up from their drawings. "High taxes and no one to work the places anymore."

"Oh, at Shady Oaks everyone pitched in. Mm-hmm, the annual hog slaughter was not to be missed."

I held out my hand. "I'm Dash Gallagher, attorney. How may I help you, Mr. Wyngate?" *First, be professional, and then make with the questions.*

He shook his head. "As delightful as that sounds, Mrs. Gallagher, I am here to see Lucinda." He poked his head into the room and looked around. "I thought I saw her walk in here. Must have been mistaken."

Teddie jumped to her feet and gave the man a broad smile. "She was here. She came to see us, but just for a minute." Teddie held her skirt and simpered around a bit in a fair imitation of the woman. "Then she was gone."

Beau smiled at Teddie and then at me, with a wink going to Jinxie and a nod to Evangeline along the way. "I'm sorry to have troubled you."

"Oh, no problem at all." Evangeline piped up. She stood and gave the hot, wet air a wave. "I was just wondering why your family came out to our building."

Behind my back, I gave her the thumbs-up sign. I hoped the window behind us did not reflect this back to Beau.

Beau gave a shrug and then patted his cravat back into place. "To protect the family honor. That's what they always do."

"From Lucinda?" I asked. I did not even try to sound casual.

Beau raised his eyebrows.

I smiled. I might as well give information to try to get some. "She seemed very flustered when she was in here. She seemed to be hiding from you."

"Surely not me," Beau said. "Maybe from my mother, maybe from Abelard, and she's always been terrified of my father, for some reason, but no one fears me."

No one feared the prostitute's murderer, and no one suspected.

I took a short gasp at the thought of someone so sick and twisted wandering through the crowds in even the disreputable parts of town and no one stopping the person.

I think everyone stared at me. I know a clammy silence descended.

"I expect an important man like your father can be frightening," Evangeline said. I suspected her words were only uttered to end the silence, and I felt her worried eyes on me even though I saw her large lips flash into a smile.

Beau frowned at her and the perpetual smile on his lips drooped slightly in what looked like thought. A hard blink came, and then another so strong, I thought the effort might damage his eyes. "Why fear him more than Sextus? She always seemed fond of my big brother."

I thought of Sextus, and although I knew he was the head of a huge corporation involving banks and railroads, I held no impression of him from my short meeting, nothing more than the husband of that small blonde woman who appeared to be a gasp away from falling into a faint.

I saw a blur in black wool burst from Barker's office and tear down the steps. Probably Sextus.

With a rustle of purple taffeta I would have deemed too heavy for the sultry days of summer, Miss Alice strolled down the stairs to stand beside Beau. Her long neck extended well past the purple ruffles and black stripes of her shirtwaist and showed posture that may even have been better than Barker's.

He turned to look at her with an affectionate smile. "Mama." His pronunciation accented the second syllable in a vaguely French sound. "You remember Winnie's friend, Mrs. Gallagher. She is working in Winnie's interest."

I smiled at Beau. He might not be the best at accounting, but he knew his way around a woman.

"Yes, aren't we all working in her interest?" Miss Alice said. Although her dark gray eyes darted around the office, she extended a hand to mine, one even longer than my own and with such a firm grip, I doubted that this woman believed in subtlety.

"Thank you," I said. "I hope that you are doing well throughout this ordeal." And I would love to know what happened in Barker's office to make you cry out.

In my peripheral vision, I saw Evangeline looking down at her hands. She wasn't about to say anything. She might pipe up to a wayward son, but she knew a matriarch when she saw one and said nothing.

The telephone rang, and Evangeline was out in the hall to answer even before it completed my ring.

Beau shot his mother a glance and then looked at me. "Did you know Lucinda was here a few moments ago, Mama?"

Alice's deep gray eyes flicked over me for an instant before taking in the office, the girls, and the items on my desk.

"She seemed to have been watching us," Beau explained. "But she ran from the building before making contact with us. I wonder if the summer heat has left us particularly odiferous."

She gave him a slap on the arm that was too firm to be playful, but too quick to be angry. She looked out the window with a frown, as though she were trying to spot Lucinda somewhere out in the streets between here and the harbor. "I tell you, that girl has been jumpy as a cat since she came back." She shot a glance to me and then back out the window. "Haven't had a chance to say so much as 'hello' to her since her return."

Is that why you went to see Barker? Did you want him to get information on Lucinda if she wouldn't give it herself?

Miss Alice heaved her broad shoulders in a sigh and turned to leave, but stopped when she almost ran into the tall, narrow form of Abelard.

Beau's shoulders still pointed toward me, but his neck craned around to face his brother. "Hunting for Lucinda. We thought she was here."

Abelard pinched his long, narrow nose in long, narrow fingers and rolled his deep-set blue eyes. "'Hunting for Lucinda.' That almost killed me after the storm, and now I see I must do it again . . . for the rest of my days?"

Beau patted his brother's sleeve. "Sorry, old man."

"Well," Miss Alice said. "We've taken up enough of this nice lady's time. We should be going."

The girls filed out past the Wyngates, but only to go to Evangeline on the landing.

"If there's anything I can do . . ." My words fell on Alice's departing back without acknowledgement. Abelard jogged down the stairs, and Beau turned to tip his hat before he left.

A man with rosy cheeks behind a silver handlebar mustache made his way through the departing Wyngates. He tipped his bowler hat at me. "Looks like I'm late again to the party."

"How do you do, Mr. Wyngate?" I extended my hand. "I'm Winnie's friend and attorney, Dash Gallagher."

He grabbed my hand, but did not shake it. He held it, smiled into my eyes, and sauntered closer to me. "And what a lovely friend you are." His eyes dropped to my bodice. He wasn't even subtle about it. He was close enough for his legs to thrust my petticoats against me.

"Oh, I didn't realize you still had someone in the office," Evangeline said. She slipped past the elder Wyngate, captain of industry, who looked as though he now wanted to captain me.

I yanked my hand free and stepped back until a potted palm stood between us. I looked out to the landing to make sure my daughters hadn't seen this, but they sat on the green velvet visitor's bench and stared out the front window to the street.

"I'm sorry if you got the wrong impression," he said. He took a step toward me. "I'm a man who appreciates the beauty of art and femininity." He turned to Evangeline. "And who is this lovely lady?"

"She works for me," I said in a voice I tried to make sound sweet. "And she's very busy."

He gave a shrug but did not leave. I wondered if I would have to encourage him out at the point of a hat pin.

Miss Alice reappeared in the doorway. "My dear, we're leaving now." She extended her hand. He gave a little shrug and then took it.

Evangeline and I stood in silence until they were well down the stairs. I think she held her breath, as I did. She gave a little peek through the doorway to make sure a wayward Wyngate would not reappear, and she said, "That was your housekeeper. She said you and the girls need to get home right away."

CHAPTER 8

"I expect she's just miffed at us being late for dinner," I said over the slight streetcar noise.

Teddie gave a little sigh that said she was having none of it.

"It's twelve-thirty now, and she expected us right at twelve." I pointed to the diamond-covered watch pinned to my shirtwaist, the only item I had salvaged from a case that went very wrong.

Jinxie looked at the little watch as though it were some foreign and dangerous elf carving. She hadn't mastered time-telling yet, and I feared my tutoring sessions had not helped.

Teddie started tapping one foot and then the other, as though impatience would propel the trolley faster down the street.

I leaned as the electric car curved around the smooth stone and brass statues of men and women who formed the Texas Heroes monument. The marble still showed the dark mark about twelve feet up where the storm waters had come to rest, drowning much of the island.

I opened my mouth, closed it, and reminded myself that I was the mother and needed to deal with this sort of thing. "Teddie, did you talk about ghosts at Sunday School?"

"Spirits," she said. I wished she would look at me when she spoke, but I didn't want to grab her face and feel the resistance. Even when I ducked down to her eye level, she cast her eyes lower.

"So, you spoke about spirits."

She looked at the street beyond, where a mansion of stone towers stood with broken windows and a parched lawn. "I talked to the other kids about a book I read."

I rubbed her back. I had read to her and encouraged her to read, something her original parents must not have had time to do, since the girls were way behind their age group in language skills. I wouldn't chastise her for what she read as long as she was reading. "You did fine, honey."

"I thought, maybe, people come back."

"They don't, dear."

"Maybe." She insisted. "Maybe they light up someone else."

Someone like Lucinda? Not hardly.

The streetcar jangled to a stop, and I put my hand out to help the girls from the car. "She never likes it when we're late for dinner." The girls hopped off, Jinxie raising her skirts to get as much loft as she could.

We walked at a quick pace, and I kept making it quicker every time I saw the girls swish around in what was a fair imitation of Lucinda. We rounded the corner where the remnants of two houses leaned against each other and past a large Queen Anne style home of clean lines, except for the round tower on one side. We saw our red house with green shutters.

Built in a high Victorian style, it had a wedding cake's worth of fripperies in the woodwork of the double galleries of shaded balconies and gabled tower on the other side. The air was still and hot.

I opened the screen door and ushered the girls in with a wave. The house was dark and held its usual smell of the cedar-like pine that made up the floorboards, carved moldings, and beadboard. Another, harsher smell filled the air--probably beef soup.

In the large archway to the front parlor, Winnie stood just behind Aunt Cornelia.

Jinxie grabbed Aunt Cornelia around her skirt at about knee height and mumbled something into the fabric that sounded like, "I love you, Mama."

I caught Winnie around the waist and whispered, "Did my daughter just call the housekeeper 'Mama?' "

"Could have been 'ma'am?' " Winnie followed me into the parlor.

Teddie said, "Hello," without looking up from the rug.

Jinxie put her arms around Winnie, just above the knees. "I love you."

"Jinxie!" I said in a voice loud for the still room. "You can't love someone you don't even know."

The girls, Winnie, and even Aunt Cornelia, who carried a silver tray adorned with some quivering mass of meat, looked at me. No one said anything.

These women had called me today, both seemed to have wanted to talk to me, but now, they stood as still and as silent as the hitching post out front.

I stared at Winnie to wear her down until she volunteered information.

Aunt Cornelia took her burden through the front parlor to the dining room. "Better come eat," she said. "Before everything melts."

"Melts?" I asked. I followed her into the dining room, where the mahogany table was set for four with the second-best red transfer-ware china and the silver plate.

"Tongue in aspic, jellied eggs, and blancmange," Aunt Cornelia said.

"All sounds rather jiggly," I said. I took my seat at the side of the table and fluffed my napkin.

"The girl who helps out," Aunt Cornelia said. "I'm teaching her to cook. Today was gelatin." That was why the house smelled funny; they had spent the morning rendering gelatin from bones and cartilage.

I nodded and slid into my chair. I might sneak a sandwich home on the day the lesson turned to tripe.

Winnie sat opposite me.

The girls whispered at the end of the table. I gave them a sharp look, but they did not seem to notice me.

Aunt Cornelia served a shivery plate to Winnie. "How are you holding up, girl?" Before Winnie could answer, she turned to me. "I said she could stay. That's why I called you. That and you needed to get here before the whole thing turned to goo."

I looked at the plate she handed me. The tomato aspic surrounding the hard-boiled eggs was sweating profusely, and pieces of tongue protruded from the receding tide of aspic.

Winnie perched on the edge of her chair. "Okay."

"Mama, can we eat on the back porch?" Teddie turned toward the back porch to point as if I might not know where it lurked.

I wanted to say, "No! I'm your mother. Come sit by me and like my friend," but I knew that wouldn't help at all. I nodded, and the girls took their slippery meal to where a slight sea breeze moved the hot, damp air around and their dinner might stay solid a little longer. Mine was at the point where I would need a spoon to eat it, or possibly a straw.

Jinxie hugged me, and then Teddie did.

Teddie turned to Winnie and said, "She's not wearing the same thing she was when she left the house." Then, she took her plate and headed for the back of the house.

Winnie pursed her lips and looked down her nose through her pince-nez at me.

I stabbed a bit of tongue and ate it before I could think about the less-than-congealed gelatin around it. "If you must know, I couldn't wear my other dress any longer on account of it being covered with the blood of a prostitute."

Winnie's lips remained pursed; her eyes did not grow larger. "That could be messy."

My fork clattered to the plate. I rubbed my napkin on the back of my neck beneath the wide swirls of hair that I attempted to keep fashionable despite the East Texas humidity. "I'm sure you'll read about it in the paper."

"I expect I will." Winnie sliced and ate her meal as though it were something other than dripping blobs of meat and egg. Winnie had the soul of a librarian. She didn't press for information, but waited until you offered details; then she would help.

"Aunt Cornelia said I could stay," Winnie said. "I called you, but she said I didn't need to."

"She came with the house," I said. This wouldn't have made much sense to Winnie, but it did to me. Aunt Cornelia had taken care of my late mother-in-law and had not adapted to a new, younger mistress of the house. "But I'm glad you're here."

"Thanks for letting me stay. Abelard said I could stay with him since Miss Alice insisted the returning prodigal stay at her place, but I needed to get away."

I looked up from my plate to smile at Winnie.

"I won't be here for long, I promise." Winnie leaned back an inch, reared the chair back, and stiffened. "Just until I figure out something to do."

I picked up my fork and set it back down. "I don't think I can eat another bite."

"Does it have hemlock in it?" Winnie made a jab at what remained of her tongue with her fork. "That might help." She took the last bite. "I doubt it would." She smiled at Aunt Cornelia, who took her plate and passed a smaller one to her and to me. This plate held a cream-colored dome with fruit sprayed on top. "Unless you sent it to Lulu."

Aunt Cornelia muttered, "Amen to that," on her way toward the stairs.

"Lulu?"

"My pet name for Lucinda." Winnie hacked a strawberry to a red sluice with her fork. "Would a jury convict someone of murder if the person were already declared dead?"

"As your attorney, I say they shouldn't." I flapped my napkin at her. "But I doubt she would eat something we sent her."

"Damn." Winnie looked up until her glasses glinted with the afternoon sunlight through the lace curtains. "Toilet paper. Nobody pays any attention to that. Maybe we can get some of that to her coated with something."

I held my hand before my mouth as I laughed with a mouthful of blancmange. I wanted to laugh at anything I could. "I've got an ointment that does nothing but cause itching."

"That sounds good."

"We're pathetic." I set my fork on my plate. I could get a sardine sandwich from the bakery near the office. "We try to plan a murder, and the best we can do is an itchy backside."

"Besides. You're no accomplice."

"Wha--"

"I'd be in the court, brazening it out, and you'd pop up in the crowd, waving your hand and saying, 'Excuse me, Mr. Judge. I want to confess. Oh, and apologize.' " Winnie stood. "Thanks for everything. I'll help clean up and then go up to my room. I think I want to cry myself into a stupor."

I got up from the table and gave her a hug. "I've got some ideas, I'll do the research, and, well, I've got a lead that I need to follow up on."

"You don't have to--"

"Yes," I said. "I'm your attorney." And I watched her walk upstairs without mentioning anything about fees, money, or professional relationships. I assured myself this wasn't the time for negotiations.

Winnie turned back to me. "I got an invitation. I was thinking maybe, I don't know."

She started up the stairs again.

I hiked my skirts up and raced to catch up with her before she made it to the solitude of the guest room.

CHAPTER 9

I leaned against the banister at the top of the stairs for a moment to cool myself. I only had a few moments, since I didn't want to be late. Not that we could be late to a tea dance to which I had not been invited. Winnie was a half-day from being a Wyngate when she got the invitation she told me about last night. Still, I figured punctuality might endear us. The heat seemed to have pooled in steamy clouds at the top floor of my home. I walked into my bedroom. The space was cluttered with crystal dishes, china angels, and inartistic doilies on every surface in an extravaganza of the old-lady taste. This lair of my late mother-in-law was far too cute and dainty for me to feel comfortable.

I grabbed the newspaper from where I had left it on the nightstand between a ceramic dog and a frog made of seashells. I sat on the marble top of my vanity. A single-sentence article caught my attention and annoyed me enough to throw the paper to the floor.

"Does the paper have anything about the tea dance?" Winnie asked. She walked into the room with a swish of her tea gown of apricot stripes separated by lace insets, with pale green velvet ribbon at the waist and the sleeves. I was still in my underwear, having made my change from my work clothes only halfway into what I planned to wear to the Wyngate tea dance. "They may have cancelled it, but I doubt Miss Alice would do that since it didn't have to do with the wedding. Thanks for coming with me."

"Sure," I said. "I'm your friend--and your attorney. We need to keep an eye on Lucinda and find out what the family has planned." Money, I should ask for money. "And as your attorney--"

"You're going to see Miss Lucinda?" Teddie asked from outside my bedroom. She leaned against the scuffed beadboard in the hall. Her voice held a ring of excitement as though I were meeting Sarah Bernhardt, Alice Roosevelt, and the Princess of Wales rolled into one.

I held my finger up to Teddie to tell her to wait until I finished before she spoke. "And as I said, as your attorney . . ." I didn't think I could ask for money in front of my daughters, who filed in to sit on the coverlet as white as their lacy dresses. "We'll need to see how the Wyngates are accepting the return of the prodigal." I turned a smile to the girls on my bed. "Yes, I'm going to see Miss Lucinda today. I want to ask her about going to Louisiana. You see, she left on the day after the storm."

Teddie's eyes wandered around the room, and Jinxie's finger traced the pattern of lace on her skirt. Louisiana probably meant little more than the moon to them.

"I just want you girls to know that I don't think Miss Lucinda is the most honest person in the world." I pointed at Jinxie's feet and pointed to the side so she would get her shoes off my bedspread. She and her sister shuffled to the edge of the bed so their kid boots hung over the edge.

Teddie eyeballed me but did not say anything that could get her switched. Jinxie had become transfixed by a walnut shelf on the wall with a small surface crowded by a sleeping cherub, a hobnail milk pitcher, and a rooster who appeared to have lost a section of his beak in a bar fight. "I'm going to find out everything I can about Miss Lucinda, but don't worry. If it's good, I'll tell it also."

Winnie made a tiny sneer, but the smile that followed it showed she only jested.

"I'm not going to hide anything about her from you," I told the girls. I stared at them, waiting for a reply.

They said nothing. Jinxie still stared at the battered china rooster.

"You'll have to trust me," I said.

Eyes downcast, Teddie gave a shrug so small it didn't even make it to both shoulders and said, "Okay, we trust you."

Jinxie turned to me and nodded.

I slipped on my dimity tea dress of gray and white stripes interrupted by red flowers and trimmed with cherry-colored ribbons. I sniffed and pretended not to feel tears sting the back of my eyes, but the girls seemed to trust me and that made me misty. Before Winnie could do up my buttons, I rushed to the bed, grabbed both girls, and hugged them. I said nothing of what I felt, nothing except, "I love you. I love you both so much."

"So, you got a plan?" Winnie twisted the doorbell. She approached this house with an ease I did not feel. This was my second time here, and I had the same feeling that I needed to look around to see who stared at me.

The ring sounded throughout the large house.

"Mingle, drink some tea, pass around a few compliments," I said. "And get Lulu aside to ask a few questions." I hoped there were people within and a party. The social embarrassment of arriving a second time when everyone had been uninvited would sting, and even as loose of a plan as mine would fall apart if we were not welcomed into the house with partygoers.

The old black man answered the door. He once probably filled out his morning coat, but now it draped in the shoulders and gaped around the neck. He gave a moderately toothless smile to Winnie and stepped back to let us in.

I put my visiting card on the heaping stack of them in the carved box on a stand. The wide doors between the dining room and front parlor had been left open and furniture cleared away to make a large dance floor. A pianist and violinist in the corner worked away on the "Dance of the Hours" as conversation swelled and dropped around the buffet table. No one danced, at least not yet, but instead clustered around the massive silver trays and china plates laden with crustless sandwiches, croquettes, and smoked oysters.

Winnie walked over the parquetry of the floor and stopped in the center of the room, swaying from side to side as she peered through her pince-nez at who had showed.

I caught her elbow and hustled her toward the crowd. "We can spot folks as we go."

I didn't recognize anyone yet, but most people had their backs to me. Breaking into them and looking as though I were an invited guest would be difficult, but I had Winnie at my side. She had an invitation, and that gave legitimacy to my dance slippers creaking across the wood floor.

I saw many women in white dresses and a few sprinkles of color, but I didn't see Lucinda.

"There he is," Winnie whispered. I think she caught sight of a wave of hair that stood high above the rest of the crowd clustered around the carved walnut sideboard. The sideboard boasted Battenberg lace doilies, crystal candelabra, and delicate china with hand-painted roses and forget-me-nots.

Abelard wended his way through the people and caught Winnie's elbows. His narrow tanned face creased in a smile that extended from his mouth to his eyes and even to his crows' feet. His hooded blue eyes lingered on Winnie as though nothing--or no one--else were in the room.

Winnie gave him a shy smile and leaned toward him, as though hoping he might give her a kiss, but then thought better of it and stopped.

"I don't care what anyone says," Abelard said. His voice was a little loud, as though talking to people outside his classroom was unusual for him. "I'm going to dance with you."

She bit her lip, but then pulled it free into a smile at me.

I nodded my approval. Let people see him in the arms of the fiancée who remembered him rather than the wife who did not.

He slid one arm up to her shoulder and the other down to her hand to spin her onto the area cleared for a dance floor. He might have wanted to hold her close in a waltz, but with a couple of dashes across the violin strings, the orchestra started a stately Lancer's Quadrille, and he dropped his hands to hers as they greeted the other couples on the floor.

"I'm so glad you came," Abelard said to Winnie in what he probably thought was a whisper. Another couple followed them onto the floor, and then another.

Her reply was too soft for me to hear, but she said it through a smile.

I had to figure out what to do besides stand alone near the dance floor. I looked around and saw no Lucinda. I figured she was someone I knew with whom I could strike up a conversation. And I would question and question until she threw a cup of tea in my face, but I would smile and act cordially.

"Not exactly respectable," I heard a woman whisper behind me. I turned for a quick glance back to see an elegant, narrow woman with dark eyes following the moves of the dancers. I recognized her companion, the little rosy-cheeked woman with blonde hair haloing her head. She was the one married to Sextus. The brunette said to her, "Eula Rose, you must have been shocked when he didn't even wait a year to remarry."

I turned away far enough to offer an innocent glance at a potted palm while I listened to them.

"His little boy needs a mommy," Eula Rose said. Her voice had a slightly pinched tone that veered toward baby talk when she spoke of the child.

"And where is his mommy?" the woman said. Her scoffing tone made me turn to face them. I saw she looked past me to where men walked down the wide hall with a rear door open to bring in the breeze off the Gulf.

I heard no reply, so I smiled at the dark-haired woman. "Have you seen Lucinda?" She looked at Eula Rose.

I also looked at the diminutive woman in ruffles and roses. She didn't look at either of us but stared at the dancers as though she did not see our gaze. Her flush and fidget showed that she had heard me. This silence thing sometimes worked for me, so I kept staring until I bore a hole or got an answer.

Eula Rose turned toward me with a blink of surprise as though she hadn't seen me before. "May I help you?"

"We were just wondering whether you'd seen Lucinda." I gestured toward the brunette to try to draw her in as an ally.

She took a step back and bumped into Beau. He gave a gracious smile before turning back to the sideboard, laden with raised china stands bearing food.

Eula Rose tilted her head and looked up at me. "You're the attorney lady working for Winnie, aren't you?"

"Well, today I'm here as her friend."

Eula's glance strayed to the dance floor, as did the brunette's. I looked and saw Winnie and the other women skip between the male dancers before Abelard caught her around the waist rather than just hold hands for the promenade.

By the time I turned back, I saw the brunette and Eula Rose had walked to the arched doorway to continue their conversation on the terrace.

The music stopped and a few people applauded.

Winnie walked up to me and slid her arm around my waist. She smiled at me. "You look like you've been losing weight, so you must be hungry." She steered me toward the stands of diminutive sandwiches, cakes, and scones.

I took a slice of salmon on dark bread and put it on a little plate with bouquets of forget-me-nots painted over the gold-rimmed surface.

Winnie took a scone and covered it with a dollop of clotted cream. "Did you realize Jack the Ripper wasn't the only maniac like that in London at the time?" She took a bite of a petit four and gave a nod that she would explain as soon as she finished chewing. "You were looking at the china. It's beautiful. The whole display is."

I nodded, figuring this was the best way to get her to explain why fine china made her think of a brutal murder.

"Miss Alice collected all of it--and I think her love of afternoon tea--when the family lived in England." Winnie took another bite and looked around the room. She must have spied Abelard, since she smiled and gave a little wave of her lacy glove. "Ask Abelard about it. He was studying there and said that bodies kept washing up from the Thames--that's why the china reminded me. Also, that item in the paper today."

"Fascinating," I said to the sandwiches I piled on my plate. I did not look at Winnie or let her see my face flush at the mention of that article in the paper.

"You know," Winnie said. "The one about the prostitute's body found in the alley, her throat cut. Was that the one you said got blood on your skirt?"

I took a bite of a small sandwich filled with nutmeats. "Officer of the court, you know I can't say anymore."

The newspaper article had been two sentences and half of it lies, I didn't have a client involved, but I felt the need to stay quiet.

Winnie's chewing slowed as she became thoughtful, an abstract academian who could talk about the details of a murder over canapés. "Actually, it was just parts of bodies that washed up."

An older woman reached for a scone, turned a pinched frown on Winnie and me, and moved away without any food.

I poured myself a cup of tea and stood very still to keep the cup from rattling on the saucer. "I never heard about that," I said. "I just heard about the prostitutes that were victims of the Ripper."

"These were prostitutes, too." Winnie used the tongs to add a cube of sugar to her tea.

"Just body parts? How did they know the women were--"

"Tattoos. Prostitutes tend to have them." Winnie took a bite of a roast beef and cucumber sandwich and straightened her pince-nez as she looked over the offerings on the food table. "Abelard studied the case. He figures that prostitutes tend to be victims because they lose the fight or flight response that the rest of us have. Ask him about his theories sometime."

And how I would!

"Oh," Winnie said. "We're going to dance again. He says he doesn't care that his mother and Eula Rose look as though they're trying to kill us with their eyes." Her index and middle finger traced the invisible magic beams from her own eyes to those across the room. She smiled at a maid and handed her the empty plate.

Abelard darted to her side and smiled at her with a loving look, holding his eyes on her.

She gave a shy smile in return and let him take her out to the dance floor.

I looked around and saw no one I knew. I didn't feel like engaging in conversation with any of the ladies standing nearby who heard us talking about tattooed body parts. Down the wide hallway beyond this room, Sextus spoke with another man in an unseasonably dark suit.

I finished my sandwiches and stalked behind them. I could head toward the powder room and get a little eavesdropping in.

"Storm scare," the man with Sextus said. He echoed the news reports of people fearing another deadly hurricane almost a year after over 8,000 were killed, and life for us survivors was changed by the Great Storm. "Got all sorts of people leaving town, leaving it and taking their money."

Sextus' raised his shoulders in a shrug. "I hear things are bound to get better. I don't see it." He put his hand on the man's shoulder and steered him through the gentlemen's parlor and out the oak door to the smoking porch.

On light steps, I walked down the hall. The space was dark with only a single gaslight protruding from the black walnut, carved with acorns and acanthus leaves. I assumed a powder room would be back here somewhere. I passed the dining room with its massive chandelier over a carved mahogany table and then the narrow butler's pantry with a plain oak dumbwaiter and longleaf pine counters behind it. The room was empty and, although clean, dust motes floated in the still air. I walked farther down the empty hall and away from the music and chatter in the main parlor.

"Please," someone whispered.

A very slight whisper. I realized I shouldn't have heard it over the talk, laughter, and music from the ballroom, but I was sure I had heard it.

"Please," it whispered again. I couldn't get a direction on the sound. It might have been in my head.

CHAPTER 10

      I walked back to the butler's pantry. No one was within. No one could have been there to ask me, "Please," and then run away without my seeing them in the hall.

      Stepping into the small room, I smelled the acrid dust, and then something else, a slight, tart smell, like lemon verbena. That smell was gone in an instant and the room quiet.

      "A room with a presence, is it not?" a woman asked behind me, making me jump and gasp.

      I turned to see a handsome, buxom woman with dark hair, dark eyes, and elegantly long nose.

      She was swathed in lavender and purple silk from high neckline to lengthy train and held up a hand with a flutter of fabric and oriental-spiced perfume. "A thin place." She turned a smile on me that spread across her face but did not light her cheeks or those sad, dark eyes.

      "Thin place?"

      "The Celtic Christians, ancient folk, believed heaven and earth were only three feet apart." She raised her head and gave the air a deep sniff. "In some places, that distance all but disappears." She moved her hands slowly above her face as though feeling for the thin spots. "Those are thin places." She extended a hand to me. "Hello, I am Madame Sylvie."

Not wanting to be in that creepy room with an equally creepy woman, I smiled and slipped past her back into the hallway.

"I am a psychic medium," Madame Sylvie said.

"Oh, are you now?" I raised an eyebrow.

"Yes, I also was called here by the vibrations." She looked toward the ceiling and took a deep breath.

"Vibrations?" I was more comfortable as a smirking skeptic than as a wide-eyed devotee of the realms of magic. If anything was trapped in there from another realm, it would have to be evil to have the power--and even the desire--to come to earth.

"Yes," Madame Sylvie said. "Through the thinness in this place, those ones you felt." She skewered me with her dark eyes. "Or heard, you heard them." She gave a satisfied nod at her diagnosis and turned away.

I stumbled back into the ballroom. I smoothed my sleeves and bodice as though that would ease the jitters in my mind.

Something had said, "Please," to me. I could not imagine what. Actually, I did not want to imagine what, but I could not help but look over my shoulder to see if something was gaining on me as I walked down that corridor that seemed to grow longer with each step. Even the sound of the orchestra and the trill of a woman's voice were slow and labored sounds in my ears.

"Please," the whisper came again from back down the hall.

I forced myself to concentrate on something else. I wondered about Lucinda, where she was and if she knew that prostitute who had come to Galveston at the same time as she. Why wasn't Lucinda here? Was she out with the Guy of the love letter and the prostitute's tattoo? Was she hiding from the intimidating Wyngates? Why had she returned to Galveston?

My thoughts had taken me to no discovery, but I was back in the ballroom, and there was music. The violin and clarinet started, and then the rest of the band joined in the swirling waltz from Gounod's *Romeo and Juliet*. I knew it, since I had a gramophone cylinder with it at home. The live music was more beautiful and so romantic that I felt myself sway.

A couple bumped into me. They were so young his collar left ample room around his Adam's apple, and she had ringlets. She giggled out an, "Excuse me," and danced on.

"You're standing in the middle of the dance floor," Barker said. "Dancing alone."

I looked around and saw that my steps fleeing from whatever had spooked me in the hall had driven me all the way out to the center of the dance floor. I could not contrive an explanation that would get anything other than a laugh from Barker, so I gave him a little shrug that gave a little flutter of gossamer fabric. I looked into his deep blue eyes and wondered what a practical, evidence-loving man like Barker would say about the conversation I had with Madame Sylvie.

"Oh, very well." He gave me a curt bow and took my hand. He slid his arm around my back and took my hand. He was close enough that I could smell a little Florida Water and enough exertion to reveal he was a man, but not to offend.

Barker spun through the steps of a waltz with a grace I had not expected of him. I considered saying this, but he spoke before I could. "The Wyngates want me to find out where Lucinda was these past few months."

"Thank you for telling me, Barker."

"No matter, my client said I could."

"But you asked."

"Because I knew you'd want to know." His arm on my waist gripped tighter as he navigated our way around the fireplace and andirons, edging the dance floor.

I frowned at the realization that he wasn't giving me anything information-wise and was certainly not offering to help me make Winnie's case legally, but I brightened at another thought. "So, you're free to tell me why Alice screamed? She did, when you were in your office, I heard her make a loud gaspy-scream."

"Gaspy-scream?"

"Yes." I stiffened, which made me stumble. "Somewhere between the two."

Barker pulled me so close that I rested against his chest as he navigated his way around a potted palm and back to the dance floor. "What you heard was her reaction when I suggested blackmail."

"Blackmail?"

"Aye, I made a wee mention of blackmail." He raised his hand and led me through a quick spin with a swish of my skirts.

"And they still hired you?" I laughed.

"Remember, Molly's maid suspected Lucinda."

"Yes, yes, of course. What did she--did Alice--say?"

"Didn't want to give too much information. So I just asked if she knew anything about blackmail. 'My husband would never do such a thing.' "

"Strange response. What did her husband say about that?"

Barker smiled at me as we spun in the sunshine from the windows. "So, are you officially working on Abelard's divorce petition yet?"

I looked away from his face, but managed to see the crinkle of a smile at the edge of his eye. "No," I said. "No, I haven't talked to anyone about money yet."

"Then you're not really on the case," he whispered in my ear.

Closing my eyes, I leaned into him and felt his arms around me. I did like the feel of the man.

Stop it! I blinked my eyes open so fast, Barker pulled far enough away to look at me in concern.

"Have you heard of a Celtic belief about some places being close to the spirit world because the air is thin there?" I blurted. "Or something? You're a Celt. I thought you might."

"Did you see a ghost, Mrs. Gallagher?" His smile was large, and his eyes twinkled in a way I could never distinguish between good-natured teasing and nasty mocking.

"I heard something," I admitted.

He said nothing, but spun me in an elegant move. In response to my smile he said, "I prefer an eightsome reel, but this will do. So, tell me what you heard."

"A noise, a person who wasn't there."

"Intriguing."

"Not really," I said. "Some people here, well, they don't want to think of so many loved ones being gone. I mean, dead children and everything. I can see how people want to believe that some part of them might linger." I pressed close to him again, allowing myself the comfort of his muscular body. "But I'm a Christian. I believe that if something does come back, it hasn't come from the nice part of the spiritual world."

I expected Barker to give some scoffing reply that reflected the fashionable man's acceptance of science as a religion, but he gave a thoughtful look and said, "The disciples thought Jesus a ghost when He appeared after the resurrection. They knew what a ghost would be." He gave that teasing-mocking smile again. "No doubt, they knew about those thin places."

I shot a glance toward the hallway and saw what it was: an empty hallway, with no life and no death within.

The waltz ended with a few closing plucks of the violin. Barker released me from his grasp and walked away without a word.

"There you are, Mrs. Gallagher," Miss Alice said. She extended one of her long hands, and I shook it. "Would you do a favor for me?"

I smiled. I never had been able to commit to doing something before I heard what it was, even for someone as formidable as Miss Alice. "What do you need?"

I drifted to sleep after tossing in bed and having to unwind myself from the sheets a couple of times.

Once again, thoughts of a prostitute's dead eyes staring at me and intestines hanging like curtain swags kept jolting me to a wakeful state. I must have drifted to sleep, because my mind wandered to the Wyngate Mansion.

The front door gaped, and I walked through. The butler was not in the entryway; no one was. I wandered over Persian rugs and past carved furniture. I was alone. I stood and listened. I heard nothing, but I felt a breeze on my skin, a light breeze that seemed to come down the huge, carved staircase toward me. I grabbed the banister and felt the dark, cool wood slide through my hand.

I walked upstairs, not sure what I would see, but sure that I would find something.

The breeze grew strong enough to give a slow flutter to the tapestry hanging along the stairway and bring a faint, sweet-sour smell, like freesias. I walked over the boards of the upstairs corridor and heard them creak beneath my feet.

The door to the balcony was probably open. Mansion or shack, that was how most of us cooled the house this time of year, by opening the back and front doors to allow the ocean wind through the center of the house and trapping the air to provide a little cooler temperature in the heat of midday.

This floor was also empty. I walked through the corridor, past bedroom doors hanging open. Above the doors, transoms tilted open to catch the breeze, but the windowed door to the back balcony remained closed and still.

I stumbled, a bit unsure. I was not quite scared, but some emotion, some hesitation swelled within me.

Where was the breeze from? The blow was not strong, but it was so constant, it billowed my skirts and threatened to raise me from the floor.

I reached the end of the hallway and looked out the window, but saw nothing out there. Everything was blurred, and I could not clear my eyes. I fought to clear my vision and see out the window, but some pull--someone pulling on me--tore me from the window.

In an instant, I was outside, far above the house. Then, I was up another staircase, a narrow spiral staircase. I was within the tower. I tried fighting against the pull but could not. I was exhausted and out of breath. My energy flagged, and I realized I was still moving. I stopped struggling and felt an ease. I floated up the stairs toward the closed door to the round room at the top of the tower.

A man--I did not see his face--walked toward me and did not stop. He walked through me.

I felt myself overcome with goose bumps at the feeling of a man brushing through me, but continued up toward the small room at the top of a tower where a black-haired woman had her back to me. She leaned over something that I could not see.

I climbed the narrow stairs toward her.

She turned to me. She was a black woman with a kind smile showing her beautiful, white teeth. She rubbed her stomach in the manner of a pregnant woman, although she was slender with a tight waist beneath her white apron and black dress. Her smile stretched until it was a rictus of death. It stretched farther until the skin slid from her nose and eye sockets. She was death, one of the dead bodies I had seen wash back on shore after being dropped at sea after the Great Storm.

I drew away from her. Fear filled me and cut off my breath. I felt myself fall through the shadowy house and kept falling until I saw the darkness of earth around me. No, not earth: I was in the water. I heard the roar of wind and was in the Great Storm, but this was not where I had experienced the storm. I was not bracing within my large, columned house that spun off its foundation, but was still in the Wyngates' mansion. I was in the basement and saw the half-windows above the ground crack to let muddy water ooze in.

My skirts caught on some piece of furniture, and I went under. I saw the woman's face again. She must have just died, since she hung there in the murky water, her large eyes hanging open and her mouth drooping. Behind her was the dumbwaiter that I had seen open to the butler's pantry a floor above.

My lungs hurt, but I still had some breath. I yanked my skirts. Nothing happened. I yanked them again and was free. I swam to the surface and took a gulp of breath. I was only a couple of inches from the brick ceiling.

The window glass shattered, and water blasted through the opening. I struggled to find any space above the water. I took the last breath I could find and swam toward the drowned woman. I pressed her aside to climb into the large dumbwaiter. If I could work it, I could get to safety on one of the floors above.

I pulled my body into the dumbwaiter and grabbed the rope controlling it but could not make it budge. Bubbles of spent air poured from me. I pulled again, but it did not move. I eased the remaining air from my lungs and felt the turgid water fill me. I stopped struggling and felt death float through me.

    The dead black woman's hand grabbed my shoulder.

CHAPTER II

I sat up and took a deep breath in the darkness of my bedroom. A dream, it had been a dream, but I gasped for breath and felt my arms covered with goose bumps. I'd never had a dream that did gave me a physical response, like goose bumps, but it was also the first dream in which I'd ever felt things and even smelled them.

I got up to get some water or go to the bathroom, anything to dispel that dream. I felt shaken. I could not see anything in the dark. I heard rain pound against the house.

Footsteps rubbed the lacquered wood of the stairs.

I reached across my bed and felt through the darkness for the nightstand drawer. My eyes were not becoming accustomed to the dark. I realized this was because the night was cloudy and moonless. I felt through the powder compress and medicine bottles, but found nothing. I remembered that I no longer had a gun. I grabbed the rooster with a broken beak. I figured I could throw it and use it as a distraction to get to the girls. I crept from the bed and opened the door a crack.

Winnie waved at me. She still wore her street clothes: yellow dotted fabric, corseted shape, and all.

"Couldn't sleep?" I looked at the clock and made out three o'clock.

Winnie shook her head. "And I've always been something of a night owl. I thought a walk might cool me off."

I climbed back in my bed, flipped over the sweat-covered pillow, and fell into a dreamless asleep in moments.

I woke before the alarm. I braced for it to ring, since that often happened just moments after I woke. I always wondered what caused that. In an instant, I realized what made me wake. The telephone in the alcove below the stairs rang. Two long, one short, three long. That was my ring, but I had never received a call this early in the morning.

"Hello, hello," I practiced, then grabbed the candlestick telephone and answered. "Hello, this is Mrs. Gallagher."

"This is Mrs. Wyngate." The telephone made a human voice sound like something from a can of peaches, but I thought it sounded like Miss Alice.

"Yes, Ma'am, I'll be there today. I promise."

"Thank you, dear. I'd like to speak to Winnie." I held the receiver to my breast and called to my friend in my loudest voice.

Teddie looked outside her sister's room.

"Good morning, darling."

She ducked back into the room. Jinxie came out to blow a kiss toward me and then sank back inside.

Winnie wandered from her bedroom with Dewey the cat in her arms. A messy braid sat over the shoulder of her lacy nightgown. Her eyes were red, but she saw the telephone I held toward her. She kissed the top of Dewey's head, set him down, and took the telephone.

"Hello?" she mumbled. She listened. She nodded several times. "Thank you for letting me know . . . Do you know why? Hmm . . . Bye-bye." She hung up and looked at me. She opened her mouth in an attempt to say something, but no words came out.

I dashed into the dining room, filled a small glass from a decanter that had been half-full since my mother-in-law had the place, and took it to Winnie. "I hope this hasn't turned to vinegar."

Winnie took a small sip, gave a little wince, and then drank a little more. "That was Miss Alice."

I nodded.

Winnie yawned widely enough for me to see a gold tooth at the back of her molars. "Lucinda didn't come home yesterday."

"Oh," I said. I worked out a scenario where this helped Winnie by ceasing the interference from an estranged wife, and another scenario where it caused tie-ups because abandonment would be harder to prove if the abandoner showed up and then disappeared. "Oh."

"Miss Alice thinks she's run off again. Seems Lucinda's been afraid of Mr. Wyngate for a long time."

"Yes, randy old fellow," I said from the dining room where I filled my own small glass with claret that seemed to have grown thicker over time. The taste was sweet, almost like drinking corn syrup, but not too bad.

"Oh, you know him," Winnie said. She forced a little smile at me as I walked back in the room. She blinked her nearsighted eyes at me. "I've always found him harmless, but Abelard says that's because he knows a woman who could cause him grievous harm."

I laughed. Winnie didn't, but some people didn't when they joked. I could never tell when people were joking, so I just laughed at what I thought was funny. I thought of Winnie and her interest in dismembered bodies and stopped laughing.

"He made a grab for Lucinda at supper the night before last--the night before the tea dance--and she stormed out. They haven't seen her since."

I set the claret glass down on the sideboard. I had only had one sip, but I had to get to the office and get some work done before I performed the favor I had promised to Miss Alice.

I opened my parasol toward the sun, straightened the short, speckled necktie I had affixed to my shirtwaist, and took a place before the steps of the stone church. Last night might have howled with rain so hard, it reminded everyone of the power of the Gulf, but today shone with a hot clear sun.

Behind me, I glanced to where a great bell tower once soared skyward. Now, the roof held only an expanse of oilskin tarpaulin that rippled like waves on the Gulf, in the same hue of greenish brown.

Memories of my time in Russia before I was adopted by an American family blurred together into colors, a curve of architecture, the pain of a stone curb when I remembered sleeping in the street, and a snatch of conversation when a woman said, "Rain on a wedding--new enterprise--is lucky." I don't know what sunshine on a thwarted wedding day meant.

I looked down the street. Good, no one was here.

Miss Alice had made calls on most of the guests and told them not to expect a wedding, but she had not been able to catch everyone. She said I could reach her at the bank if I had any trouble shooing people away.

I wasn't sure what words to use if someone did walk up the sidewalk expecting a wedding and breakfast after, but I didn't expect to have any trouble. I wanted to ask Alice why she would go to the bank. Was she also a woman in business as I was? But the Wyngates did not seem to encourage questioning.

I looked at the small watch under a diamond bow, pinned to my red and blue-trimmed dress. The wedding would have started in twenty minutes. I figured I should have arrived here early to hit some especially eager types, and there was always the lonely dowager or two who didn't know anyone but went to any wedding they saw advertised in the paper.

An older couple--a short, curved woman leaning against her husband, who was wearing a morning coat and top hat--made a slow progression to the church.

I lit from the last step. "There isn't to be a wedding this morning." I ventured a slight smile without teeth. "It's been . . . uh . . . postponed."

The old woman looked at me from beneath the large, black plume of her hat. "What?"

"We're just going for a walk." The man straightened up and looked as if he might beat me off with his walking stick if I spoke to him any more of marriage or such things.

I twirled my parasol in my hand and walked back and forth the length of my selected step. I figured that made me look a little less predatory to anyone else who happened to be just taking his or her morning constitutional.

"You here to shoo any stray guests away?"

I turned and saw MJ standing behind me. She wore a hat of feathers, veiling, and straw of a green so deep and still so bright that all spring seemed to burst forth, tipped there on her red hair, and her lawn muslin had sprigs of an only slightly tamer green.

"Yes." I stepped up to her. "Someone was supposed to be here from the groom's side as well, but I don't think he was needed."

"You can hold back the screaming hordes?"

I grinned. "I've already scared off a charming elderly couple."

MJ leaned past me to see the couple still visibly making their slow progress down the street. "They'll survive." She sat on the steps and waved a glove to indicate I should sit beside her. "I'm here to help, ducky," MJ said. "I've done the research on our bolting friend, Lucinda. You were right."

"She was right?" Winnie said. She raised the skirt of her white linen dress to walk up the steps to join us. "Strange things do happen." She shook her head at me. "Remember that thing I told you about called 'joking?' "

"That was it?"

Winnie sat beside me and patted my arm. "You just go on thinking that." She puffed out an "Oh" at what must have been the look on my face and said, "Yes, that was kidding."

MJ looked past me to Winnie. "Look at the three of us sitting here. We'll see no wedding, hear no wedding, and damn, no wedding."

Winnie forced a little laugh.

"You don't have to be here," MJ said.

She let out a sigh and looked down the street. "I didn't have anything else to do."

"So what was I right about?" I asked. I remembered having called MJ a few days ago to see whether she could find out anything about Lucinda just having come from Louisiana. "She just came in from Louisiana."

MJ put a finger on the tip of her nose, pointed another at me, and gave a wink. "An unescorted woman on September twelfth took the *Mexican* to New Orleans." MJ pulled a leather notebook from her petit point chatelaine purse. She thumbed through a few pages. "The 'Miss Smith' paid for her passage in gold coins, one of the crewmen remembers. A diminutive woman with long, brown hair."

"That was her," Winnie said. "Or no."

MJ and I both looked at her.

"That was she," Winnie corrected herself.

MJ turned to the next page in her notebook. "Newspaper shows what we all know and love about her: charity fundraiser, patron of the Confederate Home, and lunch companion to the city's elite, but I talked to a reporter who interviewed her mother once." MJ looked up from the notebook to squint at the sky for a memory. "Seems the paper sent someone out to talk to her after there was a run on the Wyngate bank. The Wyngates all went into hiding, and the closest they could get to someone involved was Lucinda's mother." MJ flipped through a number of pages. "And did that woman ever love to talk! One of the gems she tossed out there that didn't make the print was that Lucinda ran away as a sixteen-year-old."

"So, this wasn't her first bolt," I said.

MJ nodded. "Seems no one knows where she was for a couple of years after the father died. Mother--Mrs. Dumont--told the nice young reporter she was worried because Lucinda was always off to find adventure of some type. No telling what 'adventure' meant to mother or to the bumptious girl."

Winnie gave a conspiratorial squint. "I'd say it was raw, fresh sex."

"I'd say it was eating her salad with the dinner fork," MJ said. "The reporter who talked to Mrs. Dumont said she had standards. Such standards that even her standards had standards. And none of them ever had any fun."

I ventured, "Could she have been a . . . a soiled dove?" That would make a connection between her and the dead prostitute.

Winnie raised her eyebrows high above her glasses.

"Not likely!" MJ turned another page. "When she came back, she was an actress with a successful road company performing *East Lynne*."

"Not everyone can hold the lofty profession of librarian," Winnie said.

"Yes, but during that first absence, she was a magician's assistant for a while."

"Really?" I asked.

"Yes, a fellow who said he'd found where the Confederate gold was buried and would tell all to those who came to his performance." She turned back a page in the notebook. "Nothing about him after that."

"Of course not," Winnie said. "He's probably lying low abroad with all those gold bars."

I laughed first, and then the other two did.

MJ ran her finger down the small page of her notebook. "Well, if he found anything, he didn't share it with Lucinda Dumont, because she became a dancer in vaudeville." MJ flashed a smile. "That one was hard to find. It only came up because the theater where she was working burned, and she was one of three girls rescued from a second-floor dressing room."

"May have worked burlesque," I said. Lucinda was the only person I knew to have any relation to that prostitute at all. Maybe the association was more than just having come to town on the same ship.

MJ nodded, but waved off my train of thought with a smirk. "But that's still not being a prostitute. We show many theater jobs to cover that time, with almost no gaps where she would have had to go on the gay. Besides, when she came back, all was right with the world. She and mother had a charming reunion--which made page six of our beloved news--and then ensued a serious round of husband-hunting when mother caught Abelard Wyngate in her sights and held onto him until the young couple fell in love, or at least said that they did."

"Anything on where she was on the current outing?" I asked.

MJ gave a little nod and turned another page. "New Orleans theater company had a pirate evening last year to raise money for charity, and the leading lady, Lucinda Dumont, told how she was an expert at pirate lore and had been to places along the Gulf of Mexico where the pieces of eight float up onshore every day." She smirked. "Seems she wished the doubloons would wash ashore to fund the boys' and girls' club. Isn't that just precious?"

"Amazing you found all that," I said. "Thank you."

"Thank Winnie."

Winnie, who had been staring up at a bird's nest in the damaged and neglected church steeple, swiveled her head around like a cocker spaniel trying to determine from whence Master had called.

"The woman who catalogues people by their names guards that information as if it were the treasure the forty thieves told her no one could see, but she is a librarian. Once she heard you were one as well, the whole Moroccan-bound sisterhood kicked in, and she was all, all too happy to help."

"We're like that. We're working up a handshake." Her hands made little chopping motions.

I drawled out a sentence that I hoped would ride gently on the breeze and not startle anyone. "Do you think Lucinda could have been involved in something, say, like blackmail?"

An old man at the sidewalk gave a big smile.

I returned the smile, but did not approach him until he ascended the steps. "The wedding has been postponed. They'll send out a notice when they reschedule."

"Winnie, you came to your senses and fled?"

I gave a polite laugh.

MJ folded her arms across her chest. "You're obviously from the bride's side."

"Don't be so sure." He winked at her and then hopped down the steps and away.

MJ and I looked to Winnie, who shrugged. "Not a clue." Winnie peered at me through her glasses. "You think someone might have been blackmailing Lucinda?"

"No," I said. I did a quick assessment of what would be secret since I had been hired by Molly Perkins. "I was wondering if you thought she might have the sand to do that to someone."

Winnie smiled and made a quick, quiet series of claps.

MJ gave me a sideways glance and only after a moment remembered to tip her head back to make her nose look straighter. "Something like that wouldn't go well in her social circle. She'd be ostracized."

"Might even have to end up bolting," I said.

MJ and Winnie looked at me, but I offered no more information.

A small woman bobbed up the steps to us with prominent eyes behind pale lashes and china rose cheeks: Eula Rose.

"Mrs. Wyngate." MJ stepped in front of me and extended a lacy gloved hand.

Eula Rose gave out a sigh. "I thought Sextus would be here. He . . . he had to work. I'd have been here sooner, but Alois wanted to talk, and I just didn't have the heart to tell him no after what he's going through."

Alois? I knew who he was because of the slump of Winnie's shoulders. He was Abelard's young son whom Winnie had cared for since the storm, the boy I knew she loved as much as his father. This would be far worse than what my daughters were going through as they adjusted to being my daughters.

"She's a reporter." I jabbed my parasol toward MJ. "MJ Quackenbush."

Young Mrs. Wyngate's big eyes scrunched into a frown.

I stood and dusted off my backside. "Hello. I'm--"

"Mrs. Gallagher, the attorney." She slid a glance down at Winnie. "I remember meeting you. Both of you." She gave out a sound that was as much bitter sigh as mirthful laugh.

Winnie stepped up to her. "How is the boy doing?"

She shrugged and turned away from us to look down the street. A drayman on a lazy horse clopped along the side street, but nothing else moved on this morning.

MJ clambered to her feet. "Yes, how is he? He's about the age of your son, isn't he?"

Eula Rose replied, "He doesn't know everything yet. I don't even know how much he would understand. He's only four." She gave Winnie a smile. "Abelard is . . ." She shot a glance at MJ.

MJ turned her back on us to examine a section of the church where once a spire stood, but now a tarp covered the uneven opening.

Eula Rose turned those round eyes back to me. "The man had his whole world changed. He's bearing up as well as can be expected. I think he just wants to be left alone."

I thought of my daughters, of their new speculation that their original mother was somehow not dead but impressing her personality on someone, and of their obsession with Lucinda. I wanted her gone because of my limited association. Abelard must be desperate to get rid of her. "If I were in that situation, I expect I would be apoplectic."

MJ turned a green eye toward me, but then looked past. "Isn't that your Mr. Barker?"

"He's hardly my . . . where?" I forced myself not to spin around in search of him.

She tipped an eyebrow toward the intersection.

I turned around and saw the fast stride and straight posture of my office landlord.

MJ started forward, but then felt my parasol block her path.

"The detective?" Eula Rose also craned to see. "I heard he explored for the source of the Nile. Is he a friend of the bride's? Oh, of yours, Mrs. Gallagher? I keep forgetting you're here. It's such a surprise to see you in such a place."

"He's a man I know." A man who gave me his best Saturday-night kiss and now acts as though I shot his dog.

A young couple holding hands strolled up to the steps. Eula Rose walked down the steps to them before any of the rest of us could.

Barker did not turn off on another street but instead continued up to the steps. He stood an inch or two below me.

"How did you find me here?" I fought the grin tugging at my mouth.

'You told me." His overhanging brow furrowed. "Twice, and you left a note."

"Yes, if you found something out." I gave a twitch of the thumb toward Winnie. "Since I'm her attorney, investigating a divorce petition in her honor."

Winnie sat staring at the ground below the steps.

"Have you found something out, Barker?" I stood still, but acknowledged MJ by scrunching my mouth in that direction.

"Come with me, Dash." He tipped his hat to MJ and to Eula Rose.

CHAPTER 12

I looked at the watch pinned to my shirtwaist.

"Go on." Eula Rose waved me away. "I can handle it if anyone else comes." She pasted a smile on her face.

I started to say goodbye, but she was already down the steps and a couple yards away to talk to a middle-aged woman with two young girls, all three with the same round face.

MJ stood beside me. "Mrs. Wyngate there is a member of the cream of New York society. She should be able to keep the wedding guests at bay." She whispered in my ear. "And let me know what Barker is up to."

Barker walked half a block in silence until the houses and churches gave way to cafes and shops. "Another grisly occurrence, I fear."

I attempted a whisper but instead mouthed, "Murder?"

He nodded.

I put my parasol on my shoulder, then above my head, then beside my ear to find the best place to block the sun from between the buildings. I attempted to hold it before my face when Barker grabbed it and shepherded it to my other shoulder. "A murder like that," I said. "It was horrible. Like Jack the Ripper. You don't think . . ."

"I think more than one human heart holds that manner of darkness. These cases come up every few years around the world. I'm sure you've seen something of it in the papers."

I stopped as the evil in the world seemed to swallow me up there on the uneven cobblestones of the street that still bore the marks of where the Gulf of Mexico had roared through the streets.

He took my arm to lead me up a street of brick buildings and metal awnings that held merchants, banks, and a livery stable.

"No, I hadn't." I said. "That would have been before the flood. I read the fashion or gardening section, and that was about it, then."

Barker's mouth held a trace of smile at the edges. "And now you've learned there's a world outside of Denver Resurvey."

"Sometimes a very evil one." I allowed him to steer me around a corner, and then I stopped.

He nodded. "If you don't want to see the body, that's fine."

I did not want to see the work of some madman. I did not want to know what evil lurked in the streets, yet I could not look away. Someone, something might be waiting for a moment to come after my daughters and me.

I walked beside Barker in a neighborhood near the water. Once, houses of millwork and clapboard lined these streets with only four feet between them, but the Great Storm left only stacks of wood with the dead tangled beneath. The wood had been cleared away, and the occasional house stood alone for several miles.

Rows of canvas tents and a few storm-wood shacks leaned against the sea wind. No plants grew in the red dust. Across the dirt road, a black man in overalls made from flour sacks with a starburst pattern stared at us for a moment and then wandered back into a tent where a plank stretched across a pair of barrels. A man in a dirty apron poured beer in glasses for the customers sitting there at midday.

Saloons were probably the first businesses to come back after the tragedy. People used to say Galveston ran out of corner saloons because we ran out of street corners.

I felt as aimless and as expectant as those men within who glanced around, drank beer, but did not relax their standing posture by taking one of the rickety chairs by the pale canvas. I had no idea where we were going, and Barker had offered no explanation.

We passed a building made of mismatched lengths of whitewashed storm-wood with a scruffy brown dog sitting beside the spittoon at the door. Another saloon.

"A dead man?" I asked. This thought did not please me, but it lessened my feelings of vulnerability.

"No," he said. "My, um, friend on the police force told me it was a woman and that I should come."

"So that's why I'm here, your link to the distaff side of things."

Barker frowned at me and then looked at the dirt at his feet rather than answer.

I looked around again. "What would a woman have been doing here?" I didn't even see any prostitutes. The only female I had seen may not have been such, but rather a man in overalls who could only find a gingham bonnet to shield him from the sun.

"Not picking out a china pattern." Barker pulled his pocket watch from his vest, looked at it, and put it back. "She was found two hours and forty-five minutes ago. I imagine they would have figured a time of death by now."

We walked toward the blue-uniformed police officer with a large mustache on his round face standing outside of a tent.

Barker nodded to him.

"What are you doing here, Mr. Barker?"

"I heard you gentlemen found a body this morning." He wedged his thumbs in the armpits of his red-striped vest and rocked on his heels.

The policeman shook his head until the pointed cap on his head looked as though it might rattle free. "Bad business, that."

"Aye." Barker gave a little nod as if he knew what had happened.

"But we're taking care of--"

Barker pulled a thumb from his vest to gesture at me. "I believe she can help you identify the body."

I stiffened and then tried to affix an almost bored expression on my face so as not to let anyone know that I had.

"You want to see it, step inside." The policeman swept his hands to the side near the flap in the tent. "But I don't think the lady wants to see something like that."

"As though I haven't seen a mutilated body," I said.

The policeman gave a slow, sad nod.

"She died in there?" Barker peered at the tent, across the street to the saloon where two men took a plank from the street to augment their bar, and across the intersection to a lot piled with storm debris.

"No," he said. "Over there." He pointed across the street to the empty lot filled with dry, whitewashed boards, water-logged brown wood, broken metal railings, and part of a floor lamp that had been dumped either by the storm or its survivors.

I smiled at the policeman. "You moved the body?"

" 'Tis all right." Barker moved his straw hat back on his head. "The crime was of the nature of Jack the Ripper, too horrible to just leave her exposed as she was, inside and out. They did send a photographer around to take pictures, though."

"How did you know that, Barker?" The policeman frowned, drawing his mouth to one side.

Barker removed his hand from his pocket and pointed to the street before the lot. "Indentations indicate the tripod of the police photographer. In the site, you can see the boards have been turned over-- they're darker and wetter on the bottom. That shows you had to look far to find all the parts of the body. And the fact you took it away rather than just rest that sheet over it there all show that it was a murder most brutal." He looked at the policeman. They may have been the same height, but Barker's straight posture made him loom over the man. "And it was a woman who had been done indecently, so you could not risk people even in this neighborhood, where I ken they see a murder now and then, happening upon the body." He pointed to the corner where the men dragged the cedar plank to the bar. "You set the camera tripod on that plank to steady it."

I looked at the policeman. The furrows of his brow extended down to his cheeks.

Barker gave a nod to the policeman and stepped through the tent flap.

I followed, but the policeman blocked my path. I opened my mouth to speak.

He shook his head.

I arched an eyebrow. "Now, Barker asked me to come here for a purpose."

"I'm sorry." The policeman gave his head a slow shake. "But that's no fit sight for a lady."

I gave him my visiting card. He gave it a glance before pocketing it. He smiled at me. "A missus, huh?" His eyes glanced to the crepe ribbon around my sleeve.

"A widow. A storm widow."

Barker slapped the tent flap open and said, "Officer, there seems to be a button missing from her clothes. Did you find that?"

The policemen gave a series of frowns with eyebrows down, eyebrows up, and eyebrows furrowed together.

"I imagine you'll want to find it in the lot." A smile slid across Barker's face of square jaw and high cheekbones.

The policeman stood outside the tent and stared at him.

"It could be evidence. Maybe the killer took a souvenir. You'll want to know."

The policeman did not move, did not speak.

"I promise she will not come inside the tent." Barker flicked his head toward me.

The policeman turned back to me as if he had to see of whom Barker spoke.

"I'm sure that's what is keeping you from doing that investigation." Barker's accent smoothed the command in his statement. "And you have my word." Barker stared at him.

"She can't go in there." The policeman gave me a smile, and then a frown consumed him as he crossed the street.

Barker slid the toe of his brogue through the dirt at the edge of the tent. "You aren't to cross that line." He tied the flap back. "Be warned. This is grim."

"Ridiculous!" I stepped forward until the pointed toes of my satin shoes were just outside the line.

Inside, the tent held a table with a woman's body in a ripped dress and pointed shoes laid out on it. A rusty, old smell filled the air, and I held my gloved hand over my nose.

I looked at the pieces of her dress, brown with tiny gold chevrons, and got accustomed to the sight of torn, jagged fabric before I could bring myself to look at the rest. My angle could not reveal everything, but it was enough for me to see some of the horror.

The woman was stretched out on a table that ran the length of the back wall. Brown hair flowed over the edge of the camp bed. I knew that long hair with now-tangled curls. The top of her head had been bashed in on one side. Brain and bone pieces matted into her hair. Her face was worse. Her pale, thick skin gave way to a horrible red slash where her nose was sliced off. Like the prostitute, her throat was slashed in a wide gash.

Her shoulder was crushed in, and a dark stain swelled down her chest. The skirt had been ripped away to reveal a sliced abdomen.

"No defensive wounds," Barker said. He slipped his blue spectacles over his ears and pointed to the gashes on her face. "Knife--perhaps a razor--attacked her. She bled, so they were before death, so she had time to fight, but didn't . . . didn't expect to be killed."

I shuddered.

Barker looped his handkerchief around his hand and worked her stiff hand away from the side of her body. "Clean hands. No defense wounds. Not even something under the fingernails."

"The prostitute was murdered right away--but she still fought. Why didn't this respectable woman?"

Barker looked at me. "Respectable woman? You're sure?"

"Yes," I said. "She might have been a horrible woman who abandoned her son, but there's no evidence that she ever did anything to harm her reputation." I met his eyes. "It's Lucinda. I've met her. I'm sure." I looked away from the body within the tent to where the policeman now walked over the uneven surface of the lot. "The family last saw her at supper the day before yesterday."

Barker stared at me.

"I'm sure, Barker. Half her face is missing, but those are her brown eyes, her slender body, and her brown hair. Yes, I'm sure."

"She was killed there," Barker said with a nod to the lot he could not see through the canvas of the tent. "She didn't fight against her killer, and I don't see her being caught by surprise in that empty lot. They cut her face and slit her throat." He picked something up from the sandy floor of the tent and tossed it out to the rubble at the curb. It was a brown button.

"Do you think it was the same killer as the prostitute?"

He pushed his head forward on his neck, as though trying to keep his thoughts from wandering. "Gash goes the other way from the prostitute's. Also, goes up, not down at the end."

"A second maniac?"

"Same knowledge of anatomy--what would kill and how to slice out the intestines--and neither victim was stripped naked." I thought of the intestines draped over the window at the brothel. "Same . . . sense of décor."

I took a gulp of air, realized how putrid the smell was, and turned away from the tent to gag. "And now he--or someone like him--is going after respectable women."

He said, "Eyes have clouded, blood has settled in the lower portion of the body, and rigor mortis is just setting in. In this heat, I'd say she's been dead around five hours, maybe less, but no longer." He drew his hand across the air in a series of quick blows. "One blow, then a second while facing her to kill her. Looking at her face, the killer wanted her dead."

I looked at my pin watch. That would put the time of death around two o'clock in the morning. I drew in a breath and realized it was full of a stench from the sea. I closed my eyes to suppress a gag, since I also didn't want Barker slicing me out of my corset here on the street. My head cleared a little, and I thought of something. "The prostitute full of the hop was killed from behind, yet she fought. Lucinda looked at her killer and didn't."

"An important difference," Barker said.

I tried to put my mind in that of a murderer, to see the madman's logic, but all I could see was the madman's danger. "Do you think we could possibly . . . that Jack the Ripper . . . in Texas?"

Barker turned around and trained those deep blue eyes on me. "We must be going."

I turned back to see the policeman walking in our direction.

Barker pulled down the tent flap, walked past me, and said, "Thank you."

I opened my mouth to tell the policeman, "Lucinda Wyngate," but he did not seem interested in anything but the button he found in the rubble.

Barker nodded to the policeman. "You have any leads?"

"A few months ago, a similar . . ." He shot a sideways eye at me. "Incident out in Gonzales."

I had read about that. A prostitute was shot on the street, and in the same night, the daughter of a prominent family was shot dead through her bedroom window. At the time, the police doubted they would be able to find the maniac, and no follow-up appeared in the paper.

"We're thinking it's the same fellow." The policeman looked away from Barker and shifted his feet in the dirt.

I may not be a great detective, but I could tell when a man didn't believe what he said. This crime looked nothing like that one and he knew it.

Handing his business card to the policeman, Barker said, "If you can send me the coroner's report, I'll offer any help I can."

The policeman's head shook, he bit his lip and then said, "We don't want any trouble with this. Don't want to scare people."

Barker walked away down the tent-lined street.

The policeman smiled at me and gave a wave.

I waved back and stepped up to Barker's rapid pace as he crossed the street toward the empty lot. He slowed at the saloon. He stood just inside the opening, and I stepped back so the men within would know I was not joining them. His head darted a look around the tent and then settled on the wall closest to the empty lot, a wall left blank except for the lantern hanging within an amplifying tin plate.

Barker stepped back onto the dirt and loose bricks that once made a sidewalk. I stepped up to be at his side when we rounded the corner toward the beach road.

"No one would have seen them from here, and the lantern from the saloon reflects in. They wouldn't even have seen shadows out here." He looked around. "No street lights."

He looked across the street, pivoted right, and then left.

"A woman meeting someone late at night." I looked at the saloon. "One who doesn't seem suicidal would stick with the light, especially around here."

"Not here at all." Barker squinted toward the beach where rubble gave way to sand.

"Pier they're rebuilding down there." I was a little out of breath, but I liked drawing in the clean air of this street a short way from the beach. I pointed to a string of incandescent lights around a pile of rubble more organized than the other piles of debris around us, loose stacks of woods and pylons in rows. "They work night and day. The lights stay on, and it would be a landmark if she met someone." I looked from side to side, accidentally smacking my parasol into Barker.

He grabbed the shaft and gently guided it over my head to my other shoulder. "The lights are on now. You can see. They wouldn't have worked last night in the rain--couldn't have--but the lights would have been on."

I started to cross the street to the empty lot near the pier rebuilding, but Barker's arm stopped me like my mother's used to if she thought I were about to lunge in front of a speeding carriage.

He looked at the mud and crossed the street. At least he crossed most of it, but stopped three feet from the broken concrete of the far curb. He reached into his vest pocket, pulled out his blue-tinted glasses, and wrapped them around his ears.

"Rain last night was heavy," I said. In response to Barker's look at my meteorological confidence, I said, "I was awake at that time last night, and I noticed the weather."

Barker pointed one of those thick fingers toward a spot on the mud. It was just a spot and a point. Yes, a triangle in the muck.

"Shoe," I fought the desire to hop up and down and clap at getting something right, but I couldn't resist bobbing on my heels. "That was her pointy shoe, Lucinda's."

"Aye," Barker said. He crouched over the mud. "And what else?"

I looked at the ripples in the mud in front of the partial shoe print where the tip of her foot stepped off the herringbone brick that remained of sidewalk. The mud was thick before the faint mark, but blurred behind. I traced all the marks with my eyes and my mind. "Nothing. I don't see anything else." Anything else was gone with the rain.

"Exactly." He pointed in front of the shoeprint. Barker looked up at me with a smile. He had straight, white teeth, at least for a British person. "The nothing in front." He stood. "See, there's nothing there, nothing that would have made an imprint as great as a small woman's shoe. But someone scuffed through the mud behind." He smiled so big, someone might have given him free candy.

I looked. "Yes," I drawled out, desperately trying to think of what was so exciting. "Nothing. I do see noth--oh wait. That means no one was in front of her, not here. She walked in front of the other person and they mucked the mud to hide the footprints. What's that?"

A few feet away, footprints slid and blurred. "Some activity. I can't make it out."

"Her shoes move this way." He pointed his fountain pen counterclockwise over the dirt. "On the side."

He grabbed my shoulders and kissed my cheek, which oddly startled and delighted me all at the same time. He pulled away and pointed at a spot to the side of the shoe print and a little behind. "Blood."

Yes, the mud was darker in what could be splatters extending under the planks of debris.

In the street, I stepped beside the shoe print so my laced boots would be just as far apart.

A horse cart clopped behind me. The drover said, "Get out of the street, lady," but I snapped my parasol closed and swung it for him to go past. I gave Barker a nod.

He stepped behind me, standing so close that I could feel his body against mine and his breath on my hair. He grabbed my shoulder with his left hand and spun me to face him. His right hand slid across my throat. "Her throat was slit from the front, that's why the cut was up and to the left." He pointed to a spot where plaster dust and rubble had a slight indent. "The murderer tossed her down then and then smashed her head in . . ." He looked around the rubble, crouching, but being careful not to touch anything. "Smashed her head in while she was still alive--the blood oozed from her onto her hair. Smashed her head. There." He pointed to a brick with darker flecks in the mortar.

"Yes," I said. "More blood. I would never have noticed if I didn't know we were looking for it."

Barker stood and quick-marched down the street toward the incandescent lights. I clambered over the sand behind him.

"Her killer could have killed her from behind," I said. "They killed the prostitute that way, but they wanted to see her."

"You said that before, but why?" He chopped his hand toward places in the sandy soil of the road. "Pointy shoes, pointy shoes, yes, Lucinda was here. She met . . . hello." He went to the wooden railing around the construction site. In the gutter, I saw something tucked under a wood trench. A small, dirty piece of paper fluttered on the slurry of storm runoff.

I frowned. "Because she knew her killer, trusted them. At least, trusted them not to kill her in a public street."

Barker plucked the paper, gave it a quick look, and put it in his pocket.

"Does your friend have an alibi for last night? Say, around two or three o'clock?"

"I'm her attorney. I can't divulge that one way or the other." I slipped a glance at him and gave him a smile I hoped he would find companionable, because a flirty smile would probably irk him. "I would be much obliged, however, if you could tell me whether she needs one or not."

"Which wanders around the point in the way of all women and means she does not."

"Wanders around? All women?"

"Aye, I'm surprised you didn't mention your shoes or hair tongs."

I snapped my parasol open and wedged it on the shoulder between Barker and me.

He said, "She was out walking last night."

"How did you know that? Did you have your man spying at my house again?"

"No, you're not in danger. However, your friend--your client--could be in trouble now."

"You're guessing."

Barker frowned at this accusation. "You know I would not."

"And why in perdition do you think that?"

"From you. I saw your look of panic when you found out the time of death. You knew Winifred wasn't at your home then."

"I don't even know how you knew she was at my home. Oh, not that I'm confirming your suspicions."

"Not suspicions. Deductive reasoning."

"Inductive," I muttered. "What you can't see."

Barker may have rolled his eyes, but I did not have a clear view of his face with my head tilted down to the dirt road.

"Winnie could never have done something so horrible." I stopped at the corner. "She's been my friend for years. I'd know. Wouldn't I know?"

Barker stared at his shoes crunching over the dirt.

I wanted to walk to the streetcar stop. I wanted to get home so I could talk to Winnie and make sure she had not done anything, leastways not anything wrong.

"You coming with me, Daria?"

CHAPTER 13

The porch on Old Red, the main building of the medical school, was almost finished, almost back to the rusticated stone in gothic-arched glamour that it had before the storm. I took Barker's arm to walk past the workmen with buckets and trowels to the large studded door of the medical school.

"Do you think?" I asked Barker.

He nodded. "His schedule had him getting married today. He didn't have to do that, so I think the man would want to work."

Old Red had high stone arches within also. I heard the drone of at least one lecturer behind the inner doors. A pair of classroom chairs and a plain desk were the only furniture here. The desk held an older woman looking down at something on the gleaming surface of the desk.

"Professor Wyngate, please," Barker announced in that accent that tended to charm people.

The plump older woman behind the desk gave Barker a slight shake of her head, though it might only have been a mild tic. She looked up at me and then back down to where she set an accordion folder atop a small railroad timetable on her desk.

A pair of young men in lab coats walked through from the back door of the entrance building and then past the small fence that separated her area from where Barker and I stood. Medical students, I assumed.

Barker turned from the desk to look at a chart on the wall beside the large wooden door.

"So," I murmured to Barker's profile, "what was on that piece of paper you found?"

Barker gave a little jerk of his head toward the woman and winked at me.

The woman trained a glare on the medical students, then looked at the clock high on the tiled wall and smiled at them.

I stepped up to her desk, adopting a slight tremor and a tiny smile. "I hope Professor Wyngate can see me. I don't know whether he has a class or not." I gave a tremble to the hands carrying my parasol and looked out the window to the red-and-white buildings of the medical school. "Oh," I said. "Where are my manners?" I pulled a visiting card from my purse and handed it to her.

"It's not our policy to admit visitors."

I would have bet that was a policy she made up just now.

"But I have to see him. My friend, Winnie . . ." I broke off to keep from lying about how she had sent us or something, but the plump woman turned out to have sharp eyes, and they were turned on me. "She's just the nicest. This whole business has been so hard on her. I imagine it has been for Abelard as well."

"Sad business, isn't it?"

I nodded. "Thank you."

"He should be out soon." The woman made no move to get her white lace-up shoes out from behind the desk and where she could get a message to Abelard

Wyngate. Unless we used telepathy, I doubted he would know to come out here and look for anyone.

Barker stepped beside me. He smiled at the woman. "You being his favorite and all, you should be able to bring him out right away."

I stepped back and smiled to let Barker work his magic.

"Oh!" She gave a shy laugh. "What makes you say that?"

"You know his schedule well enough to tell whether he will be out or not. You know the students who just got out of his class and even have a soft spot for them, and you accepted a small gift from him--I imagine the old timetable for his family's rolling stock is for a relative or . . . someone who collects such things."

"My brother." She blushed. "I'm not married."

Barker took a step closer. "Such a sad business for Abelard. I hope he's holding up well."

"He's doing fine. I mean, he's always a bit preoccupied and absent-minded, but it seems even worse now. He was standing on a podium in a lecture hall and didn't even notice the edge of the thing. He fell off into the first row of students." She gave a sympathetic little nod. "Good thing he'd dropped the scalpel."

I had met Abelard a couple of times. This might not have been the first dive he took off of a podium.

"He's not having a class this afternoon. Just took a little time to help some of the fellows with a little extra anatomy study." She stood. "I'll just go get him for you. Stay right there."

I winked at Barker. "Good work."

He took out his pocket watch and wound the stem. "He doesn't know his wife is dead. At least, he doesn't if he didn't kill her."

I opened my mouth with a question but said nothing when Barker shook his head.

"Data, we need more data before we can determine a thesis on the killer. Don't tip him off that we know Lucinda is dead."

I gave him a narrow-eyed scowl. "I may not be the crack investigator that you are, but I'm far from a blithering moron."

He gave me a "good girl" nod.

I fought a little cringe. "I hope he doesn't come in wearing a bloody apron, looking like something out of Robert Louis Stevenson."

"A fine Edinburgh author." He pronounced the city name something like "Edinburuh."

"He--Abelard--was in Britain at the time of the Ripper murders. So were his parents."

"As was I," Barker said. I noticed a dimple creased his cheek.

"He studied them and some other murders at the time."

"As did I."

"And he's an expert on human anatomy."

The anatomist walked in with the plump woman. He wore a suit: no butcher's apron.

He shook a clean hand with Barker and turned to me. He clasped both his hands around one of mine. "Winnie?"

I shook my head.

"You don't know how she's doing?" He took one hand from mine to jab his bony hand into his waves of pale brown hair. "You're her friend."

The woman at the desk looked around his shoulder. "He's a little out of sorts."

Abelard turned back to her with a nervous laugh. "Yes, of course." He still had my hand. "Thank you so much for being with her through this."

I nodded. I wondered what "this" was to him. "I've been researching your wife's whereabouts so we can proceed with a divorce petition based on abandonment." Not that we would need that now. "I haven't asked for payment from Winnie, and she is my friend, but after everything is finished, well, I figured we could sort something out." I was babbling. I was babbling about anything I could discuss other than the lifeless, deformed body of his dead wife.

Barker gestured for Abelard to walk out of the building and before us into the courtyard of stumps from trees that had died in the storm.

Abelard's gait held fits and starts with frequent looks back to see whether we were following.

"Nice to get out of town this time of year." Barker caught up to him quickly. "So, where are you going?"

Abelard's thin lips gaped open. He ran his hand through his hair, dragging its waves straight up. "I'm taking my son camping, maybe in the hill country. I thought he would do well to get away from things. How did you know?" Abelard looked down his nose at me, and I shook my head in a way that I hoped looked as though I did not know Barker's intuition rather than as if I were just plain stupid.

"You released your class early and are already in street clothes. You gave the train timetable to the receptionist for her brother. You had that because you've looked into the family's train recently. Why would you do that? You're not a manager of the company."

"No." Abelard thrust his hands out as though pushing away the horde of those trying to put him in the seat of family power.

Barker turned to me. "That indicates he is traveling."

"Yes." Abelard's vigorous nod knocked his glasses farther down his nose, and he shoved them back up. He messed with his hair again. "He's right."

"I figured he would be." I opened my parasol and made sure to put it on the shoulder away from both men.

Barker held a finger up and looked to the sky as though a memory hovered at the edge of the clouds. "I remember reading something by a Dr. Wyngate in Britain. A monograph a few years ago."

Abelard gave a toss of his head in a nod. "In the *London Times*. I took those reporters to task who insisted that the Ripper had an expert knowledge of anatomy. Yes, he knew the map of the body, and he knew how to puncture and slice, but so would any man working at your corner butcher shop."

Lucky guess, Barker. Although Barker would never admit to guessing. It had to have been a hypothesis.

Abelard turned toward me again. "How is Winnie? I know she went to stay with you. I haven't heard from her in . . . in a couple days."

"Yes, I was there when your wife came back from the dead. I think you were too busy to notice me."

"I remember that Winnie had her friends with her. I remember which one you are."

Barker leaned his head forward but still kept his back straight. I didn't think the man could slouch. "So, Lucinda stays with your parents, but you still stay at your home with your son."

"Yes." Abelard said. "I am arranging for Lucinda to see Alois, but I'm not ready yet. I need to explain things to the boy."

"No," I said. "I wouldn't rush things."

Barker took my arm. His touch was gentle except for a distinct nudge.

Barker nodded. "Did you visit her?"

In answer to Abelard's rapid headshake no, Barker said, "Lucinda, not Winnie."

"Oh, yes." Abelard nodded so hard, his hair, forced straight up, shook with the effort. "I came over to see her, to work things out. The first night she was there." He blinked several times. "Seems so long ago. I told her that many things happened while she was gone and that I was marrying someone else. She took that hard. She cried . . . and ran upstairs. I started up after her, but my mother said she locked herself in her room."

I put a hand on Barker's arm to keep him from talking when I noticed something. "What did she say about Alois?"

Abelard shook his head. "We didn't get to that."

"Did you think it strange she didn't say anything about the boy?"

His hands pivoted, rose, and then fell to his sides. "I think everything about Lucinda is strange. She came back. I don't know why. She left--well, I didn't know she had left. I thought she was dead. I wanted to die."

I frowned at Barker.

Barker nodded at me and said to Abelard. "But you planned to remarry after only a few months."

Abelard smiled. "You Scots are a direct lot."

Barker leaned toward Abelard with a smile and said, "I thought I was applying finesse."

"Yes, I did marry fast. I've known Winnie for a very long time as a friend, never anything inappropriate. Not while my wife was alive." He shook his head. "Before, I thought she was dead. I believed she was gone. I never expected . . ."

"Yes," I said. "I lost a husband. I knew he was gone, although they never found the body."

Abelard smiled at me with lips pressed thin and white against his teeth. "Your world is destroyed, but then, it was the same for others around us. You move on, and I couldn't let my family raise my son."

I held my breath so as not to spook him. I didn't dare look at Barker, but I didn't think I felt any more movement from him than I would have from one of the anatomist's corpses.

Abelard drew his hands up on either side of his head and rattled them a few inches from his ears. "My family is very successful, but they are not people with whom I enjoy spending an evening."

"Were they hard on Lucinda?" Dang! I just spoke about her in the past tense. "I heard she went missing after dinner the night before last."

"She did?" Abelard asked. One of his hands fell to his side, the other strayed up to run through his hair and pull the waves up.

"According to your mother." Barker said.

My head stuttered through a nod. I didn't want to give away the farm by speaking again.

Abelard's thin eyelids slid over his eyes, a sigh blew out, and he opened his eyes wide to say, "Lucinda dreamt. After Alois was born, it was more pronounced then. She was different, given to unrealistic schemes. She was emotional. I couldn't comfort her. She had ideas, strange ideas."

He turned as though to walk away from us.

"Like what?" Barker asked.

His hands wandered through the air into a shrug. "She was afraid of my father and clung to my mother to protect her." He looked to the both of us when we failed to see how ridiculous this was. "She feared he would kill her. That's insane." He nodded. "I have no idea how anyone would ever consider my father a danger. Yes, she had to have been insane. I was not surprised to find that she ended up at the state home."

I didn't tell him that she had been in Louisiana taking the rabbits some man pulled from a hat or dressing up like a female Jean Lafitte, and I didn't mention that now she was dead.

Abelard gave us a nod and then started toward the street.

Barker leaned against a waist-high stump and asked in a light tone, "What were you doing last night?"

"Last night? I was home with my son." Abelard looked from Barker to me and back. "He was asleep, though, he wouldn't remember."

Barker examined a tree trunk. He ran a fingernail over a loose bit of bark. "Asleep all night?"

"Yes."

"And you?"

"I slept." He nodded with such enthusiasm, his waves of hair tussled around on his head. "Yes, I slept, too."

Barker examined the tree and pulled a dead leaf from where it was trapped in a crevice. He tossed it to the ground. "Except when you met with Winnie."

Abelard opened his mouth and stared at me for help.

I looked at Barker. Square jaw set firm, eyes unblinking. Yes, he was sure.

Barker crossed one foot over the other and leaned on the tree. "You could not know your son slept without waking through the entire night if you also slept. You had to remind yourself to say you had not seen Winnie in two days, and, as an honorable man, you are a bad liar."

Abelard gave Barker an angry shake of his head.

Barker looked to the administration building with the large stone entryway as though he could see not only the students within, but also what secrets lurked in their souls. "I expect you had a willing ally who could get a message to Winnie at her library to tell you to meet."

That woman at the desk did dote on the narrow professor.

"We just walked. She and I walked around the city. We wanted to meet and talk, but just didn't have words." He looked at me. "She's all right, isn't she?"

On the stairs last night, she lied to me! "Yes, she's fine." I smiled at him. "She's as upset as you are, but she's fine."

He sighed. "I need to get going. My son is waiting, and he's excited."

"Yes," Barker said. "That would be best."

Abelard started back toward the main entrance of stone steps and archway.

"Oh." Barker raised a thick finger at the thought that had occurred to him. "You said Lucinda ran upstairs and locked herself in her room."

"Yes, do you think that's relevant?"

"At this point, I know little of what is relevant and what isn't." Barker gave a shrug that took up his shoulders, but not his face with the alert blue eyes. "She had a key to the room her parents had given her?"

"They just leave them in the locks, like most people do. At least in the bedrooms."

"A bedroom near the stairs?"

"Probably the guest room right at the top of the stairs. Why?"

"Did she know the room? Had she stayed there before?"

Abelard closed his eyes and ran a hand through his straight-up hair again. "Before we were married, I think she might have spent the night there. It is my parents' main guest room."

Barker shrugged again. He did not want to give any more information. "We'll be going now. Thank you for your time, Dr. Wyngate."

As the anatomist walked away, I opened my mouth to let one of so many questions tumble out: Would you mind if your wife were dead? Did you know a prostitute at Molly Perkin's bordello?

Barker grabbed my elbow and turned me around toward the street. "Another time. Now, he sees you as an ally. You push with too many questions at once, you lose that."

"Where now?" I asked once we were on the street.

"I am going to my office to do work unrelated to this case. I suggest you go home."

I slowed my pace. The horror of what I had seen descended on me. Even worse, the realization descended of the wedge Lucinda's return had driven between my daughters and me. "My daughters think their original parents might have survived. Now, they're going to think they might have survived and might be in danger."

Barker kicked a pebble into the street. "I don't know if I can find proof of their deaths--so many died that we just don't know--but I can make some inquiries, if you would like."

I shook my head. "I don't *want* you to do that, but I think you should. Thank you."

He moved his hand behind my back either to pat me or give me a sideways hug, but the hand dropped before any contact was made.

"He was with Winnie," I said. I kept pace with Barker's long strides.

"Yes, I heard."

"That gives each one an alibi."

"Or an accomplice."

I stopped at the streetcar sign. With the overhead wire, they were now electric everywhere in the city. The mules had been retired. "How much of what we heard can I tell Winnie?"

"I know enough of women to know not to stop one from gossiping."

I turned toward him with a sour sneer and saw he was smiling back at me. "You were teasing, weren't you? I'm no good at that."

A trolley rumbled to a stop before us.

He said nothing, but he handed me the crumpled, damp piece of paper he had found near the incandescent lights.

"Goodbye, Daria." Barker tipped his hat, but then leaned down and whispered in my ear. "I'll see you tonight. Around eleven-thirty."

"Where? What are we . . ."

I expected Barker to walk away after he bade me goodbye, but he escorted me to a seat on the green and gold trolley and sat beside me.

I looked at the piece of paper. The ink was smeared, but block-printed black letters could be made out that said:

L--Meet me--G

I looked at Barker. "Not exactly a treasure map, is it?"

He shook his head.

"But it is a clue." I leaned back against the wooden bench. "The man named Guy that the prostitute knew?"

" 'Tis an avenue to investigate."

"But what avenue? Where does it go? We don't know anything to help us find this man."

Barker frowned at me. "We use what clues we have, follow those, and see where they lead."

On the ride back to our office near the Strand, I told Barker everything MJ had told me about Lucinda's history, finishing with a question: "So, any clues on Guy in there?"

"I fancy there is," Barker said.

I knew not to ask him anything until I figured something out on my own.

CHAPTER 14

Evening brought a return of the breeze and a lightening of my mood; there might be a monster on the loose in the city, my daughters or I might be in danger, but at least Winnie and Abelard had no impediment to their marriage.

I nodded to the Irish woman beating rugs on the steps of her massive yellow boarding house.

No impediment, unless they were Lucinda's killers. I couldn't believe Winnie would do something like that, but I would never have expected her to lie to me when I found her on the stairs.

I rounded the corner past the derelict homes and walked toward my house.

I found the girls playing within the picket fence of the yard. I kissed them both. Jinxie returned my hug and held on tight. Teddie gave me an anemic hug without looking up to see me.

Iron, she probably needed some iron. I'd make sure she got a spoonful of elixir at bedtime along with the normal dose of cod liver oil.

I walked inside. "Hello!" I called.

I heard the pleasant tinkling of laughter from my living room. I walked in to see Winnie with a teacup balanced on her knee sitting in the chair in the corner. Giggles vibrated through her and rattled the cup. On the table beside her sat a teapot and a short stack of saucers and cups.

Across from her on the couch, MJ sat with a cup on the end table. "I get the tea shipped from England. It's the same that Princess Alexandra drinks." She turned to me. "Hiya, Toots. You and the delicious Mr. Barker find adventure on the storm-tossed streets?"

I had no intention of telling her what I found. I wanted the representative of the press out of here so I could talk to Winnie. I asked, "Isn't she Queen Alexandra now?"

MJ shook her head. "Nope, not until the coronation."

This made Winnie erupt in even more giggles.

MJ joined her with a husky laugh.

"MJ was telling me the peculiarities of the royals. Did you know the princess gets her face enameled? Lead-white make-up covered with a pink tint." She giggled again. "Then, they draw little blue veins under her eyes."

"Women of society do it to hide what time does to the face. Same procedure folks use who are trying to pass as white." MJ glanced at me. "Know anyone who might be like that?"

"Who knows?"

MJ stared at me. "I would love to be a society columnist in London. They've got real scandals."

"And Jack the Ripper." I dashed to the teapot and poured myself a cup. I splashed in some milk.

Winnie's giggles died. She stared at me.

MJ eyed me over her teacup.

I drank a sip of tea and sat on the platform rocker. Normally, the gentle motions and high, spindled arms felt comforting. Now, it felt confining and like it was oscillating on its own rather than at my command.

The only sound in the room was the ticking of the small pendulum clock on the mantle.

I lifted the lace curtain to look outside at the girls.

"They've been good," Winnie ventured.

"I'm so glad." I smiled at her. "I'm their legal mother now. I have to figure out how to be their mother emotionally."

"They've been angels, in fact." Winnie said. "Although my idea of an angel child is one that doesn't come at me with a sharp knife."

"Children don't need sharp knives." MJ set her teacup on the table to gesture. "They should all learn to kill someone with a pencil like I did."

The girls squealed as raindrops hit them, and they ran inside the house. Aunt Cornelia corralled them long enough to pat them dry and then released them to run upstairs.

"A pencil?" Winnie questioned in a loud, flat voice.

MJ nodded. "Applied beside the windpipe at an angle, the pencil can be taken up through the brain, killing someone instantly. Daddy was a sheriff. He might not be good for many things, but teaching a lady to defend herself, that was his skill."

Winnie smiled.

For an instant, I wondered if Winnie might be keeping this information for future reference. No, I couldn't believe my friend had killed anyone, not even the rival for everything she wanted in life, Lucinda. To cut off these thoughts, I entered the conversation. "It's not as easy as it sounds." Months ago, I had tried to kill a man with a shard of glass that way. "If the person moves, you're out of luck." This made me think about Lucinda and the dead prostitute. They appeared to have been killed by the same person. The prostitute had fought, but Lucinda didn't. One knew their assailant and one didn't.

Someone who could kill so horribly was someone Lucinda knew. Barker would tell me to consider the madman's logic. What did they want?

Winnie gave one of her pinched little smiles and jerked her head toward me. "Sounds like someone has a little more ghoul in her than expected."

Because Lucinda had a tendency to come back. The murderer wanted to make sure Lucinda never came back again. I felt my face pull into a frown. I wondered how many more people, how many other sectors of society would the murderer prey on, before being caught.

I felt the silence as Winnie and MJ saw my frown.

MJ leaned toward me. "Your girls really are charmers. They've been through so much recently; you have, too. Let me know if you want me to take the girls, just for a few days."

"Why would I?"

MJ shrugged. "Just a little reprieve. A chance to give you some room for a few days and to have someone else work on their society skills."

I pressed my lips together. I made no secret of the fact I wanted my daughters to climb social rungs to find whatever they wanted--a husband, a career, whatever it was they wanted. I wanted them to have a chance, like the one I was given, so I never had to sleep on the streets of St. Petersburg again. Maybe more than a chance. I wanted them to be accepted by the wealthiest and most glittering of society. MJ did have access to these people. She did have affection for my girls and wanted to introduce them, but there was something more.

I took a silent sip of tea. It was so hot that it hurt my tongue and made my throat ache. "They did it again, didn't they? Talked about Lucinda, about their dead mother coming back."

"They're coming around to you," MJ said. "They just need time."

The pendulum clock beat out all other sound for a few minutes.

"Okay, now I'm curious." Winnie frowned at me. Her glasses reflected distant lightning that lit up the window. "What did this Mr. Barker want with you? Another dead prostitute?"

MJ's green gimlet eyes bore into Winnie to see whether she told the truth. "That Mr. Barker does know how to show a lady an interesting time."

"Another murder." I ventured. I was working my way up to telling Winnie how I had seen Lucinda or actually if I should tell her. "This one was not one of Molly's girls."

MJ looked as though she would sputter her tea, but managed to swallow. "Molly Perkins?"

"Yes," I said, glad for the distraction. "Big, expensive house."

"She might have some interesting scandals for you to put in the paper," Winnie said.

MJ shook her head so hard a lock of her wiry red hair flew loose, hairpin and all. "I wouldn't cross Molly Perkins."

I knew I hadn't, but I also had no idea what Molly perceived as a slight.

Winnie poured herself the rest of what was in the teapot, making half a cup, and smacked the silver strainer over the slop bowl. "Do you think the murders are connected?"

"Yes, both were brutal and done by someone very sick. Why, I can't tell you. There's so much I don't know about these killings, so much I don't know about these women."

Aunt Cornelia waddled into the sitting room and gave us a jerk of the head to indicate dinner was served.

Over dinner, the girls chatted. We did not speak of death, either in high society or low prostitution. Aunt Cornelia seemed especially to enjoy the company and allowed us to eat pie in the parlor after the girls went to bed.

MJ turned down a piece, but enjoyed a brandy with Winnie and me.

MJ swirled her drink around in the rose-colored cut-glass snifter that had once belonged to my long-dead father-in-law. "So, you want to tell the nice reporter lady all about your plans for the future?"

Winnie snickered until a frown and wet, sad eyes took over her expression. "I'll let you know when I have plans. Right now, well, there's been a terrible fuss, and there are a lot of people who just don't know what to do."

MJ gave a sympathetic nod.

"Oh my! Did you realize it's almost eleven o'clock?"

"You about to turn into a pumpkin or something?" MJ swirled the dark liquid in her glass and took a sip. "You've been looking at that clock every five minutes since nine."

Damn! That woman had the eyes of a weasel in a henhouse at night.

I feigned a stretch. "I think I need to hit the sack now."

MJ scrunched her face toward me as though I spoke some strange dialect only known to the moon men in an H. G. Wells story.

"I have to work tomorrow."

"So do I." Winnie walked over to where MJ sat and gave her a pat on the shoulder. "Nice talking to you. Hey, maybe we can do it again someday when my life didn't fall apart."

MJ gave her a smile but did not get up. "Why are you sending me to walk home in the rain?"

"Because I need some time alone." I wished my voice hadn't come out as a cat hiss.

MJ stood. "Mr. Barker going to whisk you away to elope on this rainy night?"

"Of course not. He's not the type to--"

"But this is about Barker."

Winnie closed in. "You are going to meet him? You need me to make myself scarce?"

Of course, she would think I was trotting off to meet a man in the middle of the night. She had. I didn't think about the fact that I was about to do so. I did it for a very different reason than she did.

MJ grabbed my hand. "I know you are slap-happy about this fellow, but you've just lost your husband. You're not over it yet. Don't let this man pull you into a world where you don't belong."

I said nothing. I did not want to give her any clue to help her figure out what I was doing.

"All right. I'm going." She strode to the door and left without an umbrella.

"I'm going up to bed, too." Winnie pointed up the stairs in case I had forgotten the house layout.

Sometimes, having friends could be a pain in the ass.

I emptied my full brandy glass back into the bottle. I did not want to be off my skills when Barker came. I waited in the parlor, listened to the hot rain, and glanced at a book.

CHAPTER 15

At twelve o'clock, I climbed the tall, narrow steps to go to bed.

I must have misunderstood Barker.

I unbuttoned the neck of my dress--my borrowed dress--and fumbled for the laces. I wouldn't wake Aunt Cornelia to help me with this, and I didn't want to face Winnie until tomorrow. I had made a little progress before I reached my bedroom at the top of the stairs.

"You'll need to wear something comfortable," a man's voice said.

I jumped and let out a sound somewhere between scream and gasp. I felt a body against my back, a head craned to whisper in my ear. I smelled the slight scent of soap and Florida Water that Barker wore.

He whispered. "Be still. If someone hears, I'll hide; you say it was a mouse."

I pulled away from him and closed the door.

A mouse. As if I would be afraid of a mouse! The man didn't know me.

Barker stood before me, there in my own bedroom of French mahogany furniture and flowered wallpaper. He wore black dungarees and a black sweater. He must have been stewing in the heat and humidity. He had a large leather case at his feet, almost large enough to be a salesman's grip full of samples.

"No," I shook my head and whispered with a hiss. "This isn't what you're supposed to do. Not in a lady's house."

"We don't want to be seen. I want you to be safe. I've no designs on your person. I shall avert my eyes while you dress."

"Undo my laces first."

Barker's hands slid over the lacing at the back of the dress, and it fell to my feet.

"While you're averting your eyes, can you find my bicycling suit in the wardrobe?"

"I don't much care what you wear, but it has to be black."

He didn't remember my bicycling suit and that it was black. He was a man, a very observant one, but a man after all. He wouldn't remember a woman's clothing.

I slipped off my petticoats and the rigid health corset with stays to thrust my chest forward.

"Good, you're losing the stays. Most practical of you."

"That doesn't sound like you averting your eyes." I was uncomfortable with Barker seeing me like this, not because of anything to do with Barker, but because of what he was not. My husband had initially craved to see me undress and would get in the way, which alternated between being annoying and charming. Later, my husband did not seem to notice me clothed or naked. When I did try to get his attention, he told me I embarrassed him by trying to be provocative.

Barker laid the suit of black corduroy bloomers with buckles below the knees and matching jacket on the bed. He looked at the jacket and hung it back up. He pulled a man's black turtleneck from his case.

From a drawer, I grabbed a red satin ribbon corset and buttoned the front around me. "Here, I'll need you to tighten this.

"I said no--"

"This doesn't have stays. But I need it to fit into the bloomers."

He grumbled--all I could make out was "women," "inefficient," and "devil's own"--but laced me in.

I was in the bloomers and pulling the turtleneck gently over my puffy hairstyle before he could complain again. A glance in the mirror showed that I looked like someone escaped from a women's calisthenics class, the night course. I started toward the front door, but Barker grabbed me around the waist. "Out the way I came. We don't want your neighbors seeing."

I wondered what his way into the house was.

He opened the window. Out over the bay, lightning flashed across the sky. No rain made it to the island, but a wind blew so strongly, I felt it might knock me down.

Barker was outside before I saw anything else. I ran to the window and saw him hanging below. Then he swung out and dropped to the shed.

"Your turn."

I looked out.

"I'll catch you."

I sat on the window sill and mumbled "Ladder? You couldn't find a ladder?" I slipped down against the clapboard of the house and dropped.

I prayed Barker would catch me.

CHAPTER 16

I fell through the rain and darkness.

Barker wrapped his arms around me in a tight grip that kept me from hitting the ground and made me think of things removed from where we were and what we were doing.

I did have a crush on the man, damn it.

I shook my head to clear these thoughts when I needed to concentrate on our mission ahead. I had no idea why Barker would ask me to come on a quest so perilous, but I was glad he had.

He slid me through his arms to the wet ground, then jumped from the shed.

Dewey, my three-legged cat, could not have hit the ground with such silence.

Barker stepped over the short fence to a dark backyard behind a house that had been vacant and derelict since the storm. The older couple who lived there had been trapped in the rubble when the back of the house fell. They had not been able to get out and had died of starvation and thirst. They may have had relations in other parts of the country, but no one came to claim the house. Storm death just seemed worse than the type one normally found in a home.

Barker walked to the side street and looked both ways, even though he did not cross. We followed the sidewalk for about a quarter of a mile and then turned one street over from Broadway, where the Wyngate mansion loomed. We would have about a mile and a half to walk from here. The wind tore at us and made every step an effort.

I avoided the puddles the best I could, but my laced boots still slogged with each soggy step.

"Hurry," Barker said. "Wyngates won't be at the opera all night."

Lightning laced across the sky and fell to earth in a series of angry bolts.

We took shelter under the awning of a closed furniture store from a heavier gust that might have washed us off our feet.

I leaned toward Barker. "You heard Abelard say that Lucinda didn't care about seeing her only child?"

"Not exactly what the man said."

Thunder rocked around us.

"But that's the impression any mother would get. Why wasn't Alois her first concern? Didn't she even want to know? Why did she go to the Wyngate parents and not her husband?"

"Last one I can answer. Abelard lost his house in the storm. She would not have known where he lived."

"Still, it seems very strange."

"Aye. Let's get going." Barker stepped out first and shielded me from view on the street.

Barker turned down an alley.

Above trees that bowed to the wind, I made out the shape of the three-story Wyngate mansion.

He whispered in my ear. "Come." He led me over a hedge to the neighbor's yard.

Of course, we wouldn't want to approach from the back because that's where the servant's quarters were, and those would be populated right now.

We slipped between the houses, over the neighbor's wet grass.

I grabbed Barker. "Maybe a side window. Do we want to be seen from the street?"

"In this dark, folks won't see much of anything." His accent was so strong, most words just ended in the back of his throat.

I imagined the increase in Scottishness was due to apprehension. I knew my heart pounded in ragtime.

He pointed up to the second-story veranda. It was dark, made darker because the entire area was screened in from round copula to ionic columns.

He took his hand down fast, probably so rain wouldn't get up his sleeve. He grabbed my waist to get close to my ear. I could feel his lips on my ear. They were warm, though just as wet as mine. "I get down, you get on my shoulders. You can stand on that bit of ledge. Then, come down and open this side window for me."

So that's why I was here. He needed a monkey to get through the window.

He pointed again to the window on the first floor. Galveston houses had tall windows, long enough to step through. Some said this was because property taxes had been based on the number of rooms and doors, but I tended to think it was for ventilation.

Barker handed me his pocket knife and crouched down.

I said a quick prayer and asked the Almighty to overlook the fact that I was committing a crime.

I wrapped my legs around his neck.

He started to stand, and I wobbled. I drew in a deep breath to keep from screaming. He grabbed my legs and got me level. He stood to full height.

I grabbed the roof and felt my hands rub over rough shingles as they slid off. I dried my hands as best I could on my wet sweater and grabbed again. I caught. I slid one leg up until my foot was on Barker's shoulder.

I heard him grunt with the burden of my weight, but he did not cry out. If I hurried this too much, I would fall, break something, and probably get sent to prison.

I stretched the other leg up until I stood on his shoulders and gripped the small stretch of roof below the terrace. I slid my hands farther up. I felt the wet, rough surface for a handhold. There. I got my hands around a column.

I pulled myself onto the roof.

I felt at the screen to find an opening I could unlatch.

My feet slid on the uneven roof.

I took out the pocket knife and sliced along the edge of the screen.

My feet gave again. I grabbed the edge of the railing. I heard the screen rip beneath my grasp. The pocket knife slid from the roof and fell. I hoped it hadn't injured Barker.

I stepped over the railing and through the sliced and torn screen.

Oh no. I had no knife now to slide up the latch.

I felt in my bloomer pocket and found a fountain pen, an old candy, and an envelope I knew to be my water bill. I took the envelope and slid it through the crack between the windows. It didn't catch, but bent up against the latch.

I pulled it free, folded it over to make a crisp mark, and slid again. This time, I felt the latch lift. The window did not open at my pull. I slide the water bill a little farther.

The window shuddered open, and I stepped through.

Darkness, but at least the room was warm and dry. After a second, I made out the shape of round, stuffed couches and books on the wall. This was a study, probably that of the elder Mr. Wyngate. The desk showed nothing of the man. In fact, nothing littered the surface at all.

I walked toward the door, past the desk. I tugged the bottom desk drawer, and it slid open easily. Through the dark, I could see a thick stack of magazines. I opened one on the top. In the darkness, I could make out the white flesh of a naked woman. I think she lay in chains while a masked man flogged her and another woman slid a hand to the inside of her thigh.

I closed the drawer fast. I needed to let Barker in, and those reminded me of the many magazines, postcards, and stereopticon slides that my husband had been romancing rather than me in the five years between when he learned that I could not bear children and when he died in the storm.

I slipped down the hall--the hall I remembered from my dream--and was thankful for the Persian carpet running the narrow length since it muffled the sound of my steps. Just as in my dream, the doors along the left were open. I looked to the left and saw a reflection of light come through two large windows. One window showed only a lace curtain battered in the wind. The other had the same lace curtain and a silhouette of a woman. Her dress was loose, but caught at the waist, and her head round, as though in a pompadour. Her posture curved, as though bending slightly to look in a window under curtains that no longer hung there, or as though she were a mother leaning over a cradle.

I assumed the shape was my own form and darted to the side to keep from casting a shadow someone in the house could see, but the shadow did not follow me.

I turned to look into the room, where the windows would have been the source of the shadow. The windows were shuttered, and the only light was a tiny bit of starlight leaking between the slats.

I looked at the wall and saw no reflection. I knew I had seen her and felt a slight sadness that she was no longer there. This shape of the woman had not frightened me, but rather had brought comfort.

The wind, I told myself. It plays with things outside and distorts the light.

I heard a noise. Inside the house, not the wind. I stopped. I held my breath so I could hear without any other sound.

Wind, thunder, and yes, a deep rattle.

A room at the back, probably the master bedroom, had a small light stretching through the open doorway.

I considered darting back to the office and the way I had come in, but after an instant, I calmed and walked to the open door. A single candle offered light and long, flickering shadows.

This was probably Miss Alice's room, with maroon silk walls showing scenes of Japanese villages and a four-poster bed with ostrich plumes at each high corner. In an ornate chair with gilt edge at the foot of the bed, the servant, Joe, lay atop the coverlet with legs stretched straight and eyes closed. The candle sat on a jacquard-covered end table beside him.

Joe drew in a deep breath and let out another deep snore.

I raced past the doorway. I grabbed the low, thick wood of the carved staircase and bolted downstairs.

I remembered what I thought to be the room outside of which Barker waited and tried the window. It was no simple latch--of course not, or Barker could have opened it from the outside as I did the upstairs window--but a knob and lock. It did not budge, and no key was nearby.

I hurried before Joe awoke and I found myself trapped down here.

I rushed to the front door and opened it.

Through the rain, I saw what may have been a shrub, or may have been the still form of Barker. I waved.

Barker ran from beside the house to where I stood. He started in the front door, but I stopped him with a hand to his chest.

I mouthed "Joe" and pointed upstairs. I shook my head and mouthed, "No Wyngates."

Barker gave my arm a pat and marched ahead of me.

I left the studded walnut front door ajar. Barker moved up the stairs without noise while I was sure my shoes gave out an echoing squeak as I ascended.

He gave a quick point to a room opposite the way we had come in.

He walked across the landing past the open bedroom door, took a quick look in at the snoring servant, and walked past. He gestured for me to follow.

I did not like this.

I closed my eyes as I walked across the doorway, for fear the light might bounce off my retinas and back into the room.

Barker inched a door open, peered inside, and gestured me to follow as though I might stay in the hallway dancing with invisible ghosts all night.

I walked in after him and closed the door behind me, even though that extinguished what little light we got from Joe's candle.

Barker pulled his flashlight from his pocket, the long silver cylinder that cast a beam of light when cranked.

He cranked, and I realized the loud rain had subsided since I could hear the whir of each crank. I hoped Joe did not waken because of the change and hear the same.

He flashed the light around the room and showed the heavy walnut molding over moiré wall fabric. A pair of narrow beds with arched wooden headboards sat against one wall, and a nightstand with nothing on the

red marble top made me wonder whether we were in the right room. There wasn't anything here.
    I stepped back.
    Nothing in here except that steamer trunk.

CHAPTER 17

Before Barker could lunge for it, I opened the unlocked trunk. A black dress, a red dress, a corset, and two shirtwaists, one of taffeta with fashionable narrow sleeves and the other of a blousy cotton. Two petticoats and a worn skirt that looked as if it might be used as a petticoat in colder climates. A length of curled brown hair had been secured to a small comb. On the other side of the trunk lay a notebook.

Barker opened it to show a single page with writing. It had a drawing of a fence, similar to the metal fences you find in front of all the nice houses of Galveston, and an address on Ship Mechanic's Row that was crossed out with the word "farm" written in.

The flashlight began to dim, so I cranked it.

Barker jotted the address in his notebook.

I picked up a copy of *The Cosmopolitan* magazine from the trunk and thumbed through the pages. I gave Barker a preemptory glare in case he thought I was taking time to read a short story. Stuck between the pages of "The Influence of Beauty on Love" and beside the image of an actress dressed as Joan of Arc, lay a folded, yellowed piece of paper.

I opened it.

Barker cranked the flashlight and held it over the paper I unfolded. A map of Galveston with Campeche marked where piers now lined Galveston Bay.

Barker frowned. He made a couple notes in his notebook and then folded it back.

I took out a couple of playbills. The first contained nothing, but the second had a magazine sketch of a necklace of large stones and waving bands of diamond-studded metal. Beneath the sketch was scribbled, "British Necklace."

Barker reached past me and felt the flowered lining of the trunk. His hand pressed against the curve. Then, he grabbed at the corner.

I leaned to whisper in his ear. "She's got nothing of--"

He silenced me with a raised hand.

Footsteps sounded outside the room. The light from Joe's candle lit the underside of the door.

Oh no!

Barker held his hand before me, as if to keep me from bolting or perhaps to keep Joe from leaping toward me.

The footsteps continued.

My mind flashed through a horrible succession of ideas: maybe he went up the hall and saw some trace of my footsteps; maybe I'd left the window open to the balcony; maybe he heard Barker and me in here. Any of these could end up getting me sent to prison. What kind of mother would I be to my girls in prison?

Joe's footsteps sounded down the stairs.

I closed my eyes for an instant and stifled the noise of a sigh. Then I remembered I had left the door ajar.

Joe might figure out what was wrong. He could hear things now that the wind had eased.

I grabbed Barker's arm.

He nodded to me and then stopped moving entirely.

Panic seized me, and all I could think about was that I wouldn't be able to drive the girls to the children's dance Saturday night at the park pavilion if I got arrested. I bit my lip to keep from whimpering.

Downstairs, the cathedral-sized door swung closed. The footsteps sounded away from the stairs and disappeared. We needed to get out of here. What if Joe had gone to call the police?

Barker continued clawing at the trunk lining. He pulled it away to reveal a cloth bag. He pulled out a handful of round metal disks. He put one in his pocket, the rest back in the bag, and then put the bag back in the trunk lining.

I thought of the girls again. I thought of Jinxie's bloomers and the jacks, balls, and rocks I often pulled out of those before handing them over to the girl who does the laundry.

I rifled through the skirts, shirtwaists, and dresses. Yes, I grabbed the petticoat. I pulled one out and felt along the side. There it was: a pocket. I took out a handful of hairpins, a small key, and a visiting card.

Barker gave the flashlight a crank and wrote what he read on the card:

Madame Sylvie
Trance Medium
Discreet

He pocketed the key and gestured for me to put the rest back in the pocket.

I gave Barker a frown that must have shown my anguish even in the dim light.

He nodded and pressed the trunk lining back in place.

I folded up the under-things and placed them inside as best as I could remember where they had been. Barker put the other things back and closed the lid.

Now, we had to get out.

He rose, put the flashlight in his pocket, and peered out the door. He reached back, yanked me to my feet, and ran across the landing. He did not go for the front door, but for Mr. Wyngate's study.

I allowed a quick look back as we entered the study.

Joe was in the main entrance hall downstairs speaking to a man I could not see, other than the top of a hat and a jacket with a bulge that might have been a gun.

We ran on silent feet through the study and out the window.

Barker had a knife and managed to knock down the latch after we were on the screened-in terrace. Barker slipped through the opening in the screen and stood on the slanted shingles of the roof. He beckoned for me to join him.

I slid out as fast as I could silently. The farther I was from inside that house was the closer I came to being free.

Barker grabbed the column beside me and leaned past me to wedge the screen back into place. He used his pocket knife to jam the last bit.

The wind had dropped to an irritating breeze that offered no comfort but flapped loose hairs against my face. It was not enough to hide the noise we made on the slate tile.

Barker pocketed his knife, slid down from the roof, gripped the rain-gutter for a second, and dropped to the ground.

I slid down to do the same, but caught a wet spot on the roof, shredding the flesh of my hands, and plummeted face-first off of the high roof.

Barker caught me. The force of my fall sent him to the wet grass and mud. I was able to get my hands out and suffered from only sparks of pain through my wrists.

I stood and took his arm.

We ran between the houses and back to the alley. The alley did not have gas lamps, so it was dark.

I started back toward my house, but Barker steered me in the other direction. I didn't care where we ran. I just wanted to get away.

We stopped at Post Office Street. I groaned, but I followed Barker to his house.

"She wasn't in those plays, but they were from this year." I spoke between pants and deep breaths. I did not slow my pace no matter how tired I was. "Any Guy listed in them?"

Barker kept up beside me.

"They were the same theatrical company, one out of New Orleans." He took the keys from his pocket and opened his front door. "One that the article stated was headed for Houston when they closed in New Orleans, but the article didn't list the names of the company other than the leading lady."

Down the street, music played, but it was too far away to be loud or for people in those lighted buildings to see two disheveled people in the dark.

"Nothing in that notebook with a name and address for Guy." I walked to the kitchen.

"Haven't figured out what we know about finding him, have you?"

"Damn!" I hopped on one foot to pluck the cockleburs caught on the soles of my boots. I heard Barker snicker in the other room. "But it looks as though she wasn't at the loony bin."

Barker walked into the room carrying a bundle of folded cotton petticoats, my petticoats. The ones I had left here the other day. "I washed them for you, don't worry. I thought you'd like to get into something dry before you go home."

I smiled at him.

"And your dress."

I shuddered, even though the night was hot and humid.

"I washed it. No blood." He set the petticoats and under-things on the table. He walked past me to the service porch and returned with my dress, cleaned and pressed with an even greater skill on the ruffles and sashes than the rather gifted girl who does my laundry shows with the iron.

I pulled my boots from my feet and shook them over the waste bin. "So, what do I know about Lucinda? She was an actress. She may have been crazy."

"Good start." Barker smiled at me and for a moment I forgot I was sweaty, dirty, and probably scraped up.

"She ran from what sounds like a lifeless marriage," Barker added.

"But then she came back. Why did she come back?"

"What interested her? What did she like here?" Barker swept the floor around me where I must have shed twigs, roof debris, and more cockleburs.

"She liked being a society wife, and she liked working for charities."

"Charities?"

I sifted through memories. "Charity. The Confederate Home. That can't be important, can it?"

" 'Tis the only direction we have to go, so we might want to try."

Although he had seen me in my under-things twice in the last two days, I made a spinning gesture with my finger to let him know he needed to turn around before I yanked the sweater over my head.

"Barker, she doesn't have any keepsakes or anything."

"The woman traveled light." Barker turned his back to me.

I pulled the turtleneck over my head and flung it into the sink. "Too light. There was nothing of her son. She wouldn't do that if she loved him."

"There was nothing of any life, not even her own." Barker stood with his back to me and reached into his pocket. He pulled out a disk-shaped object of black and silver. "She never intended to stay here. She came back for something."

"So we don't know what she did care about." I slid off my bloomers and tossed them in the sink. "But we know she didn't come back to see him--her own child."

"She came back for some other reason." Barker, with his back still turned toward me, tossed a towel onto the table beside me. "Why?"

You're asking me? I smiled. Yes, he was. He respected my judgment. "She didn't have much stuff. As women go through life, we tend to collect things. I think she was poor. Maybe she had become desperate, and that's why she came back."

"Would you use your brain and think, woman?"

I stiffened, but he didn't know that because he had his back to where I stood in my corset and combination garment. "So, what is it you figured out and want me to guess?"

"I want you to remember what interested her."

"Magic, acting, pirates."

"Aye." He turned and looked at my face, but turned back right away.

"What do you think that key was for?"

"Padlock. What it's on, I'm not a mind reader." And the sandpaper gruffness of his tone indicated he was not pleased with my answer, either.

I sneered at him, which he must have felt because he stiffened even with his back to me.

"What do you think her interest was in pirates?"

Barker whirled around.

I gasped and pulled my dress before me.

He smiled and held up what he had taken from the pouch tucked in the lining of her trunk. He held a gold doubloon.

"Campeche!" I whispered. "That was a treasure map. She was after treasure." I brought my hand to my face and had to reach to catch my dress before it fell. "That's all she was ever after. The Confederates. She wanted the Confederate gold."

CHAPTER 18

I rounded the corner of the derelict houses heading toward my clapboard home where the girls' white bloomers flapped in the breeze of the upstairs gallery, beneath the rows of beaded millwork. My stomach fluttered at the thought of going home for midday supper.

I started toward the steps, saw a man beside me, and turned with a start.

Barker raised his gray bowler to me and opened the garden gate. "You'll have to be more observant," he chided with a gentle smile, "if you don't want someone to sneak up on you."

"Barker, I read contract bids for dry dock construction all morning." I raised my skirt high enough not to trip on the steps. "I doubt I could recognize anything that didn't pump, winch, or lift."

"Then you might not be much assistance in an interrogation." His mouth screwed up into what I would have called a huff in another man.

I smiled and gave a quick bat of my eyelashes. "I take this to mean you like my help."

He raised an eyebrow.

I unlocked the door and gestured him into the entryway of my house. "Mr. Barker, do come in."

"I want to talk to your friend."

"Yes, I know." I had come home late and left the house early to keep from talking to Winnie, now that I knew she had lied to me.

Barker doffed his bowler and put it on one of the few free hooks of the hall tree not covered with my parasol, Winnie's parasol, umbrellas, scarves, and the girls' hats. The little table held a vase painted with dying flowers and a book with a streetcar ticket inserted as a bookmark. "That must be Winnie's," I said, tapping the book.

Oh no! I just claimed ownership of all the clutter. Well, it did belong to me, if only by default from my late mother-in-law.

"Oh, stay for supper, please." I didn't want to face Winnie without company. "There's always more than enough, even if it might be a bit wiggly."

"How can I refuse such an offer?" Barker's feet creaked over the floorboards to the parlor.

Winnie pushed open the swinging door from the kitchen. She kicked her cotton skirt out of the way as her black boots pounded the floor until china on uneven tables tinkled. When she came to a stop between the shuttered side windows, her redoubtable footwear was visible beneath the soft white fabric of her skirt.

I would not question anyone's fashion choices; I wore a floaty dress of white muslin and lace insets with a black satin mourning band around the puffy sleeve.

She held a teacup on a saucer. "Hello," she extended a hand to Barker. "You must be Dash's Mr. Barker. I'm Winnie."

I walked into the front parlor so they would not see my blush at Barker being described as mine.

"I'm glad I caught you while you're still here, Miss Winnie." Barker squinted at her. "You plan to move very soon. Perhaps to some property owned by your library?"

Winnie looked at me.

I shook my head. *I'm not helping you. I didn't know you were bolting.* "Let him explain the inductive reasoning to you."

"You have the glasses and expression of an academic." Barker looked at her with blue eyes turned even bluer by those colored spectacles he wore to see in greater detail. "There is a stain of blue ink on your finger--that could indicate someone working in an office--but that additional bluing on your palm indicates you stamp books for a living. Hence, a librarian."

Winnie looked at her hand and then waved it at Barker as if he were a cab she had hailed.

I had forgotten that Barker had not yet met Winnie and knew little about her.

She nodded to him. "Impressive. How did you know I was on my way out the door?"

Barker turned back toward the vestibule with the hall tree. "You had your parasol ready to go, with a streetcar ticket and a book to read on the journey."

"That just shows she's going somewhere across the island." I said to Barker. "What makes you think she's moving?" I turned to Winnie. "She hasn't told me she's moving out, but then, I guess there's much she doesn't tell me."

She puckered her lips in a confused frown.

"Her shoes." He pointed at her feet, and even Winnie looked at her boots. "She wears boots larger than women usually wear this time of year. That indicates they did not fit into her suitcase, but smaller shoes did."

"Wow!" Winnie showed the first big smile I had seen since everything had gone wrong in the last few days.

Barker squinted at Winnie. "You are still here to say goodbye to your friend, but also to have one last cup of tea in a china cup. Clearly, you are going someplace without such amenities, and I would not expect any niceties in the sort of apartment a municipal institution like a library would offer."

"Janitor's shed?" I grimaced.

"It's really nicer than that." Winnie enforced her words with a series of short nods. "More of a shack." She ran to the hall toward the kitchen. "Here, I'll get you both some tea."

"Don't go," I said.

She stopped in the hallway. Her arm wandered up until it pointed toward the kitchen.

"I mean to the shed." I sat on the chaise lounge covered with fabric depicting blossoming and dying hydrangeas. "Especially not after what's happened."

Winnie was so fast, she probably hadn't heard me, but she went back into the kitchen and returned almost immediately with a tea pot in one hand and a clattering stack of two saucers and two cups in the other.

"Aunt Cornelia said to say that dinner will be salad and roast leg of lamb with potatoes and gravy." Winnie set the tea items on the marble-topped end table. "Just the thing for a man."

"And I suspect few wiggles," Barker said.

Winnie looked at me. Behind her glasses, her soft, brown eyes contacted mine as though nothing had happened. "The girls are helping Aunt Cornelia."

"If the girls are in the kitchen," I called out in a voice loud enough to be heard in the kitchen, in the shed beyond, and probably in the tumbledown stable in the alley, "then they need to come out and say hello to the mama who is home from work." The mama who now breathed in short, angry breaths and caused Baker and Winnie to inch away from her across the front parlor.

I needed to get a hold of myself. I would ruin the interrogation and scare the girls.

"What's happened, Mr. Barker?" Winnie asked. "Does that mean something new happened? Something new and bad?" She looked at me.

Bad? I'm not sure I'd say "bad." But I wasn't sure Winnie had an alibi.

Teddie, with Jinxie just behind, raced into the parlor and gave me a limp hug. Jinxie's arms got tangled in Teddie's as the older girl attempted to slip free.

Teddie shoved her sister, and Jinxie stomped her sister's foot.

I gave them a warning growl while I filled a cup of tea. This might not have been a technique I read about in *A Guide for the Mother*, but it worked for Dewey.

The girls scrambled back into the kitchen, leaving the door to swing back and forth behind them.

I handed the cup and saucer to Barker and poured one for myself.

Barker took the cup and saucer. He gave a dip of his head that looked as though it could be a nod. "The police have found Mrs. Wyngate's body."

Winnie pointed toward the telephone in the alcove. "But I just spoke with her--"

I shook my head. "Not that Wyngate. Lulu."

"Lulu?" She just breathed the name. Her face fell into a confused furrow, a flicker of what may have been either a smile or a frown at the one side, and the confused furrow fell into a frown. She left the room with a clop of her boots and entered again with the silver cream and sugar holders. "Body? She's dead? How did she . . .?"

I hopped to my feet and stood straight and tall. "Mr. Barker, anything my client says right now is privileged information." I let a gesture fly toward Winnie. "Yes, she might be a liar, but she's still my friend and my client."

Winnie set down the tray. "What are you--"

"She will pay you for your services, and you are under moral obligation to tell nothing she reveals to the police."

Barker lifted his eyebrows over his nose that was well shaped even if large and looked at Winnie from lowered lids. I didn't know if I had done anything to merit getting paid by Winnie, but that wouldn't stop me from asking for money for Barker's investigation.

Winnie scowled at me. "What's going on?"

Barker gave a look down the hall. Aunt Cornelia walked into the dining room and slid closed the ten-foot wooden pocket doors between the dining room and front parlor.

"Lucinda Wyngate was killed last night two miles from here." Barker watched me watch him over the rim of my tea cup.

"What time last night?" Winnie asked. She steadied herself against the wall. "I was out walking around one or two in the morning. That could have been me killed."

"Walking, huh?" I stood with hands on hips. "Just out, all alone in the night?"

Winnie scowled at me with her arms folded across her chest.

I glared back with my hands on my hips.

"Abelard said he was with you late last night," Barker said.

"Yes," Winnie said. "We met at the library, but he was late. Raining like a son-of-a--very hard--so I almost left before he came. He was soaked when he did arrive." She leaned forward to pick up the cup on her lap, but decided not to engage her arms and instead leaned back. She looked up at me through the shiny lenses of her glasses. "I didn't mention that Abelard was along for my walk when I saw you night before last, but that's hardly lying."

"Meeting up with your fiancé while his wife gets murdered," I said in a voice loud enough that my mother would have said it belonged outside. My fists pressed against the side of my corset. "Yes, I'd say that's different from a walk in--"

"Murdered?" Winnie asked Barker.

He gave a little nod and a silent sip of his tea.

She looked at the teapot. "I made tea because I'm not very good at making coffee. Abelard says I make 'tea-sippers coffee.' " She pulled off her pince-nez and rubbed her index finger along her nose.

"You still angry?" I asked her.

"Yes," she said to the cup on her lap.

"Me too." My fists were starting to grow numb against the stays of my corset.

Barker's cup clanked onto his saucer. "So, Miss Winnie, would you say--"

"I'm trying to help you," I said.

"By accusing me of lying?" Winnie looked down at her tea cup for a very long time. Her shoulders shuddered, but she made no noise. She might have been holding her breath.

Barker said, "What can you tell me about--"

"Lucinda was murdered by the same maniac who killed that prostitute in the alley." I dropped onto the sofa and picked up my tea cup. "You need to tell me the whole truth."

Winnie drew in a deep breath and looked up at the starry sky of the ceiling fresco. "This is just too much for me."

Beyond the parlor in the dining room, the smack of china and silverware on the table vied with our volume.

"Daria," Barker said. "Perhaps you could help me with questions or you could go away for a while?"

I sipped tea. In the heat of the day, it remained close to boiling.

I heard what I believed to be a fork hitting the wood floor and then being dropped back onto the table.

Still looking up to the ceiling, Winnie pulled a handkerchief from her sleeve and dabbed her eyes.

When she looked at me, her eyes were red, but no tears remained pooled in them.

I heaved out a sigh. "I'm sorry. I shouldn't have called you a liar."

"You always apologize if I wait long enough." Winnie smiled, but she also gave a sad sniff. She put her pince-nez back on her nose. "I did lie. I'm sorry."

"I'm so glad," Barker said. "Would you say the Wyngates--"

"Do you know anything about someone dying in the Wyngate house during the storm?" I asked. I looked at Winnie and did not venture a look at Barker, who probably would laugh at this inquiry. "A ghost."

Winnie shook her head. "I don't know much about Abelard's family. We always kept to ourselves. The three of us." She smiled at my frown. "Alois. Oh dear, we hadn't told him yet about Lulu coming back. I'm not sure how to approach telling him that she came back and then died."

Another fork rattled to the floor.

"When you have seen them," Barker said, "what was your impression?"

Winnie shrugged. "Eccentric."

"Many monied families are," Barker said. "Could you be specific?"

Winnie shook her head. "Not 'dress up the cats' eccentric."

"Then what type of eccentric?" Barker held his teacup, although I could see it was empty.

"Dinner," Aunt Cornelia announced from the dining room as she yanked the pocket doors open a few inches.

The table was set for five with fine china at the edges and the silver dome in the center over the main course. The girls stood behind seats at the side of the table, Barker held a chair opposite them, and Winnie and I took the head and foot of the table.

"Beautiful table, girls," I said. I sat and felt Barker help me with my chair. I tried to move smoothly, but my late husband had never done that when we sat down to dinner.

Barker helped Winnie with her chair. The girls were in their chairs before he had a chance.

From the corner of my eye, I thought I caught a wink from him to the girls.

"What I've seen of Miss Alice," I said as I flapped my napkin loose, "I've liked."

Barker looked at a portrait of a large woman with inexpert swirls of hair and ruffles of black dress that had been painted by one of my long-dead in-laws.

Winnie nodded. "She's given to moods now and then."

Barker took the dome from the roast and sliced some of the tender meat.

If the laundry girl was still learning to cook, she was doing well.

"Sometimes, or so I've heard at least, Miss Alice puts on an old sunbonnet."

"I've seen women wear them here," Barker said.

I shook my head. Barker sure didn't know women. "Not someone like Miss Alice, unless she's working in her garden."

"I don't think so," Winnie said. She took a small piece of meat, an even smaller bit of salad, and executed the fastest pour of gravy that was humanly possible. "She puts on an old sunbonnet and sits out by the fountain, watching the water. I've never gone near her when she's like that, because the family--Eula Rose--said 'Don't approach her when she's like that. You try to talk to her, and she'll bite your head off and spit it out in the dirt.' "

I laughed.

Teddie and Jinxie stared at Winnie.

I gestured toward their plates.

Barker asked, "Eula Rose said it just like that?"

Winnie's mouth bubbled with a giggle. "Maybe a little differently. I guess I came up with that interpretation because I did walk by Miss Alice once when she was like that. Her eyes looked beady and puffy."

"Wonder what bothered her?" I was thinking it could have been marriage to that hound, but I said nothing.

"You never saw her in one of her moods." Winnie shrugged. "Mother of three boys, I can see that happening. I have my hands full with just Alois." She dropped her knife and stroked it a few times before picking it up again.

"What about the husband?" Barker said.

"Mr. Wyngate?" Winnie's thoughts showed with her furrowed brow. "I admit I get along with him better. Maybe because I'm the only one who hasn't heard all his old jokes." She shrugged. "Or at least pretends she hasn't. He's happy not having to run the railroad or bank anymore. Although he says the family empire is more of a 'postage-stamp republic' these days."

"Sextus Wyngate oversees all of that?"

"Not without help." Winnie smirked. "His father started it and then just got tired." Winnie nodded in agreement with a thought she did not share. "I like the old guy."

"You do," I sliced my meat. "Abelard says he's harmless, and yet Lucinda seems to be scared to death of him."

"According to Abelard quoting his mother," Barker said.

Did he suspect Abelard? Miss Alice? I looked at his strong profile. *Yes, and probably every person in the city without an alibi.*

"I wouldn't question Miss Alice," Winnie said. "No one ever dares to question Miss Alice. Not that she isn't nice. She's been wonderful to me even though things are, well, what they are now. I like her."

"Sounds like you don't like Sextus," Barker said.

"He's a bit of a weasel." She wrinkled her nose at the girls. "Nice when talking to you, but then Eula Rose would say he wasn't happy about something. But I don't think he'll be a bad brother-in-law." She set down her cutlery and took a sip of water. "Oh, not that he'll be . . . oh, I just don't know what's going to . . ." A sob came out of her, but she pressed it back in with the napkin to her lips. "If you'll excuse me, I'd like to be alone for a moment. I'll go upstairs." She ran from the room in those heavy boots, clomping through the hall and up the stairs.

I heard the door close upstairs and sobs sound through the wood.

Jinxie started to cry. She was a sensitive girl, and someone else sobbing would have that effect on her.

Teddie spun her fork around on her plate, but picked up no food.

"Darling, what's wrong?"

No reply.

I tried again and then a third time.

"Nothing," Teddie whispered.

"If there's nothing wrong, then you'd be able to look at my face."

Barker ignored us and poured himself a cup of tea. I suspected he didn't even like tea, but liked seeing our conversation even less and wanted to learn more from Winnie.

Teddie's lips trembled. "Did you kill her?"

"Teddie! No. Of course I didn't."

"That boy doesn't have a mother now."

"He didn't for the last year," I shouted at the girl. I calmed and spoke softly. I felt my eyes burn with as many tears as I heard upstairs, but I did not let them flow, not in front of Barker and not at the dinner table. I wasn't sure why the last part mattered, but somehow it did. "A mother is someone who loves you."

Teddie's eyes looked up at me, as red as I imagined Winnie's were right now. "I heard you. You planned to kill her."

Oh damn! That caught Barker's eye.

"We were joking." I turned to him. "The worst we came up with was irritating toilet paper. If her posterior was red, then maybe you can blame . . ." I remembered the state of her lower regions, and my words ended in a shiver. "If you saw what I saw today,

Teddie, you would never think that I could have done any of that." I blinked back tears again. "That was done by someone horrible, a maniac."

"And we might end up murdered in our beds," Jinxie said in a voice that was quieter than any I'd ever heard her use. At least until I realized why she said it.

"You've been talking to the madwoman across the street, haven't you?" I turned from Teddie to Barker. "That dear old scold across the street sees roving bands of murderers lurking on every corner. I wonder what she had to worry about before the storm." I held my arms out to her in hopes she would come to me for a hug. "You're safe, you're secure, and you're my daughter."

I walked over to her side of the table and kissed the top of her dark hair. "We'll solve this. We'll find out who killed her, and you'll know you're safe." I then kissed Jinxie.

We finished dinner in silence. The girls ran outside to play, and I walked Barker to the front door.

Winnie came downstairs, her face red. "I wanted to say goodbye, Mr. Barker, and thank you--you both-- for helping me."

Barker gave her a smile with a dimple and a sparkle of his blue eyes. "Can you tell us what you know about Lucinda?"

Winnie looked at her shoes on the bottom step. "Well--"

I cleared my throat. "Barker, before you ask any questions, you need to tell us whether you will ensure the confidentiality of her answers."

"Very well." Barker turned to me without any smile at all. "I assure you."

I squinted at him. "Go ahead, Winnie, answer his question."

"I never met her. I heard that she was active in charity."

"Yes," I said. "In just one, the Confederate Soldier's home and we're heading there tomorrow."

Winnie turned her black-brown eyes to Barker. "Miss Alice was close to her. The Confederate Home has always been a pet charity for Miss Alice. She funded it. You should probably talk to her about Lucinda."

"He will." I jerked a thumb toward Barker. "He just likes to get more of a perspective."

"Well, they were close. I got the feeling from what Abelard said that his mother doted on Lucinda."

Barker leaned on the newel post. "And she doesn't dote on you?"

Winnie shrugged. "She didn't have time to know me yet." She gave a timid smile and spoke in her librarian whisper. "I'd have won her over."

I smiled back.

Barker nodded.

Winnie blew out a sigh. "I thought the worst that would happen was people thinking that we hadn't waited long enough to get married. This is worse, much worse."

"Do you think you failed to wait long enough?" Barker asked.

She shook her head and nodded.

I stepped between Barker and Winnie on the staircase. "Want to do some endearing charity work tomorrow?"

"Shots cracked from every direction," the old man in the patched shirt said with an expansive gesture of quavering hands. "We had to hold our skirmish line, but we couldn't even shoot, so many shots were ringing out. Bullets, cannons, they threw everything they had at us. We lost eleven horses."

"Eleven?" Jinxie asked. Her eyes showed a concern for the horses and maybe even for the Confederate soldiers.

Her sister sat in silence on the couch and tugged at the black ribbon she had tied around the sleeve of her white, ruffled dress. They both wore mourning ribbons of their own manufacture for Lucinda. I chose to consider them emulations of my own mourning band for my husband, who had drowned in the storm when he decided to stay in a saloon rather than heed my plea for him to come home.

"There we were, dying."

"Did you die?" Teddie asked.

I looked across the lounge to give her a glare for being a wiseacre, but saw that her dark, slanting eyes shone with earnest interest. I pulled a card, and the little old fellow with a big mustache shook his head.

I sat at a wooden game table with two other men and MJ, playing whist. I liked the game, I knew the game, and I didn't like dummy telling me what to do, but I was a guest here in the large, sparse lounge of the Old Soldiers' Home. I switched to another card and gained a smile.

MJ lifted her chin and looked down the side of her nose in the way she did to make her long nose look straight. She slipped a card onto the table to take the final trick to stack with the rest of the ones she and her partner had taken. After a quick count, she said, "We win. Here, let's play again. My deal."

    I hadn't invited her. I didn't even tell her we were coming here. I think Winnie must have asked her to come in her place while she sobbed behind closed doors.

    I looked around for Barker but didn't see him. He had come with us, but I think the starched matron had spotted a man without lumbago and marched him upstairs to fix an electric light.

    Few of the veterans took refuge from the heat in this room where tall buildings on either side and to the back blocked the breeze and gave a feeling of what doctors called claustrophobia. Three men sat in wooden chairs alongside the girls on the floor, who were listening to the old Texas Guard telling tales of sieges and Confederate charges. Another one lounged on the threadbare sofa. From what Winnie had said, all the furniture in here had probably served time first in Miss Alice's mansion.

    "So," MJ said as she fanned the deck out with a swipe of her hand, stacked it again with another swipe, and shuffled with only a slight touch on the corners of the cards. "Any of you boys remember Lucinda Wyngate?"

    Little mustache man shook his head, and MJ's partner jerked awake and looked at his card.

    "What was that?" The Confederate story teller bellowed from across the room.

    "Miss Lucinda," Teddie said. She flapped her arm either to take off into asymmetrical flight or show off her scrap of black fabric on her arm. "Why we're in grieving."

Mourning, grieving, she had the right concept.

I bid, "Three uptown," and hoped this had some bearing on what the others had bid or what my cards said, because all bidding stopped after that.

"Miss Lucinda died," Jinxie said.

"I'm so sad for you," the storyteller said. "Was Miss Lucinda your dolly?"

Teddie shook her head. Jinxie got a sudden case of the shies and looked down at her crossed legs. Well, good for them to come along to cheer the men, even if they weren't crack investigators.

"Dash," MJ said. "Your lead."

I tossed a card on the table.

"Lucinda Wyngate," the old fellow sitting in one of the wooden chairs said. "The young lady you talked to, George, about the buried gold." He nodded across the room to MJ.

MJ leaned a hand on her hip and the other elbow on the table. She tossed a card out and then turned to the man.

"Buried gold?" I asked.

"Yes," the storyteller said to the girls. "When old Jeff Davis saw that the Yankees were coming, he buried all the gold from the Confederate treasury. It's out there somewhere." He gave the girls a wink. "Help me find it, and we could all be rich."

"She brought her little boy," said the man in the folding chair.

"Truly?" I tossed another card down. I think I lost the round, but I didn't care. I wanted to hear.

The guy nodded so hard, his chair squeaked. "Nice little fellow. He was walking. Kind of wobbly, but on the go, you know?"

"Yes," MJ and I both said.

"Said she would love to find that gold so he could have it."

"That's nice," I said. It was motherly and gentle. It was strange for someone who had abandoned that child and then lied about why she was gone.

"Do any of you know a fellow named Guy?" I asked.

Everyone in the room--every man, my children, and even MJ --looked at me in confusion.

"I thought he was a friend of hers I might know." I took a trick and then another. "I think he's also interested in Confederate gold."

"Nope."

"Guy? No," the little man with the big mustache said. "That would be Gee." He prolonged the hard G. "How we say it in French."

"He's a Zouave," the storyteller said, as if that explained everything.

The man on the couch opened his eyes. "The magician, came a couple of time with the charity ladies. He also liked old Harry's stories about the Confederate gold." He flapped rheumatoid fingers at the storyteller. "He came a couple days ago."

"Magician," MJ said. She played a card and lost the trick to me. "He was supposed to come yesterday also."

I gave her a "How would you know?" squint.

"I submitted the story about a talented professional doing charity work. Something about the old charities coming back now that people aren't as preoccupied with troubles from the storm."

Troubles. That word got a nod from the men who remembered even worse troubles than our own flood.

"Got an earful from my editor when he didn't show yesterday." She looked to Zouave Mustache and her own partner. "He didn't come, did he?"

Jinxie held Barker's hand, and Teddie wrapped herself around MJ's narrow arm while I walked alone across the street before the Confederate Soldier's Home. Well, I walked beside MJ, but without encumbrance.

"You're like a soldier," Jinxie told Barker. "You walk like one. Or maybe a policeman."

He smiled at her. "I like that. My father was a policeman. And I spent a wee bit of time as a soldier." He had been a member of the Gordon Highlanders in Afghanistan. I only knew because of a framed medal on his wall.

Jinxie smiled at him to show gums where her teeth had yet to come in on the top.

It's good that the girls like the people I've brought into their life. I repeated this to myself to dispel the poisoning of jealousy. I thought I was making headway when MJ frowned at me.

She whispered, "I can take the girls for a few days, give you a break. I'll teach them the important manners for society." She twitched to regain some of her arm from the child who appeared to want to run off with it to create a mother from parts out of Mary Shelley's book.

"Like not staring at people or trying to yank arms from their sockets?" I laughed.

MJ's feathered hat showed she gave an almost imperceptible nod.

"Barker," I called out in as light of a voice as I could manage. "I think we found who Guy was."

"Gee," MJ corrected.

"Magician." Barker said. "The matron told me about him when I rewired her fixture."

MJ suppressed a juvenile giggle beneath her handkerchief.

"She did?"

"Fit to be tied, she was, at him not showing. Marched out to the address he gave. No sign of him there, no sign of him having been there."

I asked MJ, "But he's been here for more than the last few days, hasn't he?" After she nodded, I said to Barker. "Looks as though the pros--soiled dove--came here to meet up with him."

"The one who ended up . . ." MJ slipped a green-eyed glance to Teddie.

"Dead in the alley?" Teddie ventured.

Apparently, I wasn't the only one who read more than the gardening section of the paper.

I gave Teddie a nod.

MJ whispered, "One of Molly's girls? I'd avoid that type of company." She yanked her arm away from Teddie so she could put her hand over the girl's ears.

"People who cross her have ended up--" She made a noise as she slid a hand across her throat.

Barker slipped a glance back to MJ, but said nothing. One of the main things he did not mention was Lucinda, whose death had not yet made the paper. He walked on a few feet before he turned back to look at MJ again. "A name, one I've seen before, came up. The matron said that Guy had worked with a spirit medium, a Madame Sylvie."

I set the draft of the bylaws for a freight company, made a series of notes for the primary counsel, and picked up the morning newspaper.

The morning newspaper held an obituary for Lucinda that explained nothing of how she died, but it also had a second-page article about the deaths:

> **Two Deaths from the Opposite Ends of Society**.
> Yesterday evening. A woman of aristocratic mien in an unfortunate part of town. Had she cried out, no one would have heard the poor creature.
> This comes after a similar murder earlier in the week of a woman, a known courtesan, who was found killed in a most brutal manner. Her body had been violated in the manner of the vilest lunatic and then dumped in an alley behind a saloon in the most boisterous part of town. The city

commission is concerned that a maniac is on the loose in our already beleaguered city.

As rail transport has been restored and enhanced since the storm, tramps and hobos can come to our city easily and leave unseen. The city police believe one of this number harbors the vilest of intentions.

Could this have been the work of a transient and a maniac? I doubted Barker thought that. His questioning of Winnie and visit to the Confederate Soldier's Home showed he believed the murderer somehow connected to Lucinda.

From the stairs, I heard the scream of a child.

"Oh no," I said to Evangeline. "I think that's mine." I ran.

"Oh, Miss Dash," Aunt Cornelia rushed up the stairs to my office and clasped her hands at the sight of me as though I were the answer to a fervent prayer. "You deal with them."

My youngest daughter, Jinxie wrapped her arms as far as she could around Aunt Cornelia, her skirt, and her petticoats.

"Hello, darling." I extended my arms and knelt down for a hug. "I'm glad to see you."

She took an instant to take her face from Aunt Cornelia's apron and notice me. Her large gray eyes were red, and tears streaked down her face. She pulled herself away from Aunt Cornelia and wrapped herself around me.

I smelled kid and soap. I was glad to be here and so glad to have her. I kissed the top of her head.

I figured a better question than "Where's your sister?" must exist. "Everything good?"

Aunt Cornelia pinched her forehead up in a concerned frown. "The girls are upset."

"Yes, I saw." I pulled Jinxie far enough away to see her face. "What happened?"

"I told them you wouldn't be happy with them--"

"Shh!" I said to Aunt Cornelia.

The girl dissolved into body-shaking tears.

"They thought they saw her." Aunt Cornelia used the slow words and frown of one breaking the news about a family member dying. "Their mother."

"But I'm here, darling."

Aunt Cornelia shook her head. "Their first mother."

Teddie stood at the top of the stairs, but did not come into the office.

I gestured to her to come downstairs with a scoop of my hand.

I looked at Jinxie and smiled at her. "You don't have to worry, darling, I'm here. I'm your mother."

Teddie walked down the stairs at execution gait. She stopped beside me.

I opened an arm to take her into the hug. "It's okay, sweetie. I love you."

She wandered into my hug. She still didn't look at me. I wanted to yank her head up so she would see me, but something told me that was a bad idea.

I rested my head between the two of theirs.

Jinxie's tears ebbed and may even have stopped.

"Girls. Your original mother was killed by the storm. You know that. I know it's sad, but I'm grateful that she brought my girls into the world." I knew this sentiment was something they wouldn't understand today, but I figured parenting was about doing things for a someday.

Teddie lifted her face to mine. Her eyes were shiny with tears. "I saw her. I saw her long hair. She was walking down the street out there."

I tightened the hug and then released them. I couldn't take myself away from them, though, and I held a hand of theirs in each of mine. "Your original parents died in the storm. That is sad, but God led you to be my girls."

"But--"

"The orphanage wouldn't have given you to me if there were any doubt."

Aunt Cornelia shook her head. "I told them you'd give them a switch if they didn't stop this."

I stood and hissed, "This isn't like stealing a cookie. It's not something that can be switched out of them." I rubbed an arm of each of the girls. "Girls, you need to understand. If they hadn't died, don't you think they would have come back for you when you were in the orphanage?"

"If I may, Miss Dash," whispered Evangeline behind me. At my nod, she said, "You argue thinking when they're feeling."

Barker might consider me a sappy woman, but I was always more comfortable with thinking than with feeling. I said nothing, but I gave a sigh.

"Miss Lucinda came back." Teddie still looked at me. Her brow furrowed with the insistence of her statement.

Jinxie shuddered with more tears.

Aunt Cornelia looked at her, then looked at me. "They heard about what was in the paper, about the two women being killed. I don't know how they found out."

Teddie let out a huff. "We can read."

Aunt Cornelia ignored her and continued speaking to me. "They think that, if their mother is back, then she--"

"She can't be back," I said.

"I know, I know she can't be, but they're afraid that man will kill her before she comes back."

I felt the breath knocked from me and could only give the barest whisper. "I'm their mother."

"I know," Aunt Cornelia reassured me with a maternal tone as if I were one of the girls.

"I'm doing what I can to solve those murders, but when I do find the killer, it won't bring your mother back."

"You'll find him?" Teddie asked.

At least she'd listened to some of what I said.

"That's a big promise," Evangeline whispered.

I took the girls' hands and walked down the stairs with them. "Things will get better," I assured them. I didn't know how, but I knew they would. "Things always get better." I kissed them both and gave them each a penny to get a cookie at the bakery that took up part of the downstairs space of Barker's building.

A pair of women rounded the corner. No, one woman in heavy mourning of black serge rounded the corner; her black veil with satin edging billowed in the intermittent breeze.

I stepped aside from a skinny man in a suit and red vest who rushed into the building--a man so narrow, his teeth seemed to be the only thing swelling his cheeks as he made slow progress on spindly legs up the stairs. He gave me a polite bow that showed how his slicked hair shined.

I gave what I hoped was a professional nod. After a kiss to each girl, I walked back inside my building. With a quick nod to the narrow man, the woman in mourning marched past him up the stairs.

A slow smile spread across the man's face, jack-o-lantern wide. He turned around at the landing and said, "Mrs. Gallagher, I'm here to see you. If we could go to your office?"

I said nothing, but walked past him to the office. I had no time for a salesman, but I'd found the best way to get rid of drummers was to sit and do my work, ignoring them.

The woman in mourning stopped outside Barker's office.

I saw her face through the veil. It was Miss Alice. She was back at Barker's office. I started after her. I had no reason to entertain this fellow's sales pitch when I wanted to know whether Alice knew anything about Lucinda's death. She had agreed to let Barker tell me of her case. She must not mind me finding things out.

Barker reached out and shook hands with the man. "I have a few moments. I can see you, Earl."

"I'm not here to see you, Mr. Barker, but your lady friend." Earl poked the air at me and gave Miss

Alice a glance and a smile that was too fast to be disrespectful.

He had a narrow face that seemed to taper to his long nose and small mouth. His dress was flashy, with a flowing red silk cravat and a suit of fawn-colored plaid with a red stripe in the design. He held a briefcase of red leather.

I'd have bet his socks were red.

I turned to Barker with a question in my eyes, but he had ushered Miss Alice into his office and closed the door.

Damn, I wanted in there! At this moment, I wondered if the only thing I could do for my daughters was solve this crime.

I turned to the man with a smile. Maybe he was a prospective client. I could use the business.

"This way, sir. I have a moment." Please, let it be only a moment.

He gave a little laugh and followed me. "I'm no 'sir,' just call me Earl."

"And she's Mrs. Gallagher." Evangeline glared at him.

Earl must also have noticed her black-brown eyes narrowing and nostrils flaring. "Do I know you?"

"Nope." Evangeline ripped a piece of paper from her typewriter, crumpled it, and tossed it into the gilt-edged rubbish can. "I've seen your kind before."

Now I narrowed my eyes toward Earl.

He put his hat on the hat rack, sat his briefcase on the visitor's chair, and spread his hands out to his sides with palms wide. "I have many types."

"What does that mean?" I folded my arms across the short jacket of my pale blue suit with yellow trim.

"People need all sorts of things." Earl flicked his head toward my door as though that might mean something to me before he pulled one of the red velvet chairs from the wall to sit close to my desk.

"I need nothing right now." I sat to face the work on my desk. Even if I did need what he sold, I had no money or patience for a drummer right now. "And I've no time for a drummer."

"Everyone needs a little something now and then. My role is to provide comfort, not to judge."

Comfort?

"Oh, I know who you are," I said. He was the man who managed the front door at Molly Perkin's whorehouse.

"I consider myself a majordomo." He crossed one ankle over the knee of the other leg to show red, green, and tan argyle socks. "I'm here because my employer wanted to retain your services, and I bring a check."

"Employer?" Evangeline meowed.

"Yes," Earl said. "Mrs. Mildred Perkins."

"Molly Perkins! You think we would do business with her?"

"Yes." I wobbled my head at Evangeline. "I did, but I don't think . . ." I remembered what MJ had said about people who cross Molly. Earl was big enough to kill someone and had a pistol bulge in his vest pocket.

Evangeline didn't look at me, but at Earl. "Is this about the girl who was killed?"

"I agreed to represent Mrs. Perkins," I told Evangeline. "I intend to give any money she gives me to charity."

"Admirable," Earl said.

I felt my hand flutter in an impatient gesture. I wanted him out of here, and not just because I wanted to barge into Barker's office.

He slid a check across the surface of my desk.

Oh my, that was a lot of money. That would pay for so much, so many ways I could help my girls.

"Thank you, Mr. . . . Earl." I rose and gave a tip of my head as I passed him on my progress to the door. "Evangeline will help you with any details." I was out the door and in front of Barker's office before I had even taken a breath.

I gave a quick rap of the knuckles on the rippled glass of Barker's door and walked inside.

In the center of the green plush settee, Miss Alice flipped back her black veil and looked toward Barker. ". . . your retainer, if you wish." She looked at me with her eyes open in surprise for an instant before she turned back to Barker and then looked out the window beyond. "But I thank you for what work you've done."

"Of course." Barker gave her a quick bow and gave an expansive gesture of his arm toward me. "Mrs. Wyngate, you've met Mrs. Gallagher."

"I figured you might want my assistance," I said to Barker.

His smile looked as though it might erupt into the laughter that twinkled in his eyes. "I'm surprised you took this long."

I fought to keep from smiling at him. "Miss Alice, you know I was assisting Winnie. Oh, and also your son, in the divorce." At least, I told him I would charge him.

"Mrs. Gallagher," Barker said, "has assisted me in learning what I told you about Lucinda."

So, he'd been through what he found out. She was a client and had paid to know. She also was a suspect, so I wondered if he'd left anything out.

"Thank you," Alice said. "You can see I'm in mourning for her."

"Yes," I said. I slid in to sit in the chair near where she sat on the settee. "Terrible, the way she died. Were you close?"

"Yes." Miss Alice looked at her gloved hands. "She doted on me. I did everything for her. For her to leave and come up with that story about--being in an asylum--well, to bring scandal on the business like that is unconscionable." She pressed a black-edged handkerchief to her face and closed her eyes to take a deep breath.

"On the business?" I repeated. "How?"

"All of the women in our family represent the business, no matter whether our husbands work there or not." She smiled at her hands. "She was always eager to help me. Being a hostess to businessmen can be tiring, and I find it too much for me sometimes. I was glad to have . . ." She frowned and drew in a deep breath. "I can't imagine why she'd run away. We did so much . . . I know she was happy."

I smiled to make my voice light and easy. "But this wasn't the first time she had left you, left Abelard."

She shot a frowning glance to me. "I can't imagine what would make her run away."

"You can't think of any reason?" I asked.

"Certainly, I don't have a clue. Not unless someone, I don't know, some pressure. Running away when she was so happy. I don't understand it."

I slipped a glance to Barker. I willed him to notice what I had. She was talking about Lucinda's leaving, not her coming back.

Barker said nothing, and I rushed to fill the gap in conversation that I, at least, found to be awkward. Winnie had told me that these are natural pauses in the flow of talk, but that was introverted thinking, and I'd have none of it. "Disappearing was dreadful. Why do you think she came back?"

"A man," Miss Alice said. Her hand slid up to cover her mouth for a moment. "Oh, God forgive me for it, but there was a man waiting for her at the edge of the garden the first night she came back. She didn't know I saw her sneak out." She looked at Barker, at me, and then back to Barker. "I should have done something, I know. I should have interfered, as the mother of her husband." Her eyes dropped beneath her lashes. "She seemed to need Abelard so much and even to need me. She depended on us. Why would she suddenly leave? Who convinced her to do such a thing?"

"Maybe she did lose her mind after the storm," I said.

"I can't believe that would happen if she thought we were alive," Miss Alice said.

"And you knew her better than anyone," Barker stated.

She looked at Barker, at me, and then out the window. "Abelard might say he knew her best, but I'm a mother. I believe I know even more than my boy, yes, even about his wife."

I smiled at her.

Her voice was warm and engaging, and she turned a sweet smile at me and gave a slow blink.

I gave her arm a gentle touch. "Forgive me. Did someone once die in your house?"

"The house has been there since before the War. Sam Houston once stayed there, as did Austin. Along with all the history, there is probably tragedy as well. I imagine someone--more than one--has."

"I mean, during the storm," I said. "That you know of."

Barker looked at me in amusement.

"Why, yes," Miss Alice said. She looked at the ceiling with a frown as she found the memory. "Not one of the family. Our maid--I don't know why--she climbed in the dumbwaiter and went down into the basement. She drowned."

I hoped I didn't show the whites of my eyes like a spooked horse, but I felt goose bumps rise on my arms.

"None of us knew why she did such a thing. We harbored so many people that night. I was so busy. I didn't know until the next day, when they found her body."

"How terrible," I said.

"I must be going." Miss Alice lowered her veil over her face. "I'm glad you understand that we want to put this whole Lucinda business to rest. This has been so difficult, so emotional for all of us."

"Yes, of course," Barker said. He extended an arm, and she rested her hand on it to rise from the seat. He walked her out of the office and down the stairs.

He came back and saw me still sitting on his settee. "What was that? That 'anyone died in your house' argy bargy?"

I shrugged.

Barker interrogated me with eyebrows raised over his glance.

I looked at my hands. "Very composed woman."

"Too composed?"

Barker was still staring at me.

"I don't think she let us see her emotions, but I don't think that means she's a killer."

Barker smiled. "Good, gather information."

"And what do you think about her?"

Barker shot a look at the door, as though to make sure she was not hovering outside. "I think she worries about money."

"From something she said before I came in?"

He shook his head and looked at me, waiting for me to come up with the right answer.

I huffed a little sigh and rolled my eyes to disguise my efforts at furious and unproductive thought. "Oh yes!" I remembered something. "All the talk about business. That was important because she is worried."

"And . . ."

"And what? Please, just tell me."

"And her whole reason for being here, lass."

I scrunched up my forehead to think. "Oh yes. To tell you she didn't want to pay you to find out about a woman who is dead."

"Why would she care about that in a time like this?"

"Either she's cheap enough to make the eagle on the coin squeak, or she's short of funds."

"They're selling off assets," Barker said. "The family isn't as wealthy as it used to be when the father ran things."

I got up to leave, but Barker placed a hand on my arm.

"So, tell me about this dead woman and you."

Words tumbled out of me about my apprehension in the Wyngate mansion, about my dream, and about the ghost I saw when we snuck into the mansion.

I ran back to my office before he could laugh at me.

Back at my office, a small blonde woman, with a gait that could not be proven to touch the floor billowed into my office. Eula Rose Wyngate. She whirled around and called to someone who must be at the bottom of the stairs. "I'll be with you in a minute, Mother Wyngate."

I had seen two women round the corner to the bakery, I realized. Eula Rose had been behind Miss Alice. She just hadn't come into the building until now, until she wanted to see me.

She gave a smile that went up to her rosy cheeks and Delft-blue eyes. She turned her gaze from Evangeline to me and back a couple more times. She proffered a visiting card.

Evangeline realized that the presence of this creature from the realms of a Pre-Raphaelite fairyland required some pageantry and strode from behind her desk to take the card and read aloud, "Mrs. Sextus Wyngate."

"Hello, Mrs. Wyngate, I'm so pleased to see you here." I stepped forward to shake her hand. She was probably the most respectable member of society ever to walk into my office. "So, you're down from the church steps."

"Pardon?" She said the word slowly, making the two syllables almost two words.

"On the church steps. The last time I saw you. The day of the wedding that wasn't to be."

"Sad business, that." She gave a sage nod, and her smile disappeared into a restrained moue. Her blue eyes hid behind the thick, pale lashes for an instant and opened bright again toward me. "Is there some place we can speak privately?"

I turned to Evangeline to gesture to the person from whom I had no secrets, but saw she pointed toward the door.

"The waiting room outside is very nice." Evangeline smiled, but not enough to show her dimples.

I led the way to the waiting room of green plush seats within the dark walnut of Gothic arch trim and a medieval-style flowered wainscot.

"You do have a nice building here," said Eula Rose. She looked out the large round window to where skeletons of buildings remained from the flood nearly a year ago and to the brown waters of the Gulf of Mexico beyond.

"Oh, it's Mr. Barker's office. I rent." I sat and bit my lip before more stupidity could belch forth from my mouth.

She nodded. She smoothed the back of her wide skirt and lowered slowly into a seat opposite me. "I was sure you wouldn't mind my making a call to your office. I knew you worked." She did not say, "I knew you had to work," but I found myself wondering if she thought that.

"I appreciate your calling on me." I considered offering her tea, but the way she fidgeted with the chain of her purse looked like the sort of impatience I felt when the pastor went on too long and I was wearing shoes that were too tight. I wouldn't prolong her stay. If it was business and not a social call, I'd learned to let people get to it on their own.

"I'm here because you left your card at my in-laws' house."

I nodded. I said nothing. I prayed she did not see the sweat I knew was glistening all over me at the thought of what she said: did she know I had burgled the house? Was she going to send me to jail? I forced a smile that iron will and clamped lips kept from shaking.

"You had come to visit them." She spoke in the distinct words of a tipsy person attempting not to slur, but the blue gaze trained on me was sober as a funeral.

I nodded.

"That was nice of you." She tipped her head and gave me a little smile. "I suppose."

I suppose? "I figured they were going through a tough time right now. All of this must be just devastating."

"Yes." Sad little moue was back. "Is that why you were there? At Mother Wyngate's?"

What did she mean? Did they realize I broke into the Wyngate mansion? I wanted to bolt into my office and declare this conversation over, but I was a logical creature, even if Barker might laugh if I told him that. Logic demanded that I tough this out and learn what she knew. Damn, I needed to say something. I remembered the last time I was officially in the Wyngate's house. "I wanted to make sure my friend, Winnie, didn't go to the tea dance alone."

A frown creased her peachy forehead and fluffed her pale eyebrows, and plunged the room into more silence filled with my own worries.

"This situation must be terribly hard for the whole family." I pressed my hand to my chest in a light gesture. "I didn't know Lucinda. Did you know her well?" I wanted to get the subject off of me.

Eula Rose gave a little shrug. "I never got to know her much."

"But she was your sister-in-law?"

She gave an impatient sigh through her nose. "She was a shy thing. I didn't pry."

I smiled. I hoped she wouldn't pry too much into my night-time activities.

She stretched her little feet forward and gave me the smile again. "I remember you from the church steps. I asked your friend from the paper, the writer gal, about what you had done for the Russian Consulate."

"Yes," I smiled. I had helped Barker on a previous case that involved Russians.

"You're from Russia, aren't you?"

"Yes." I told myself this was good that the conversation was no longer about my presence at the Wyngate mansion, but I wasn't so sure.

"And adopted by Americans?"

"Yes. Why do you ask?" Why do you pry when you won't allow me to do so?

"Oh, I find that fascinating." She gave a little laugh. "Do you remember your real parents?"

Real parents? Well, that wasn't the first time I'd heard that. Not everyone understood that my real parents were the ones who loved me, not the ones who threw me into walls when in a drunken rage or who went at each other with knives. Those people had given birth to me and nothing else.

I shook my head. "Not really."

"That's a shame."

I didn't wait for her to explain why. "You're interested in adoption?"

"No, I have children of my own. Two and . . ." She blushed to imply that she was pregnant but was too ladylike to say she was "with squirrel."

"Congratulations."

She frowned, tipped her head, and even let her little mouth gape in confusion.

I wondered whether she might know why Lucinda was in that part of town, but more than anything, I wanted to fill this silence that echoed with my stupidity. "So, you weren't close to your late sister-in-law?"

She shrugged and gave a weak shake of her head. "Do you still speak Russian?"

"Yes, why do you ask?"

"Oh, I was wondering what it sounds like. Can you say something in Russian?" The smile was back, all the way to her eyes. "Say something."

I found myself on my feet. I resisted the urge to use my knowledge of Russian to suggest she and that whore she called a mother go to hell; it is a language good at that, and living on the street, you learned that even as a child. "I must get back to work."

"Yes, of course." She looked at her purse strap that was now wound around her glove. "I wished to let you know you that don't need to call on my in-laws again." She turned those doe eyes up at me. "They aren't exactly friends of yours, are they?"

"What with me being Russian and all?"

She laughed and covered her mouth with her hand.

"Or because I was adopted?"

"Now that wasn't what I said, was it?"

I stared at her. This time the silence was working for me instead of against.

"I'll be going now." She stood.

"I'll consider your views." *In a pig's eye.*

"That's very good of you." The smile was all the way back to her eyes.

I watched her walk down the stairs and out the door. I turned and saw Evangeline behind her desk, typing at a rapid pace. I strode back into my office and kicked the door closed behind me.

I leaned on the door for a moment. I was as good as any Eula Rose Wyngate.

Hell no.

"Evangeline, send Mrs. Sextus Wyngate a bill for fifteen minutes of my time."

"Outstanding," she murmured, which made me think she had listened to the conversation.

"At the full whorehouse rate."

Evangeline giggled and had the billing form out before I finished speaking.

I went back to the trust assets I was reviewing on my desk. Eula Rose and her ilk were the guardians of the life I wanted for my daughters, the life I didn't have as a child. I might have caused harm to that goal, but I doubted being nice and taking her insults would have helped.

Leaning against the telephone niche in my hallway, I spoke into the receiver on the brass candlestick telephone. "MJ, have you heard of this Sylvie woman?"

"I have." Winnie's tea cup clattered against the saucer. She held the pot up in silent offer of a cup. "I have an appointment with her tomorrow. Abelard suggested it."

I shook my head at the teapot. "Never mind, MJ Bye-bye."

The tinny voice at the other end of the candlestick telephone cried through the static, "Wait--"

I depressed the switch hook with a satisfying click and put the earpiece back.

MJ would probably talk for another five minutes and seethe for another ten after she realized what I had done.

"Abelard?"

"He's a visionary: most men of science are."

I turned to Winnie. "So, what time tomorrow?"

She shook her head. "I thought you were a skeptic."

"I'm a Baptist."

Winnie pursed her lips and nodded. "A skeptic. I don't think going with me would suit you because, well, you aren't looking for answers." She strolled into the front parlor and sat on the couch.

I followed her and took my place on the hydrangea print of the swooning couch.

Dewey wandered into the room after us and sniffed each surface for change since his last round of sniffing in the morning.

I crossed my legs. "I don't think Dewey believes in haints, either."

"I went to a medium once before, one who specialized in figuring out where you were before this life. I figured I might have had some fascinating adventures before." Winnie took a sip of tea. "Life as a spy or a princess."

"Or a pirate?" Yes, I wondered what she knew about pirates.

"No such luck. She said, 'I see you standing in dirt. There you are, standing in dirt.' That was all she said. I don't know whether I was a farmer or what, but I seem to have been pretty dull in my past lives."

So, my attempt at subtle inquiry didn't work. I loved my friend; I cared about her. I couldn't see her as a murderer, but she had not been cleared as a suspect.

I hadn't cleared any suspects. Mr. Wyngate, his wife Miss Alice, and their sons Sextus, Abelard, and Beau all remained suspects along with the Eula Rose--although I couldn't see a motive--and of course Winnie. They hadn't been eliminated, and another had only been added with this Guy fellow.

I wished Barker had been in his office to talk to me. When I crossed the hall to find him, the door was locked, and I saw no movement behind that frosted, rippled glass.

Dewey gave Winnie's tan skirt a sniff, found nothing extraordinary, and moved on to the end table, where a cloth mouse hung on a string. He reared up on his back legs and gave the mouse a good slap with his single front paw.

I grinned. "You made a present for Dewey?"

With that schoolmarm purse to her lips, she nodded. "I am so thankful for your hospitality, but I feel I need to do something to repay you."

Now I felt like a grade-A heel for thinking of her as a potential murderer, but wouldn't a murderer work on my emotions that way? "It's okay, I like having you here."

"And I miss my cats." She beckoned to Dewey in a husky, flat tone as though she called through a bunch of crackers in her mouth.

"You can bring them here. Dewey's probably not the most charitable of hosts, but he'll adapt."

"No, I couldn't take them away from Alois right now. He's lost so much in the last few days."

Yes, an opening. "He and Abelard went camping."

"How did you know?" Pretending I didn't know something that I did just seemed dishonest, so I answered my own question by blurting, "Abelard said so."

Her mouth gave a shrug. "I didn't even know."

I patted her hand.

"I had so much to say to him. I still do, but we didn't talk at all." She looked at her toes for a moment and gave a sniff. "I don't even know when we're going to get married. I mean, if." When she looked up at me, she had fought back any tears. "Sure you don't want a cup of tea? I got some of the that stuff Alexandra of England drinks."

"Oh, stay down! I'll pour my own cup."

While I poured the tea from the pot on the end table with my back to Winnie, I heard her whisper. "I love him, and I want to say things, but I don't know what to do."

I thought of the girls, now ignoring me upstairs. "I don't know what you can do." I didn't know what I could do, either. With a clatter, I placed the china cup on the saucer. I looked down at the deep blue flowers within the gold rim. "Is Eula Rose Wyngate a conceited witch?"

"What did she do?"

"Yesterday, she came to my office to tell me I was not suitable to make a sympathy call on her in-laws."

Winnie laughed. "That sounds like something she'd do."

I had my waiting-for-an-answer tip of the head going, just like when I shepherded the girls through their homework.

Winnie looked up at the top of the ten-foot pocket door to the dining room. "No, not really. She's protective of her family. She has a sense of everything belonging in its place that can be irritating, but she's--well--I wouldn't say all right, but I'd say she's unlikely to cause too much trouble."

But would she fight or even kill if she believed someone did pose trouble for her family?

"And whom would you say," I said. "Does cause too much trouble?"

"That bitch, Lulu, who seems to be coming from beyond the grave to ruin my life."

I peered out the side window to make sure neither of the girls--or the neighbors--were close enough to hear her vulgarity.

"Miss Alice is a formidable woman." I said. "She doesn't need Eula Rose protecting her, and I don't think she'd like it one bit if she found out her daughter-in-law was doing that."

"I have no evidence for this, but I think that some of Eula Rose's properness--especially when she's telling others to be that way--is actually from Sextus. He dotes on her, but I think that's because she will tell people off and allow him to be above all that."

"Do you think Sextus had his wife tell me to back away?" Maybe he suspected I was investigating the murder and didn't want anyone getting to the crux of that.

Do you think Sextus would tell his wife to kill women? No, Eula Rose was probably the only person I could rule out as a suspect; she was too small to have made the cuts.

Winnie nodded and then shrugged. "Who knows?"

Maybe this Sylvie would know something.

Whenever I looked out into the sea, I started looking for bodies rolling in the surf until I reminded myself that would no longer happen.

I turned away from the gray ocean with the history it had swallowed and back into the present. Stepping from the trolley car, I lifted my head and felt the sleek black feathers of my hat ripple with the wind. I loved this hat, and I loved my lingerie-style dress of black lace and net over a lavender lining. The black crepe band I wore around the arm blended with the pattern.

"I figure Sylvie's place has got a sign." I said. "Or a tent with an eye painted on it or something."

Winnie held her wide straw hat and stepped from the street car with a billow of her checked, cotton dress.

On one side of the road lay the ocean, and on the other a few small buildings stood like the remaining teeth in an old-man's mouth: a bait shop with a large hook painted between the second story windows and a handful of houses made from the same weathered planks, pasted on with the haphazard hope of creating a building but without any aspirations of withstanding another great storm. These structures that could barely be called buildings were made of storm-lumber salvaged after the hurricane.

One lot held a gnarled tree that had withstood the hurricane without coming down, but then died a slow death standing in its spot, and another storm-lumber fence held in a few cows. At least they had cleared the bodies away.

My mind filled with the savaged body of the prostitute and that of Lucinda, and then I thought back to images of bodies from the storm: a woman sliced so badly from debris that she had no face, a man lying in swamp water months later with a head swollen beyond where it could be recognized as human, and bloated bodies washing back ashore.

My husband was one of those whose body was never recovered. He might have washed out to sea, but he probably was one of the thousands who were loaded onto boats and dumped in the Gulf. The corpses, then in a state of horrid decomposition, floated back onto the beaches until they were burned.

A familiar, skinny redhead walked up between us and wrapped an arm around each of us. "Or we fall into a trance and it will be suddenly revealed to us."

"Hello, MJ," Winnie said. "How did you know when we'd be here?"

I glared at the white lace glove on my black lace shoulder.

MJ tilted her head back and released her grip. "First appointment of the morning seemed her style." A jerk of the head toward me. "Now, let's go see the wonderful wizard."

"There," I announced with a point toward a small house with a veranda. Storm lumber pitched to a peak to form a roof. A sign nailed to a stick read "Mme S. by appointment only." It stood before a sandy yard with a small house. Over the red door, a transom of broken glass bore tattered bits of gold paint, remains in a ghostly form of almost all the letters needed to write, "Trance medium."

Winnie slapped down a door knocker held by screws on only one side.

The door stuttered open. Winnie turned back and fought a smile. "Oooooh!"

MJ rolled her eyes.

I bit my lip.

Winnie walked inside. "Hello? Madame Sylvie?"

The house had a small landing with a wooden floor and no furniture. Doors led in three directions and back where we came. Each door was closed.

MJ looked around with her arms folded across the chest of her pale linen suit. "So, do we wait here or open doors until a beast from the netherworld comes out? Any of them have Pandora on it, by chance?"

Winnie giggled.

"She might have another appointment," I said. "I don't want to burst in while she's in the midst of evoking material from the realm of the spirits."

MJ leaned against the doorjamb and pushed aside a velvet curtain to expose a closed door. "A couple months after the storm, a spirit medium went around town producing bits of spirits."

"Really?" Winnie asked. She looked around the corner and stepped inside.

"They said she could bring them out of any orifice. Yep, you guessed it, where she was hiding the stuff. They searched her pockets, but decorum made them leave one undiscovered until the reporter turned on a flashlight and caught her in the act of, let's call it, 'unveiling.'"

"I choose to believe one can create film from the spirit world." Winnie tilted her head up so her glasses reflected the light from the broken window. "Doesn't it make sense that, as we see the physical world around us, there should also be some proof of another realm?"

"No," I said. "That's what faith is for."

Winnie gave a slight smirk.

The door behind MJ opened. MJ turned and looked at her skirt to avoid a stumble.

Madame Sylvie stood before us, even taller and darker than I remembered from when I met her at the tea dance. She wore a long-sleeved black dress with jet beads. Even in the heat, even with all of the windows closed and a smell I figured was incense, she did not seem to sweat.

She raised a stately, slow arm to gesture behind her. I figured she must be wearing double dress shields or something. She also wore the long veil of heavy mourning.

In a rumbling voice, she said. "I am ready. You may come in, Winnie. I see you needed to bring your friends. I understand. A tough time. You need the support of those you've known the longest in your life."

Winnie nodded and walked into what looked like a dining room with a large round oak table, a hurricane lamp draped with dangling crystals hanging from the center of the ceiling, and velvet curtains over the windows.

MJ raised her eyebrows at me.

I forced myself not to hunch in my chair--at least, my health corset thrusting me forward and my will did. I didn't like this. She might be evil. She might know things that no good human could know. I was glad she had not seemed to notice me and would do all I could to keep that from happening.

Winnie smiled. "I'm so glad you could make the time to see me, Mrs. Matthews."

"Madam Sylvie." She rested a black shawl over her shoulders, as though the room's 90-degree temperature were not warm enough. She glided down to a chair of pressed-back oak. With both hands moving in a slow ceremony, she slipped the veil from her face to reveal a paler complexion than I recalled. "Winnie, dear, you were right to come to me."

Winnie took the chair opposite the medium. MJ and I pulled in on either side.

Madam Sylvie reached up and started to crank the flame down on the hurricane lamp.

"Uh, no," MJ said. "We'd like it bright and shiny in here."

Winnie slipped a half-smile at her.

"And who are you?" Sylvie asked MJ Her voice was low and rumbling. It probably sounded as though she were casting a spell when she asked the grocer for a bar of Pear's soap.

"You tell me." MJ gave her fingernails a glance. She must have also been psychic because she would have had to see through her gloves to view them.

"MJ Quackenbush, but that is because of my ability to read the newspaper, not any psychic understanding."

"From reading the paper? They don't put her picture in the society section." And if MJ's story went farther forward in the paper, she had no byline at all.

"Then perhaps it was a psychic utterance." She whipped her head toward Winnie. "We are not here for them, but for you."

Winnie smiled with pursed lips.

Sylvie took her hand. Their handhold was all that stretched across the table. "I see you are shy."

Winnie thought a moment and then nodded.

"You wish you were not . . . not the wallflower who sits before me."

"Eh?" Winnie said.

"You know you have let so many chances pass you by. You wish you could speak to people, but the words catch in your throat." Sylvie pulled Winnie's hand closer, but it jerked back even closer to Winnie than it had been. "You want so much more from life, but you are afraid. Afraid to talk to--"

Winnie jerked her hand from Sylvie's. "No, you're not even close."

"That is what the spirits say."

"Then the spirits are full of beans."

MJ leaned forward. "You do a handsome business with some of the folks that I happen to write about. They seem more taken with your skills than my friend here."

"I do not discuss my clients." She waved her hand toward MJ, but the gesture ended in the ceiling as if leaving her to deal with a higher authority.

MJ shrugged. "I'm just saying that if you gave me the odd tidbit--no names, of course--I could maybe see that the paper reimburses the spirits for their effort."

I looked at Winnie for a reaction.

She still stared at Sylvie. "If I were such a forlorn, friendless creature, would I have come here today with not one, but two friends?"

"Something for you to consider," MJ said.

Sylvie snapped her head toward MJ. "I will consider no such thing."

MJ's hands went to her hips. "See here, you cockeyed charlatan, I'm offering--"

"Nothing you've said makes any sense." Winnie said. "You just assumed that, because I'm quiet and wear glasses, that I don't have any--"

"What about Lucinda?" I asked. "She was a client, wasn't she?"

Sylvie sat a little taller. "Yes, I knew her. I knew her well. I was so sad when she plunged to her death in that bath house.

"She came back from that death," MJ said.

"I'd think you would have known that," Winnie said. "Being a psychic and all.

Sylvie closed her eyes in what looked like an attempt to shut out our noise. "She was always thinking of others. Yes, it was a luncheon to raise money, that was why she was out there in the storm. Such a woman for her spirit to go out." She looked from me, to Winnie, and then to MJ's sneer that moved around as if she chewed gum, or maybe tacks. "Yes, her spirit went out. She left this place, this spiritual place. Her body remained. It searched for something." Sylvie made an expansive gesture with both hands. "And I wonder now if her spirit continues that search from the other realms."

The curtains closed us in the room.

I couldn't detect any mechanism to pull the drapes free from their moorings in the curtain hook. I couldn't see anything. What was I looking for? I turned back to Sylvie.

The lamp died.

"Hush," Sylvie said. "All of you."

I wanted out. I wanted to stand up and walk away, but I also wanted something else: answers. "You knew Lucinda well?"

A sound. It reminded me of an inhale from one of my daughters, a sigh, perhaps. It came from above. I looked up and saw a whiteness, like a piece of gauze underwater, swirl around the room.

How could I even see this in the blackened room?

Then, the whiteness swirled and formed. It was a face: Lucinda.

I looked to Winnie but could not see her in the blackness, nor could I see MJ.

When I looked up, the face was gone, and only blackness remained.

"I never hurt you," a faint voice said. It sounded like the sweet, almost childish voice I remembered from Lucinda. "Why won't you help me?"

"How can we help?" Sylvie asked.

"Find my jewels," the ghost of Lucinda said. At least, it sure looked like the ghost of Lucinda.

I tried to tell myself it was a magic lantern projection, but why was it moving? How was it making the back of my neck prickle?

"What jewels?" I heard Winnie's voice ask.

"Those dead before me, long dead before me. They hunt me, they hurt me." A scream, Lucinda's words ended in a scream that sounded like a child's, like one of my own daughters. "Only the jewels can free me."

I felt tears sting my cheeks.

A dim yellow light glowed to life at the side of the room.

The lamplight shone in Winnie's glasses, and MJ's pale face looked white against her freckles. She blinked hard with her mouth pressed to a fine line. One side of that line opened to say, "So, Madam Sylvie, how about our deal?"

Madame Sylvie's dark eyes glared black at MJ.

"My employers can make it worth your while."

"Money! What do I need of the physical world?" Madame Sylvie stood and lowered her veil over her face.

"There are other ways to make it worth your while," MJ said. She pushed too hard. She had two styles: pushing too hard or charming to death. She smiled. "I don't know if you realize your power."

Madame Sylvie hesitated for a moment, but then continued her flounce out the door. "My servant will work out the billing with you."

An adolescent black girl stood just inside the entrance.

Winnie counted five dollars and fifty cents--enough for an expensive sewing machine--into the silent girl's hand and met us outside.

"Don't ever make me do anything like that again," I said to Winnie.

"Weird, huh?"

I doubted I had learned anything about Lucinda's connection to Madame Sylvie, and I wasn't any closer to finding the murderer. All that appointment gave me was more questions. For one of them, I thought I could get an answer.

I started toward the trolley stop and said in a soft voice so as not to frighten anyone, "What were you doing, MJ? Trying to spook the spook?"

MJ gave a dismissive slap of the air. "I don't need information from her. I just wanted to see whether she'd give any."

"Why on earth . . ?"

"Or in the spirit world," Winnie whispered.

MJ looked both ways. Since we had not made it to the street yet, I had to assume she feared eavesdroppers. "No one will say anything, blackmail being a nasty word and all, but I've heard whispers about it--just a couple--when I've asked folks about Lucinda."

"Yes," I said. I hoped she wouldn't ask what I knew about that.

I saw a question form on Winnie's lips, but before she could say anything, MJ gave first Winnie and then me a stiff hug. "I've got to be off, lambs;. A couple of the fellows at the yacht club said they'd teach me to smoke cigars."

I made a sick grimace, but she didn't notice; she bounded across the street with a wave over her shoulder.

Winnie watched her bound away. "She's just a little peppercorn." She held her hat in both hands as the wind blasted us. "But blackmail?"

"Yes," I said. "You know anything about Lucinda and blackmail?" If Abelard knew anything, he had probably told Winnie at some time.

Barker stood in the doorway of my office with hands on hips and blue eyes opened wide beneath the frown on his sloping forehead.

From my desk, I gave him a bright smile.

He said, "Why does the man I am interrogating speak of nothing but you?"

"Some think I'm lovely--many, in fact." I jabbed my pen into the crystal inkwell, wiped the sides of the nib, and gave it a little tap on the blotter before I scratched a note on the amendment. "Perhaps he's ensnared by my charms."

Evangeline's typewriter "dinged" at the end of the row. She slapped the roller to the next and continued typing without acknowledging us.

"He did not sound ensnared." Barker's Scottish accent was so strong, he barely finished each word. "He sounded bothered."

"Well, yes, I've been known to have that effect on men, too. Who is it?"

"Sextus Wyngate."

The clack of the typewriter keys stopped. Evangeline said, "Must be about the bill. Probably more

than his wife could deal with out of household funds."
She gave a couple blinks of those big, black-brown eyes.
"I sent it by messenger right away, yesterday."

"Aye, he mentioned something about that."

I covered my mouth to stifle a gasp, but then said. "There isn't anything wrong with billing someone who takes up your time. Perfectly ethical, and I don't know why his union suit is in a bind about it, and I really don't know why he told you."

"People think I'm responsible for you. I do not ken why. I rent to Mrs. Hulpke's Bakery, and no one asks me whether the rolls are fresh."

I heard a sound that could be a sniff, but I knew it was a little laugh from Evangeline.

"So what did he say about me?"

"Not a thing. Oh, aye, but he asked plenty." Barker turned around and walked back to his office, in what I considered to be the middle of the conversation, so I was sure he knew I would follow him.

I stopped him from closing the door with my hand against the glass.

He turned and gave what might have been a tic or might have been a smile with a very small part of his lips. He walked behind his desk and opened the window. I heard gulls, but I felt no breeze.

I reached forward to the framed murderess on his desk and tossed the framed picture into the leather wastebasket.

That got Barker to look up from his roll-top desk.

"So, what did he ask about me?"

"Just who you were, why you sent them a bill."

"His wife took up my time. I would think he could just ask her and have all of his questions answered." I sat in the plush chair. "Or maybe he could just have asked me. I am in the telephone directory, you know."

"His wife was arrogant, and you wanted to take the piss out of her."

I shrugged.

"An emotional response. What I would expect from a woman."

"Emotional would have been ordering her out and kicking her in the bustle as she went."

Barker looked at me, and I nodded to reinforce my point.

I thought I caught the trace of a smile. "Besides, Evangeline gave that big check from Molly Perkins to the orphanage before I could have second thoughts. I'd like to get something for my time from the Wyngates." I started for the door, but an impulse came over me, too fun to ignore. I turned to Barker with a smile. "I've got a couple hours before my next client comes in. Want to go with me to corner Sextus Wyngate?"

Barker stood. "I have an appointment to see him in fifteen minutes. I doubt I could stop you if you wanted to tag along."

That's why he came to my office. He had been baiting me to get me to go with him.

"I get it." I spoke to Barker's back as he retrieved his hat from the hall tree. "You like having me along for the ride. In case you miss something."

Barker's blue eyes flashed in a glare, but he did not stop me from walking down the marble stairs of the building with him and down the strand, past hardware shops, and to the Federal Bank Building.

I looked up at the four-story stone monument to commerce. "You know his family owns the bank as well as the railroad."

Barker walked through the brass-edged glass doors. "Ah, nice to see a captain of industry could get the electricity back on." He gestured. "The elevator."

"And fans." I looked up at the whirling black blades on the hallway of each floor. Beyond them, a central courtyard held a domed skylight. "But the railroad isn't what it once was."

We climbed into the small cage of the elevator facing each other, only two inches apart at the chest in the small conveyance. I started to look away, but Barker met my eye, so I kept my eyes on him.

He smiled. "Private car."

"Excuse me?" I didn't smile. All my energy went toward keeping my voice level, with him so close.

"They used to have the whole railroad; now I do not think they've much more than a private car."

The elevator eased to a landing on the fourth floor. Barker opened the grill, and I stepped out into the hallway with stone wall and doors on one side, ornate metal railing on the other.

Behind me, Barker said, "You did well at the Wyngates. Kept your head. I was proud of you."

I turned so fast, we collided. I had to grip the railing to keep from plunging over.

Barker grabbed my waist.

I smiled, maybe even beamed, at him. I realized why I had been mad at him. "Thank you. I wanted you to be proud of me. When you didn't seem to be, it bothered me, and that bothered me even more."

He looked at me as though I were carrying small pox. He walked past with a shake of his head and something that sounded like, "*Nae ken* lasses." He held the door open, and I glided in.

I remembered the last time Barker and I went into the office of one of the city's elite businessmen. The meeting was cordial until Barker had slammed him against the wall and demanded answers.

I wondered how this would go now.

Barker smiled at the clerk behind the desk in the large, empty room with engravings of steam engines on the walls. "We're here to see Mr. Sextus Wyngate. We have an appointment."

"Good morning, Mrs. Gallagher," a young man in a morning coat and striped trousers said from behind a glass-domed tickertape machine. He took the lengths of narrow paper but didn't read the stock prices or news releases. After cutting a three-foot length, he clipped it with other three-foot lengths on the wall.

I wonder how long that history under the clips went back.

"Hello, Beau."

Beau gave a couple of hard blinks and leaned on the clerk's desk. "Forgive me, but I don't understand why Sextus would make an appointment with a . . . "

"Consulting Detective is the term." Barker put his thumbs in his vest pockets with what looked to be pride at his chosen vocation.

The clerk left his desk and walked into an office behind a door that was glass, but crisscrossed with so much brass ornamentation that I could not see inside.

"And you used to be a captain of a smuggling ship, I heard," Beau said.

I gave Beau a smile. "I've heard all sorts of things about Mr. Barker. My favorite is the one in Greenland, where he made skis from his dogsled and carried the wounded lead dog on his back across the tundra."

"That true?" Beau asked Barker.

Barker said nothing, but said that nothing with a smile he might have learned on an adventure with the Sphinx. "Your brother is in?"

Beau gave a shrug. "You don't think they trust me with that sort of knowledge, do you?"

"So what do you do for the bank?" I asked.

"What they need me to do." He gave a shy smile and looked up at me with green eyes of an almost translucent shade for a moment before he blinked. "I'm a humble clerk, and right now my job is not to get tangled in the tickertape."

"This way, please." The clerk gestured with a sweep of his hand toward the now-open office door.

Beau went back to the length of tickertape, now winding on the floor.

I realized this was the only member of the family who had expressed any interest in me, so I doubled back to stand beside him. I held up the tape for him to cut. "Such an unfortunate affair, what with Lucinda returning to be murdered." I tried to look as though I did not study him for a reaction, but affected a smile of mild comfort.

He frowned and shook his head, and the emotion cleared. "She was always a bother to the family." He looked at the tickertape as it slid through his fingers. He pressed his mouth so tight, I knew I couldn't pry any more information from it.

I glanced at Barker. He had to have noticed that Abelard, Miss Alice, and now Beau each gave a different picture of Lucinda and all seemed honest.

I followed Barker into an office with an oak desk less ornate than my own, a bookcase of the same Sears Roebuck quality, and closed window shades that had yellowed in spots. In one corner, a pair of filing cabinets leaned against each other beneath the onslaught of piled boxes with even more files within.

"You again," Sextus said to Barker. He did not acknowledge me. Tall and lanky, he looked more like Abelard than Beau, but he also sported the little V of an imperial beard like the youngest Wyngate son. He did not have Abelard's stooped carriage or straight-up-in-the-air hair. His hair was combed down into even rows of waves that ended a razor's-width above his collar. "I don't have much time, but I'll answer what questions you can give me in that time."

He rose from his desk and shook hands with Barker. I extended my lace glove, and after a moment of confused hesitance, he accepted it and shook with a tight grip.

"Mrs. Gallagher, attorney." I slipped a visiting card onto his desk in a spot near the edge without any papers, files, or ink-covered blotter.

Sextus sat back down. He never took his eyes from me, and his eyes never lost the confused frown.

"She's a friend of mine," Barker explained.

"And of Winnie's," I added.

He took a moment to digest who Winnie was, then nodded.

Strange bunch, these Wyngates. I wondered if their wealth made them so weird or if they came by it naturally. *Are they weird enough to commit murder?*

He frowned. "Very sad business, the whole thing."

"Aye," Barker said. "That's why we would like to get it all sussed out as soon as possible."

I liked that he tossed the "we" in there and had to force myself not to smile.

Sextus slid back down into his leather-bound chair and pointed a finger at me. "I saw that bill you sent my wife. You made her cry. I'll have none of that."

"I billed for my time," I said. At a huge rate, with $9.78 for a quarter of an hour. Normally, that would pay for three hours of my time. Still, I liked the precision of the 78 cents.

I took the seat Barker held for me. "Every attorney does."

Sextus smiled enough to show healthy, if a little gray, teeth. "I have attorneys, lots of attorneys, who will take you apart if you press things, ma'am."

The "ma'am" at the end was a nice touch, I'd give him that. "You should always choose battles you know you can win." I crossed my legs and affixed a smirk that I hoped would convey I knew something more than I did. "Or don't mind losing."

"Did you know Lucinda well?" Barker leaned his hand on the back of the other wooden visitor chair.

With a shake of his head, Sextus seemed grateful to talk to Barker and not me. "She kept to herself. I don't know what she did during the day."

Barker took out his notebook, but not his pen. "You're saying she never spoke to you?"

"Not quite that." Sextus gave a laugh. It sort of creaked out, as if he were unfamiliar with the concept of mirth. "Once, she came to see me in the office. She kept to herself, as I said, but she could be, well, forceful when she wanted. She came to see me in the office."

I nodded to let him know he'd already established that.

He turned to Barker. "She had these Confederate bonds. Silly, useless stuff."

Barker opened the notebook and took out his pen.

"She had these bonds, you see." He said it louder this time.

"She volunteered at the Confederate home," I said. "Maybe one of the men gave them to her."

"Maybe." Sextus gave a shrug. He picked up his pen from the stand and dotted the tip along the blotter. Many such marks showed that this was a common act for him. Was it something he did when nervous? I didn't know the man well enough to tell. "All moldy, and I think they'd been buried. She kept talking about pirate treasure. Ridiculous stuff."

"Why are you so uncomfortable talking about your brother's late wife?" Barker said.

"I'm not uncomfortable at all."

"You are. You're also lying. You knew her well."

"How dare you--"

"I'm sure it was in a business capacity." Barker's pencil scratched along the page of the notebook as he spoke. "But you did know her well, and she came here often."

How could he possibly know that?

"She knew you," Barker said. "Quite well. Winnie and Mrs. Gallagher here say that when she sat in your parents' parlor, she called to you, expecting you to come to her."

Oh, that got me a glare from Sextus.

"That shows you knew her better than you admit. Your clerk showed no surprise at a woman coming up to meet you." He gestured to me. So that was why he let me come.

Well, I hadn't thought it was from sentimentality. Yes, I would do the same sort of thing, so I didn't mind.

"You're too practical a man to have had a love affair with your brother's wife."

"Damn right." Sextus gave me a little smirk.

"Oh, no need to apologize," I said.

"So, that leaves either a string of chorus girls coming in--something a man too busy to get his clerk in to straighten his files is unlikely to do." Barker took a couple steps toward the stacks of files piled on top of each other and atop the cabinet. "Or, you've met women on business before. You don't know many, and so that leaves your wife, your mother, and Lucinda."

Sextus sat up as he stiffened. I suspected this was nothing more than the outrage any man would feel at another mentioning the respectable women in his life.

"Your wife, "Barker said, "a charming woman, has no head for business."

Sextus smiled at the compliment. "My mother comes in now and then. She believes one business is rather like another, and she ran the family plantation, so she reminds us."

"So, what was your business with Lucinda Wyngate?" I asked.

Sextus took a deep breath and blew it out in a puff worthy of a locomotive engine. "I can't give you details. I won't, not even if I had any. I've many people to protect by keeping information private--employees, shareholders, what have you--but Lucinda, yes, I'd say she helped."

I looked around the room with the huge cornice of carved stone. This was a bank, and it looked so substantial, but it could fail no matter how it looked.

"I doubt she provided rolling stock," Barker said. "But banks are known to fail, especially private ones like this. I do wonder how a wee slip of a girl like Lucinda managed to save your floundering empire."

"Not floundering." Sextus threw the pen against the desk blotter.

"Apparently unable to pay even a small attorney bill." The bill wasn't small, and I never expected to get paid for it, but I found I enjoyed rankling him about this.

"My attorneys are all men, and as such members of the state bar association."

I uncrossed my legs and put my hands on my hips within the arms of the chair. "The gentlemen of the bar--"

"And I am about out of time," Sextus said. "You'll have to--"

"Blackmail," I said. I was playing a hunch, one that had been germinating inside me ever since drinking tea with Winnie. All I knew of blackmail among the Wyngates was what Winnie had told me: Lucinda once was yelling at Abelard because she said he liked bones more than people. He didn't know what set her off, but even Winnie realized that Abelard wasn't the best at understanding women. Lucinda had yelled at him about how hard blackmail was and what a danger it was. She started crying until she couldn't speak and never said any more about it. He had blurted this out to Winnie because they had an argument, and he had told Winnie how he appreciated that she didn't yell at him.

Barker smiled at me. He may even have chuckled.

"You can show yourselves out." Sextus spun his chair around to grab the brass-headed intercom tube. He blew into it to send a noise to the outside office and then hung it up. "I'll have my clerk cut you a check, Mrs. Gallagher, and I expect that to be the end of it."

Barker held the door to the outside world for me.

I walked through before letting the clerk slip inside. "The gentlemen of the Texas Bar association reasoned that, if women really did want the vote, wives and sweethearts would have pressured their loves to grant them that right, so women don't want suffrage. Have you ever heard anything so absurd?"

"Hardly absurd, but the analysis stems from the result rather than data," Barker whispered behind me.

"Can you imagine me joining a group with such fool notions?"

Beau snipped a length of tickertape and said, "I can't imagine you indulging in any fool notions, unless they provided lots of fun." He gave a wink in that one eye blinked a little faster than the other.

After a couple of budges, the glass and brass door to the outer office opened. The elder Mr. Wyngate rushed in with a frown. "There you are, boy. Train won't wait for us."

"Yes, father," Beau said. The flirty good nature slipped away and left him a boy staring at his shoes before his father.

"What's the matter, boy, you give up on chasing loose skirts?"

An embarrassed glance by Beau flitted to Barker and me. I didn't blame him. That was an odd thing for a father to say, and his hoot of laughter afterwards was about as endearing as a lunger's hack.

Mr. Wyngate followed Beau's glance and tipped his hat to me. "Hello there, I don't think we've met."

I gave what I suspected was a relieved smile; I didn't mind the old reprobate forgetting me.

Barker stepped forward and offered his hand in what looked like a tight handshake with Mr. Wyngate. Barker smiled and said, "Looking into what happened to Miss Lucinda. Unfortunate business, that."

Miss Lucinda? His client, Madam Molly Perkins, had hired him to find out about the death of the prostitute. He must believe that it was not only the same killer, but that the connection was through Lucinda. Did he think the prostitute's murder was to lead suspicion away from Lucinda's killer?

Mr. Wyngate frowned. "Didn't know much about her."

"So what do you remember about her?" Barker asked in the strong, clear voice he would have used to dare someone to take a swing at him.

"Scared kitten: she never let anyone close to her. Talk to Abelard, he knew her best." He scooped his arm toward Beau. "Come on, boy."

Barker said, "Enjoy your trip to New Orleans."

This was an easy one: the morning train to Houston was already gone, and only two trains would leave within the next few hours to two different places. Chasing skirts would be easier in New Orleans than in Cleveland.

Mr. Wyngate opened his eyes wide at Barker, as though the detective had the unworldly knowledge of a trance medium. Beau grabbed his hat and stick before hustling his father out the door.

The clerk walked out of the office and held a check for $9.78 toward Barker. Barker shook his head and held his hand toward me. The clerk handed the check to me so quickly, I almost dropped it, but didn't, and I snapped it into my purse.

In the elevator, Barker leaned against the cage and smiled down at me. "What did you think of his answer to your question?"

"He didn't answer."

"Indeed he didn't. Beyond that, he decided to pay you instead of answering."

"Oh, you're right. That seems so obvious now, I should have . . ."

Barker's smile evaporated.

I needed to say something clever to keep his interest. Yes, I should be above caring about keeping his interest, but inside, I was a sap. I hoped he never noticed. "Winnie told me that Lucinda once yelled at Abelard about how hard blackmail was. He didn't know what she meant."

With a soft bounce, the elevator slid to the first floor.

Barker held the door open for me. "Sextus Wyngate told us Lucinda did work for him. What do we know of the woman?"

I stepped through the vast corridor of the bank. "She liked Miss Alice and feared Mr. Wyngate. She liked looking for pirate treasure and didn't like blackmailing people, although she sure seemed to be doing it, and Sextus benefited from it."

"Aye." Barker waited for me to step through the door that the attendant held open. "Although I doubt the man would call it blackmail, just persuading investors not to make a run on the bank."

I blinked at the bright sun out on the street. "You can't trust a blackmailer, even if they're working for you. So, we've got another suspect: Sextus. Have we eliminated anyone?"

"I figure you and I have alibis," Barker said with a saucy smile.

"But you've eliminated a maniac," I said. "A crazy hobo who just wanted to kill women from every sector of society."

Barker squinted at the sunny street. He did not answer.

"So, where do the clues lead us now?" I asked and waited to see whether he dismissed my assumed "we" or would let it stand.

"Where do you think the clues lead me?" Barker helped me down off of a high curb and over a channel of dirty water running through the gutter to the sea. Since the storm, we had these all over the place, either designed by civil engineers or by nature.

I thought. "To the Wyngates."

"Aye, and . . ."

"And that Guy fellow. Oh, oh, New Orleans!"

"Would you care to accompany me on a quick trip to New Orleans, Mrs. Gallagher?"

Yes, I want to very much, and not just because your touch on my arm makes me feel safe and happy. I shook my head. "I shouldn't."

"I'd put you up at a hotel for ladies if that's--"

"No," I said. "I just need more time with the girls. I don't think they see enough of me." And I hoped spending time with me would endear me to them.

Barker walked me to my house in silence and declined my invitation to stay for noon dinner.

Before I got to the door, I could hear sounds inside.

One of the girls cried in loud sobs; I believed it was Jinxie.

"Don't be so stupid," Aunt Cornelia shouted. "You put all sorts of lumps in it."

I charged inside and down the hall to the kitchen.

The girls stood at the sink holding each other while Aunt Cornelia beat a whisk in a pot on the stove.

She muttered, "You wouldn't see the late Mrs. Gallagher putting up with this."

The laundry girl stood in the corner with arms folded, shaking her head.

The girls fell into my arms and cried gently against my skirt.

"Oh, there you are," Aunt Cornelia said. "You're late."

"And you're not to speak that way to them, to me, or to her." I raised an arm from Jinxie's head to point to the laundry girl.

Aunt Cornelia's face looked as though it boiled like the gravy in the pot. Her lips puckered and fell, and her nostrils flared to take in a deep breath. After a moment, she said, "Sure."

I rubbed Teddie's back and Jinxie's head. I steered them down the hall with me. I had a telephone call to make, a couple now that I'd made a decision.

Barker walked down the center of the concrete road to get around the crowds on either sidewalk. I took his arm and hung close to him on the cobblestone New Orleans street. I did not belong here, and I alternated between hoping that the women leaning out from hurricane shutters and the men weaving the walk of the drunkard noticed that and just as quickly hoping I blended in enough that no one noticed me.

"I thought we came to New Orleans to see the Wyngates." I spoke as lowly as I could and still be heard in this boisterous place, where we could make out ragtime played on a tinny piano whenever there was a gap in the conversations on the street. Some were in

English and some were in French with a fluid Southern accent that seemed to hang in the heavy, still air.

White men spoke to black women or white women, but black men spoke only to black women. Some rules of Southern society were relaxed in this Gomorrah with incandescent lights, but not all.

"We will, but remember, I was hired to find the murderer of the prostitute."

"And Lucinda."

"Undoubtedly." Barker steered me around a man hunched over his own knees. Once we passed, I heard the rush of food and drink exiting him.

I pulled my skirt closer to my body but made sure I did not show any ankle.

Barker's eyes scanned the street, as much on either side as on the road ahead.

We stopped at a saloon where plaster chipped off the walls to expose the bricks beneath and a row of windows at the crown of the wall. A sign of gold letters once would have read, "Storyville Inn," but now read only, "toryvil e In."

Doors, windows, and shutters gaped to catch a nonexistent breeze. Within, a set of black musicians played a soulful piano, trumpet, and string base. A small group of both black and white people listened to the music. Nearly empty tables stood in rows before the wooden bar on the other side of the room.

"I admit I'm curious about a place like this." I caught Barker's arm a little tighter. "But there's probably a reason why women--ladies--aren't supposed to go in these." I felt an exhilarating flush at doing something wicked but not bad enough to cause guilt. With my daughters safe at MJ's and away from the influences of a frustrated Aunt Cornelia, I could afford to participate in a wantonness that wouldn't cause actual trouble.

I probably wouldn't have this giddiness if I hadn't taken a paregoric to fight off the migraine that had started as soon as we got off the train in this city broiled by a sun ringed with humidity.

"Do you think I'd let anything happen to you?" Barker growled.

No, I didn't think he would if he could help it, but I wasn't going to rely on him for everything. Actually, I didn't rely on much of anyone for anything, and I liked it that way.

Taking my arm, he led me toward one of the empty tables and held out a chair.

I examined the seat for gum, crumbs, or worse. Finding none, I sat. "So, what are we doing here?"

Barker sat in the chair opposite me. "Meeting a woman."

"You didn't say a lady."

Barker leaned back in his chair, not in an effort to be comfortable, but to take in more territory when he slid glances around the room.

"Does she know where Guy is?" I figured he would be the first person we would try to find. Then, we might snoop around the house that the Wyngates had rented in the Garden District.

"I don't know. Told by a friend that I should be able to find her here."

"Friend and a client?" *Named Molly?*

Barker gave a shrug that appeared to be an affirmative.

I looked around the room. My head hurt too much to make the subtle movements that Barker did, and the effort made my head swim. I saw no one but the throng around the musicians and the bald waiter.

I daubed the perspiration from my forehead with my handkerchief. "How high on your suspect list is Guy?"

Barker looked out the door.

A man walked in with a woman in a dress so low, one sleeve fell down to expose a breast. She gave a laugh and slowly put the sleeve back in place. Her companion steered her to the table behind us.

I knew I stood out in a white muslin dress with no ornament other than the black crepe ribbon on my sleeve, but I would rather stand out than fit in here. I remembered what happened the last time I wandered into a neighborhood like this with Barker. He ended up hitting a man who grabbed at me.

A whoosh of headache and opium came over me for a moment, forcing me to close my eyes. Faces came through my mind: Sextus, who had an unholy alliance with Lucinda; Beau, the skirt-chaser who did whatever the family wanted; his mother, Alice, who valued the family and the business equally; Mr. Wyngate who was a prize ass past his prime; and Abelard, whose life would become easier because of his wife's death. The last face I saw was the black woman who had drowned in the basement.

"Miss Alice harbored over a hundred people in her house the night of the storm," I said. "But she didn't seem to notice her own maid dying in the water."

A woman in a gauzy black dress that swathed her ample figure and drew in tightly at the corseted waist came up to the spare chair.

Barker gave her a nod, but she looked past him to the table behind us.

At that table, a high-toned mulatto woman with the years settling hard on her lumpy form leaned against the table and squeaked her chair across the floor to get closer to us.

I felt myself lean away from her, but that brought me toward the woman now at our table, so I positioned myself halfway between the two.

The woman gave Barker a smile that showed good teeth in the front. She had a hairstyle of frizzed bangs that had gone out of style years ago, when the ratted and puffed pompadour most of us wore became fashionable. The light wrinkling and slight sagging indicated a woman in her fifties, but the hard look in her eyes indicated that she was younger and only looked that age. "You Barker?"

Barker gave a single nod.

"Man at the bar said you wanted to see me."

Barker gave a short wave to the bartender. The bartender waved back.

Gees, this man knew everyone.

"Mrs. Chartier." Barker pulled a pair of photographs from his pocket. One was a posed picture of Lucinda looking over her shoulder to show the wealth of curls down her back. The photograph was on thick paper stock with a scrolled frame around it. The other picture was a thin photo of the prostitute with closed eyes, her messy hair spread over the pillow. It was taken closely enough that it did not show the slashes on her neck. He held the picture of the prostitute up toward the woman. "Does this woman look at all familiar to you? She might look a little different here than you recall. Does she look at all like someone you might have known?"

Mrs. Chartier gave her mouth a sour twist. "Yeah, of course she does. You getting me a drink?" She looked up and down the length of Barker, looked at me, and then gave a look around the room.

A gust of hot, wet wind smashed into the saloon with such force, the door rattled against the wall and the glass shattered.

"We're getting a storm," I murmured. "A big one. That's why the air's been so still." Memories of the hurricane came to my mind--watching the water rise in the house and wondering whether it would stop before we drowned, the sound of ceiling tiles ripping through timber, the smells of mold and death. "That's why my head hurt. I thought it was caused by emotions, about my . . ." I sat up straight and took in as deep of a breath as my corset would allow.

A scream came from one of the people clustered before the band. Several others laughed in response. The band started a slow, stately tune.

The bartender walked from behind his bevel-edged bar toward the door. "It's going to be a bad one. They got the hurricane flag out."

A busser in a white coat brushed past the bartender and toward the door with a broom and dustpan. The bartender went back behind the bar, accepted another wave from Barker, and responded by holding up one, two, and then three glasses.

"Hurricane." I shuddered.

Mrs. Chartier gave a laugh that exposed a gap where her canine tooth should have been. "Don't stew, honey. If you were from here, you would be used to weather."

I straightened until I was half a head taller than this woman, my fashionable hairstyle of back-brushed waves taking my height up even a few more inches. "I'm from Galveston. I've seen more hurricanes than you ever have. I've seen my neighbors' bodies after they starved to death from being trapped in their homes. I've seen looters shot in the street. About the only thing I haven't seen was the body of my husband because it and so many others were never found."

The bartender set a short, wide glass before each of us. "Don't have to worry. We've never flooded."

"Oldest part of town is on high ground," Barker explained. "That would be here and in the French Quarter." He raised his glass toward me in a toast.

Wind whipped through the bar despite the busser's efforts to nail a sheet over the opening, where once had been the window with the name of the saloon in gold letters.

I tried to look unflustered by the weather, but Barker still stared at me. Eventually, he turned to the woman and asked, "So, Mrs. Chartier, you know that woman?" He continued to stare at me. Not a penetrating or angry stare, but searching and perhaps a little kind. Even so, I wished he would stare at Mrs. Chartier for a while.

The lights dimmed with a buzz, but then returned to full power.

She seemed uncomfortable even without him looking at her, but looked down at the picture of the prostitute, looked at the picture of Lucinda beside Barker's glass, and then took a swig of her own drink. With her head down like that, I saw she had a row of silver roots at the base of her chocolate-brown hair. She put her finger on the picture of the dead prostitute. "Yeah, I seen her. Yeah, she used to work for me. Nothing special. She wasn't that interesting." She frowned a glance at Barker, but he was still looking at me.

I found that I thrilled at the thought of him looking at me. That was probably just an increase of emotion borne on fear. Whatever it was, I prayed he wouldn't notice. I took a sip of my drink. Boy howdy, that was strong. There was a little lime, then the stinging licorice taste of absinthe before the kick of the high-proof spirits.

The lights went out. After a cry from someone in the dark, the band started playing again. This brought applause.

The bartender put a set of lanterns with tin bases and shades on the bar. The busser lit these and took them from table to table.

I looked away from the table and saw rain in waves outside the door. I never liked when rain came sideways. We weren't far from the river here, no matter what Barker and the bartender said. The waiter slammed closed a shutter over the open window, latched it, and then closed the other. He came in and struggled to close the door. Two patrons pulled him in.

"You've never been to my place," Mrs. Chartier said to Barker. "I'd remember a handsome fellow like you."

Mrs. Chartier tipped her head back and gave the sort of smile that showed no amusement because it had seen too much. "I cater to all kinds of needs. As a matter of fact, if someone wants something different, they come to me. I've always said, 'If a girl can get a job at a normal place, she's got no business with me.' "

"The girl in the picture?" I had a thought that took a few seconds for me to express. "What was her, um, specialty?" I wondered if it might be the sort of thing that brought out some maniac who might have killed her.

"Yes, she was one of mine." She fingered the picture of the dead prostitute and set her empty glass before Barker.

He waved to the bartender and then gave a circle over our glasses to bring an encore.

"Fact is," Mrs. Chartier said. "It changed over time. She was fresh off the train and pretty young."

"Under eighteen?" I blurted.

Mrs. Chartier laughed so hard, I saw that many of her back teeth were also missing. "Eighteen? I doubt she was even fourteen."

I set my drink onto the table and felt my stomach turn.

"Some men like that sort of thing." Mrs. Chartier gave a shrug. She stared at me.

"Stop staring." I took a small sip.

Somewhere outside, wind roared and whistled.

"I was just thinking I could find a position for you. Sometimes, men like something laced a bit too tight, like that Sunday school teacher they had a crush on as a kid."

"Please!" I gave her a glare that had made judges wilt and high-paid attorneys wither.

"You're old. Most want 'em young, but sometimes they like that."

I was in my mid thirties and had been told I looked a few years younger. What a strange world where that was "old."

"And this girl." Barker tapped the picture. "Did she have regular customers?"

I didn't ask him why he knew this. Even I had figured it out from what the woman said.

"This and that. Fact was, she'd be anything for anyone. If a fellow wanted to slap her around, she didn't mind. Certain . . ." Even Mrs. Chartier hesitated to put words to some of the practices she did. ". . . Certain bodily functions."

For an instant, I had no idea what she meant. In another instant, I longed to still have the innocence of ignorance.

Mrs. Chartier winked at the bartender who handed her a second glass and then one to me.

Surprised, I saw I had finished my drink and accepted the second with a "Thank you."

"She was a learner," she slurred. "She started out kind of coarse. She worked to get better."

Outside, a sign fell and smashed into the wall before rolling down the street.

"Regular customers," I repeated.

Mrs. Chartier shook her head. "Same ones who frequented the rest of my girls. Men come to me for the services." She gave Barker a wink. "And all of them are damn good at what they do. They don't come for any favorite girl."

"How was she involved with the girl?" Barker slid Lucinda's picture toward Mrs. Chartier.

The woman at the next wooden table with spindly chairs sat up and took a moment to focus her eyes on the thick photograph Barker held. "She's the one who sang."

"Shut up, Marie."

Marie sneered to show teeth that must have been natural because one of the two in the front twisted sideways and was a good half inch longer than any other tooth. With loose, silvering hair and rows of scallops beneath her eyes, she looked as though she were in her sixties, which probably meant her forties with a few extra decades added by the large glass of golden whiskey before her on the table.

I asked, "Lucinda was one of your girls?"

"Hell no!" She turned to the bartender and pointed at her empty glass. "She was a singer of French songs. A chanteuse."

She got the word right, but pronounced it as a rather Anglicized "chant-use."

"Not a hooker, but boy, she'd have been a great one. She had elegance about her . . . like, like . . ."

"Margaret, the girl Queen of Holland?"

"I was thinking a Floradora girl."

Barker slid the picture of Lucinda through his fingers with an affectation of casualness. "But you knew her as more than that."

"I didn't know her a damn bit."

Barker's eyes stayed on Mrs. Chartier.

She gave a huff through her nose. "She knew the girl." She tapped the picture to indicate the "girl" was the dead prostitute. "Her agent did, at least."

"Agent?" I asked. Was she using a euphemism for pimp?

"Theatrical agent," she said, syllable by syllable.

Outside, wind roared through the street.

I realized I had no idea what the prostitute's name was. I probably never would. Abused in life, she was now anonymous in death.

Barker continued to stare at Mrs. Chartier.

"That fancy woman." Mrs. Chartier gave a tap to Lucinda's picture. "She knew the girl. When I talked to her, she said she was giving the girl lessons in how to talk, how to act. That her agent wanted her to help the girl out." She snorted out a laugh at this.

Barker took a sip of his drink and gave her the wink of a co-conspirator. "That agent, Guy, he was partial to the girl."

She frowned at him. "How did you . . ."

"Just let us know where we can find Guy," Barker said in soft tones that still managed to rumble like the wind.

"You killed her!" The woman at the next table said. Her companion had left her.

One of the windows high on the wall shattered as a branch slapped against it.

"Shut up, Marie." Mrs. Chartier gave a few jerks of her thumb toward the woman at the other table, who glared at her and panted. "Squirrel-Tooth Marie. Everyone knows she's crazy."

"That singer, that elegant woman." Marie stood. Wind from the broken window billowed her wisps of curled hair. "I see her now. She walks in death." She looked at me and smiled. "I'm a seer, you know."

I looked at Barker. His smile had evaporated and been replaced with a smirk.

I took a deep breath to calm myself.

"She's a witch," the bartender said.

Mrs. Chartier stood and drained the last drop from her glass.

I stood, but Barker caught my arm. "She doesn't know where he is or she would have told us. She knows she doesn't have any information left worth another drink."

"Then that was worthless," I said. I raised my glass, coughed at the smell, and gave it to Barker.

"You're looking for Guy?" Squirrel-Tooth Marie said, giving it the French pronunciation. "I can find him for you."

Barker slid my drink before her. She grabbed it in both hands and drained it in a series of gulps.

She slid the back of her hand across her mouth and then licked her hand. "He works at the Bon Chance Tavern. Does magic." She shook her head toward me. "Not real magic like me."

"Voodoo witch!" someone called from the other side of the bar.

"She does walk in death, that one." Marie's hand made a broad arch to the door and Mrs. Chartier, who fought her way against the wind to get outside. "She does. That was why one of her girls died." Marie dragged her hand across her throat and made a gurgling cackle. She stumbled into Mrs. Chartier's chair.

The lights flickered on, but popped and died.

The bartender put a pair of lanterns on the bar and lit them. The waiter hung one on the back wall and one near us at the front.

Without looking at the bartender, Barker snapped his fingers in the air. "When?"

"Last night," she said.

My pain-clotted brain realized this was another one and not talk of the prostitute who died in Molly Perkins' Galveston brothel.

Last night? If the squirrelly old drunk could be trusted, that would rule out Beau, Sextus, and Mr. Wyngate, who were all in town this morning. Suspicion remained with Abelard, Mrs. Wyngate, and no, I hadn't seen Winnie since yesterday morning. This Guy fellow remained a suspect. If we could find him where Marie said he was, maybe we could trust her about another prostitute with a slit throat.

"Left the body at the river this morning." She grabbed the glass from the bartender. Both sides of her dress came down, exposing brown nipples. A little shrug, and then she pulled her straps back up. "Someone in a black suit, bowler hat. I saw him run out and heard the girls scream." She drained the glass and set it on the table after a couple of tries. "I, uh, spend time in that alley behind there. I saw him sneak in." She shook her head. "I was too tired to do anything. He wasn't there but a second before he came back out."

"A second?" Barker asked.

"Seemed like it to me."

A window crashed.

I leaned toward Barker and past Marie. "Sounds like the killer was interrupted before he could decorate with the prostitute's guts," I said. "As long as anything Marie says is true."

"Aye," Barker said. He may have said something more, but I could not hear him over the sound of the roof tearing from the nails that held it. "He or she. Do not dismiss the idea of a woman in a suit."

That meant he hadn't ruled out Miss Alice or Winnie.

He grabbed my arm and pulled me to my feet. He pointed toward an arch at the back of the room and bustled me into an alcove between the back door and kitchen.

I trembled, not with cold, but with memories of the Great Storm.

Within the bar, patrons talked over the sound of the wind. The band played a ragtime tune.

I stood against Barker in the dark alcove and waited, waited to die or for the storm to end.

"You need a distraction." His hand slid down my shoulder, down my arm. "No one knows you here. You don't have to be you."

A flash of lightning showed the brick buildings along the alley and the ghost of a giant box of Uneeda biscuits painted above them.

"Close your eyes," he said in the resonant tones of a carnival mesmerist. "Think of something else."

I felt my back against the warm, rough bricks that shut out the sounds of the storm. "Kiss my lips, Barker. Then no one will think I'm a prostitute."

"Don't think. Let your mind fill with colors and um, feelings."

The last word drawled out in the pronunciation of a school boy reading a foreign word for the first time in a primer.

His hands ran over my shoulders, my arms, and down my back to, well, to my small pox vaccination. Mine was not on my arm.

I kept my eyes closed. I felt my body press towards his, and my face tilted up toward his. I know his face was close to mine. I smelled him and faint, astringent male soap.

"Physical, chemical responses." His hand slid along the edge of my dress from my shoulder, across my clavicle and slightly over the gauze of my bodice. "That's all there is, that's all that's in your mind."

He was playing with me. He had no interest except perhaps to make me forget the storm. "You bastard," raced through my mind and, I suspect, from my lips. At least, part of it did. Something came and smashed the words away: his lips.

He pressed his mouth gently against mine and pulled away after a length of time just longer than my palsied Aunt Agnes would have kissed me.

My eyes flitted open.

He looked at me with the furrowed-brow study of a scientist staring at something on a microscope slide.

I grabbed the sides of his head and said, "We're here where no one knows us." I pressed my parted lips to his and said, "Almost as if we're not us."

He did the rest. His tongue slid into my mouth while suction drew mine--and almost my soul--deep into his. He might not be interested in this sort of thing, but he knew his way around an embrace.

I stopped shaking. I trembled, but no longer from terror.

The wind howled, and rain exploded against the building.

He broke away from me for an instant, and I drew close. "What's the matter, pal, afraid? Think something evil will find us?" I met his lips again with short, rapid kisses, tilting my head and exploring his mouth.

My body slid against his as the chemical responses rose through my system.

He kissed me again as though devouring my consciousness. His thick, warm lips, as strong as those big fingers, were still soft and warm. He sucked hard, sucking my tongue, lips, and teeth toward his. He broke free, but just to press hot kisses against my neck.

My hand must have slipped from the side of his head since I felt him draw it into his mouth and suck on my fingertip, first gently, then firmly, then pulling more of my index finger into his mouth against the firm, velvety surface of his tongue.

I moaned and then bit my own lip at the intoxicating pleasure of the feeling.

His one hand exchanged the finger in his mouth for the next. He kissed, nibbled, and sucked them in succession. His other hand slid over my back and pressed by body so tightly against his that the clothes I wore might as well have been made of whipped cream.

I slid upward within his grasp to kiss his ear. I bit his earlobe, heard a gasp, and then slid my tongue into his ear. I blew the slightest breath I could over the wet surface. "Do you like that?" I inhaled.

"You're a very handsome woman," he said between half-closed eyes.

I felt his chest swell against me as his hand slid over the lace of my bodice.

"Are you saying you like me?" I purred.

His hand slipped from my back and fell to his side. "Good. You've bucked up."

Bucked up?

I might be wearing a few petticoats, but I was reasonably sure you were distracted by something stiff, pal.

My thoughts must have blared at Marine-Corps-Band-plays-Sousa-march volume, for he said, "Some of your chemical impulses. Nothing more than a body responding to another body. Think nothing of it."

"Well, thank you for that. Do you think anything Marie said was true?"

"We'll find out when we see about Guy, but only after the storm dies down."

The back door sucked in, and the window cracked.

I jumped.

"Do I need to distract you again?"

"No," said what little pride I had over the hurting head and fear. "No, thank you."

I don't think Barker heard what I said because he was looking out the broken window. A series of lightning strikes lit the alley.

Barker took a step toward the back door. With wide hands spread, he motioned for me to stay in place. With a hard yank, he pulled the door open.

Rain pelting him in the face, he ran to the end of the alley.

I skidded after him, holding my hand up to keep the stinging wind at bay.

He turned to face me; needles of rain turned his face red. "Damn it, lass, I told you to stay."

I pulled my skirt up over my head to shield myself. I didn't care who saw my petticoats. "No," I said. "Do what you have to do, but I can't stay here alone. Go on."

He ran to the street and rounded the corner. Wet wind blasted us, and I smacked into a brick wall. Barker lunged forward. He grabbed a man by the shoulder.

I saw his face, and I saw his blink. It was Beau Wyngate.

"Why are you following me?" Beau trembled. The gun he held on Barker shook. His finger was on the trigger.

CHAPTER 19

"Beau," I said in a soft, husky tone. "We aren't following you." *Not any more than we are any suspect.* The rain stinging my eyes kept me from seeing him. I wondered if he could hear me over the roar of the storm, but men tended to notice a woman speaking in a low voice. I stepped forward until I was just behind Barker's shoulder.

"You're here," Beau said. He blinked hard and fast against the stinging rain. "You're after me."

Above us, angry wind tore at buildings and trees. A piece of limestone molding fell and danced through the street. Hard rain and bits of twigs, leaves, and gravel pelted us, and I struggled to stand against the squall. On my own, I couldn't, and I grabbed Barker's sleeve to keep from sliding along with the wind and rain.

I opened my mouth to speak, and water battered my lips and even went down my throat. "Don't tell him to calm down," I whispered to Barker.

I think Barker heard because he gave out a groan before he squinted at Beau. "You don't like storms, do you?"

An angry gust blew tree branches and maybe an entire tree against a lamp post, bending it.

Beau took a step back.

I watched the gun barrel bounce around, but it remained trained mostly on Barker's gut.

Barker spoke with difficulty over the angry weather. "Storms . . .they . . . remind you of her."

Beau shook even more than with the buffeting of the wind. He shook his head.

Barker whispered to me, "Black woman?"

"Yes," I whispered. I had no idea if he could hear me over the howling wind. "The black maid. She loved you. She was carrying your baby."

"I never hurt . . . I never would have . . . done . . . I loved her."

Thunder cracked.

I said over the sound of the storm and the throbbing of my headache, "You're why she drowned in the storm, aren't you?"

Beau raised the gun toward Barker's head. "I loved her."

Lightning glowed white all around us, too bright and full of clouds for me to see anything. Thunder cracked immediately.

Overhead, a power line buzzed and glowed blue.

I heard a snap and saw a flash of blue light.

Above us, the black cable snapped and half of it billowed for an instant on the wind before it snapped toward me.

Oh no, I thought. I'm dead. I still ran to get away from the falling power line before it fell on me. I ran, but I was slow, and I heard the sputter of electricity behind me.

Barker shoved me hard. I smacked onto the sidewalk and scrambled to the wall. He yanked me by the back of my clothing until I felt the wall against my face.

"Had to get you out of the water," he said.

"I know."

The cable lay in the puddle, a long, dead snake.

"Beau?" I looked around.

Bricks and gravel spewed through the air. Barker pushed me down and covered me with his own body. He buried his face in my hair until the worst of the stinging ebbed.

Nausea overcame me. I might have vomited, but with the pain creating blackness in my head, I wasn't sure.

"We'll not find him," Barker said to the howling darkness. He gave my back a couple of pats and helped me to my feet. "Come, this way."

We crossed the street and made our way past shuttered buildings that were gambling dens and cathouses a few hours ago. A hard gust knocked into me, and I slipped. Barker caught me around the waist, and we stood against the wall for a moment before he pounded on a door.

He pounded even harder, the only noise that could be heard over the howl of the storm.

A waiter opened a door and pulled us into a dim room with a single lantern illuminating a fuzzy world of cigar and cigarette smoke.

A pianist played a poignant ragtime tune. As my eyes adjusted, I saw a place nearly full of people of every color, sitting in chairs and on the floor. At the back, near the door to the kitchen, a box emblazoned with gold swirls and letters announcing "The Great Gee Whiz" stood before a man in a tail coat and tweed vest.

"Oh wait. It wasn't supposed to go like that, you see." The man in the tailcoat yanked the card from the hand of a large man.

A pair of women with the large man looked away with boredom and leaned behind their companion to whisper to each other.

Barker held up two fingers to the bartender crouched behind the marble-slab bar.

I made my way between chairs to where the magician worked. No chairs remained, so I sank to the floor.

The building shuddered and groaned.

I closed my eyes and held myself as still as possible to keep my head from throbbing.

Barker said, "Guy? May I have a word?"

I opened my eyes to see Barker sit beside me.

Guy, in the tweed vest and tailcoat, held a deck of cards to Barker. Barker shook his head.

The shutters on the window behind the bar broke away in the wind, and a wooden chair bashed against the window until it broke.

With a jangle of items in his pockets, Guy sank to the floor opposite Barker. His thinning blond hair stood up in the electric storm, and his faded brown eyes opened wide in his narrow face.

Barker said, "I work for Molly Perkins."

Guy gasped.

The bartender handed a drink to me and one to Barker.

This would probably make me feel even sicker, but the first round of alcohol had made my migraine ebb for a while. I took a swill of the harsh, brown liquor.

Barker continued: "I was wondering why you left Galveston, and so suddenly."

"I didn't kill her."

"Oh, that never sounded innocent." I thought and then realized from the two men looking at me that I had said it.

"I loved Maisie."

Maisie?

"I knew she was a prostitute. She couldn't help it. Someday, I was going to get her, well, out of the business, but she died. So I can't."

Her name was Maisie. I'd never known--and to my chagrin--had never asked.

"But you left so suddenly," I said.

Rain grew even louder than the wind.

Guy pocketed his cards. "Yes, well, I saw her. I got scared."

A gust of wind came so hard, the brick building vibrated. I prayed it would not fall apart, crushing us. I opened my eyes and saw Guy giving me a bug-eyed stare.

"I was a coward, I know, but there wasn't anything I could do for her."

"You saw her dead?" I asked. I must have swayed because I felt Barker hold me around the waist.

"I . . .I did." His pale face of thin skin twisted with misery. "She left the window open for me the first night she worked there. I thought someone watched us, just felt it, but I didn't know."

I looked at Barker who seemed to be studying the integrity of the brick columns.

"Were you followed?" I asked.

"Must have been," Guy said. "I saw someone step into the window. I was mad, but I knew she was, you know, she was paid for . . . for . . ."

"Yes, I know what she did for a living."

"Someone went in. I got sore, but went to have a beer and figured I didn't have any reason to be. When, I came back." He looked down and fumbled with his intertwined rings.

I sipped my drink. How sore did he get? Sore enough to kill her?

"You'll excuse me," he said. I don't like thinking about that. I saw her dead. I didn't even need to step inside to know."

"Lucinda," Barker said. "That's who I wanted to talk about. You were her agent."

"She's lovely, I know. Lovely, but, well, she isn't my love."

Something smashed against the building, shaking it with a roar. A window crashed and conversation stilled.

"Tell us about Lucinda," Barker said. To me, he whispered, "The prostitutes were killed only to cover the murderer's aim: Lucinda. Of that, I'm sure."

Guy's mouth wobbled as though he would cry, but then grew into a wide and wistful smile. "I knew she'd come here after the storm. I found her some good work. We shared a love, a hobby."

"And that was her only concern in life?" Barker asked. A strange question, but he must have been formulating an idea.

Glass shattered with what might have been debris or the pressure of the storm.

"And family. She has a little boy, don't you know. Well, she missed him so much. She'd tell me about him. Never talked about the rest of her family. She came from Galveston, you see, that's how she got me fixed up so quick at the Old Soldier's home, doing shows for the old boys. Poor thing, she figured her family had all died." He nodded at his own recollection. "I think she wanted them to be. I'm not sure what, but once she told me they made her do terrible things."

"Blackmail?" I asked.

"Oh, I wouldn't know. She's just the finest, sweetest thing. So sad."

Barker and I both waited to hear what Guy thought was so sad; he wouldn't know Lucinda was dead unless he killed her.

"It's her boy, you see." Guy played with the pair of intertwined rings as though beginning a magic trick he did not have the energy to complete. "She hoped the boy survived, but she didn't think she could bear knowing for sure if he hadn't."

"I'm glad to hear it," I said. I didn't agree with a woman doing that, but it meant she was a bad mother and rather than an uncaring monster.

"You know Lucinda's dead," Barker said. "Of course."

"She's dead?" Guy shouted and then quieted. "You're sure she's dead?"

A woman in an evening gown heard Guy over the storm and turned toward us for an instant before turning her attentive smile back on her companion.

"Yes," I said. "I saw the body."

Barker put his arm around me, by which I figured he was bidding me to say no more, but I hadn't planned to, anyway.

"You know, I went to Galveston because of her. Just had to go but, well, I guess it sounds silly."

"You thought you found a map to pirate treasure," Barker said.

"Not a map, a history." Guy set the magic rings on the stone floor. "Jean Lafitte, called Galveston Campeche."

"Yes, everyone knows that he had to flee and leave all his gold." I slid my head up Barker's chest to look in his eyes and waited until a loud hiss of wind grew quiet enough for me to be heard. "People have been digging for Lafitte's gold for nearly a century, and no one has even found an old coin."

"Because his men took it all," Guy said. "They were the ones who buried it, so don't you think they were the ones to dig it up?"

"I like the logic," Barker said.

"But they wouldn't have done anything to her." Guy nodded with an earnestness that could get him beaten up in this part of town.

"Her?" Barker asked.

"Lafitte's wife. You see, he gave her jewels. Well, he was given jewels by the British who wanted him to fight with them on their side . . ." He shot a weak smile at Barker in apology. "But Lafitte double-crossed them. He took the jewels and had them made into a tiara for her."

"Lucinda knew this?"

A drunk staggered over to the bar. The bartender dropped a baseball bat on the bar top. The drunk sat down.

"Yes, well, she knew about the jewels." Guy pulled his knees to his chest. "I just found out about it being made into a tiara. I thought that would bring her to Galveston. She won't be reading it now, I guess." His eyes pleaded with Barker and me.

Barker and I said nothing. Guy didn't seem to have known Lucinda had followed him out to Galveston and died there.

Guy leaned toward us. "Lucinda knew about the farm. She wanted to go there."

"Farm?" I remembered something about Lucinda's interest in a farm. My cloudy mind filled with an image of her notebook, which was where I'd seen the reference.

"Why, yes," Guy said. "You see, people always figured he buried all his gold on the island, so that's where they always looked, but he had a friend on the mainland, east of Virginia Point. Harbored the fugitive there sometimes, don't you know."

"And you think his treasure was buried there?" Barker asked.

The crash of a wave roared through the street, but I rose up to see that no flooding had come through the door.

"A building falling away," Barker whispered in my ear as an explanation.

I shivered with something. I don't know whether it was fear or a spasm from the migraine.

Barker held me tight against his body.

Barker said to Guy, "Lafitte's treasure?"

"Not his treasure, you see," Guy said. A warm smile came with the old story. "His wife. She was buried on the farm."

"Was the treasure so much that Lucinda would go back to Galveston?" Barker asked.

"Well, I don't know, but maybe for her son. She said she needed money to get him."

Barker sat very still, and I suspected he had figured something out. He murmured, "It's always been about money."

"How would money have convinced the Wyngates to let her take . . ." I may have said more, but I fell asleep, mid-thought, which is sometimes called "passing out." I thought I heard Barker say, "Because Guy would help a woman who wanted her son and not help one who was greedy."

I awoke and realized I could not open my eyes. In panic, I tried to raise my hand to open them, but I could not move my hands or arms either. I worked at my mouth to open it to cry out, but it would not move either. In the instant I realized that I was still asleep, I awoke.

Barker stood, looking behind us through the broken window to the alley. "Come, lass, we've got to go." He took my arm in what was equal parts helping me to my feet and yanking me out the back door.

My head still hurt, but the pain was not as great as it had been. The pressure of the storm must have been lessening, although the sun had not risen and the world outside was black.

Bullets of rain still hit us from the side, but the wind had subsided to a silent breeze. The sun lurked behind gray clouds instead of black. I grabbed Barker's arm and walked with him to the corner.

Black water flowed through the boulevard where horses and carriages should be. Trash, pieces of buildings, and fallen trees floated toward the river.

"We'll never make it to your hotel," Barker said. "I'll send for your things, and let's go to the train station. Come on, lass, we want to get a train before everyone else gets the idea."

CHAPTER 20

The train lunged to one side of the tracks and then the other, as if trying to find a way to free itself from the iron rails and wander out into the salt marshes and slightly dryer swamps beyond where waist-high scrub oak and mesquite presided over flat terrain.

I woke. My hair must have draggled around my head, exposing the purchased rat of hair providing puffing, and my mouth tasted like gray flannel. On the train between New Orleans and Houston, I had fixed my hair and applied a little powder, but that small mirror in the train toilet had showed me that I appeared as though I had been sleeping on the streets. I looked at the seat beside me and saw it was empty.

Barker stood, bracing himself against the beige leather seat.

Beyond him, the window showed the flat scrub between Houston and Galveston.

"None of the Wyngates talked about treasure," I voiced a thought forming in my brain. "Lucinda was obsessed with it, and none of them mentioned it. Guy did, the Confederates did, but not the Wyngates."

"Sextus did." Barker's attention was not with me, but where the small, gnarled shrubs of scenery gave way to boggy swamp. The black water in these pools was not fresh, but brackish at best, and was most likely part of the salt marsh as we neared Galveston Bay.

"Yes, but Mr. Wyngate, Beau, and Miss Alice never mentioned it. Neither did her husband."

Barker smiled at me as if to say, "Clever girl." He leaned toward the window until I thought he might have memorized the mesquite and scrub oak, then he turned to me with a frown. "I should tell you what I learned of your daughter's past."

Something about his serious frown and thrust-out chin filled me with a nervousness that came out in a high-pitched laugh. "Barker, I'm sure you'll have other opportunities to tell me."

"They lived above a saloon at the time of the storm, doing odd jobs. No one ever saw the parents sober. The girls were alone at home when the house broke apart. The parents weren't there and were never found."

"Damn," I whispered. "No answers there to give them peace." Or make them stop thinking that mother could come back. I felt a lump swell in my throat. At first, it was for the girls and what they had been through, but that fell away to self pity. *I'm the only real mother the girls ever had, why can't the girls see that?*

"Are you fit?" Barker asked.

"Yes." I drew in a deep sniff. "I'm fine. I'm just troubling trouble." I gave him a smile I knew trembled with sadness and fatigue. "Thank you for finding out."

Barker gave my arm a pat and turned toward the back of the car. "Are you coming or staying?" He put on his blue-tinted spectacles.

I followed him through the near-empty train to the door at the back. We had gotten the last couple of seats on the first train out of New Orleans. I suspected we only got those because Barker slid two silver dollars across the counter to the two clerks and said, "There's a special hurricane processing fee, I reckon."

Most of the train passengers had stayed on in Houston, and we were alone with a woman helping her boy peel an orange. She looked at us but did not say anything when Barker opened the door at the back of the train car. The chug of the wheels and blast of the steam roared out here on the tiny platform between cars.

Barker pointed in the distance. "See, a wagon there. We'll get a little closer."

I didn't see a wagon. I saw nothing more than salt grass and puddles under a sun so bright it washed away all of the colors except the deepest greens. I feared Barker was full of beans and lack of sleep. "You . . . you're going to jump off the train?"

"Aye, when the train slows on the curve. Fool thing, I know, but I want to get to Abelard before he gets back to Galveston."

"If he's there and not a bunch of bandits instead."

"We'll find out." He gave my shoulder a stern pat. "Roll on your shoulder, then curl up in a ball. Don't bite your tongue."

"Who do you think is out there?" I asked.

He looked down the length of train, pulling straight through flat grass and scrub clinging close to the brackish soil.

He kicked off from the step as though it were a pier with water below.

I heard a man's voice behind me shout, "Hey, you're not . . ."

I jumped.

CHAPTER 21

My shoulder hit the ground with a bang. Pain and moisture spread through my arm. I hoped that it was water and not blood. I held my tongue back in my mouth to keep my teeth apart so they would not chip. The side of my head hit the ground, and a wave of salt water and mud filled my mouth and nose. I rolled on my back and then over to my hands and knees. They supported me, but everything hurt, and the mud had left me feeling as though I had almost drowned. Pain radiated from my shoulder through the rest of me.

I spat. I even drooled to get the foul, muddy taste from my mouth.

Barker was already on his feet. He patted my head beneath what had to be a ruined hat and said, "Come on, lass."

With his hand on my arm, I wobbled to my feet. I tried to swallow but couldn't. I tried again, but my mouth was now too dry. I couldn't swallow. I reached down to scoop some water, but Barker grabbed my hand. He was right, the water was more salt than fresh water and would harm more than heal.

I tried to speak, but no sound came out. I felt panic vibrate through me. With the panic came memories of the storm. Our cistern had become contaminated. I had no water for over a day and thought the thirst would kill me.

I took a tottering step toward Barker and grabbed his coat to find the flask in his vest. I tried again to swallow. Nothing.

Barker grabbed his coat away. "No, Daria, that will only make you thirstier."

I didn't care about thirst; I just knew I couldn't swallow.

"You're fine, you'll be fine." He took my arm and led me through the brush and around the marsh puddles. "Your mouth feels dry, that's all. You don't need water."

I didn't try to talk, forced myself not to try to swallow. That could keep the panic away. Looking into the distance, I tried to find the wagon Barker had seen. I made out a wagon, and a horse kicking up water and mud.

That didn't look right, and I grabbed Barker's arm to let him know.

"Aye," he whispered. He crouched and pulled me down behind the scratchy branches of a mesquite thicket. He slid forward to crawl into a grove of cattails. Insects hissed, and a white egret fluttered away from where Barker had disturbed its rest in the water-plants.

Barker froze and waited until the bird had flapped well clear.

I crouched in the mesquite. The tiny, blade-shaped leaves did nothing to protect me from the angry tangle of branches.

I heard horses: fast hooves at a gallop and the voice of a man shouting, "Yah!" to increase their speed.

This wasn't an area where people went for a romp on horseback, especially away from a camp.

A gunshot cracked through the air.

I felt my breath come in short bursts as everything around me turned to a checkerboard pattern. Anxiety had consumed me, and I was about to faint.

"Come on," Barker hissed to me. He ran in a crouch. "Keep down. Stay with me."

Although I trembled, I managed to follow him as I splashed and stumbled through the wetlands. Crouched as much as my corset would allow, I followed as quickly as I could through the sticky mud. We seemed to march on forever, but the slow and painful progress--concentrating on not breaking an ankle on the shifting ground--kept me from thinking about anything that could cause panic.

Barker crouched down low and stopped me with an arm in front of my chest.

I could not see what he looked at, but I could hear the horse hooves. They ran fast and seemed to be moving away from us, growing quieter.

Barker stood and broke into a run.

In slow, painful movements, I stood and walked after him toward a wagon with a flapping canvas cover and no horses hitched to the front. Around it stood a campsite with fallen tent and broken table. Shovels, tools, pots, and pans lay around.

Barker kneeled beside a prone man.

Even at ten yards behind, I saw the blood on his shirt.

I poured on what additional speed I could manage. Panting, I crouched down.

Abelard was awake. He had torn his white shirt to make a tourniquet for his arm. His lower arm was covered with blood, but it no longer flowed. "The boy. I told him to run until he heard a shot. I told him to fall as though shot." He passed out.

Barker looked around and sprinted across a large pool. He grabbed the boy, who struggled to get out of his grasp. Barker put him under his arm and marched back to us.

I ran around the remnants of a campsite.

A pick axe . . . shovels . . . scraps of dirty muslin that bore the remnants of an old-fashioned flowered design . . .broken wood . . .ah, there it was. I found a big metal canteen. After a tiny sip, I knelt down to raise Abelard's head and offer him a sip.

He scowled at me.

Raising Abelard's shoulder gingerly, I sat and rested his head in my lap.

He slid his deep-set eyes over to his son and gave a sigh of relief. He muttered something that sounded like, "Ruthless. They would have killed him if they knew he was alive."

"You did a good job." I pointed to the tourniquet on the boy, who fought to free himself from Barker's iron grasp.

"I am an anatomist."

"What happened?" Barker called from a few feet away. The boy squirmed, and Barker shifted him to the other side.

"There were two of them. They wanted us dead, I could see it. Yes, his eyes said they wanted us dead."

"Describe them, Dr. Wyngate."

"A man, he was in charge. Tall, thin, didn't see him clear. I told Alois to run; hitting a moving target is hard, so he had to run."

"Yes," I said. "He's fine."

"They would have killed him. I knew they would try, you could see the man's eyes. They were cruel."

Barker took the small boy to where his father lay. The boy was dirty and scraped, but unhurt. "And what of the other person?"

"Voice sounded like a woman. I am not sure. She hung back."

"What did they want?" Barker asked.

"They . . . stole something from me." Abelard closed his eyes.

"Yes," I said in forced lightness. "What was it?"

Alois slipped to the ground beside his father and wailed with tears.

I reached over Abelard to pat the boy's head. He cried without noticing me, so I turned back to Abelard, whose head lolled to the side as his thin eyelids fluttered closed.

"Keep your eyes open," Barker said to Abelard. "It worries the boy."

Abelard squinted at the boy and smiled. He used his good hand to tousle the boy's hair.

Alois smiled through his tears.

Barker wandered off to look around the campsite.

"What was it?" I asked again.

"We know," Barker said. He picked up a piece of dirty, angled wood. "This was her coffin; you found the Lafitte tiara." He looked over the trampled campsite.

"This was messy, not like the murders . . . What we've seen recently."

I thought of the entrails draped over the curtains and blood. "Not what I would consider tidy."

Barker didn't look at me while he donned his blue spectacles. He said, "Messy in that the murderer didn't set the scene to make sure of the outcome."

"So this was someone else?"

Barker looked back at Abelard. "Aye."

Abelard closed his eyes and held his son to his chest. "It was just a bit of fun. Something to get the boy's mind off everything and . . . yes, to keep him from finding out his mother is back until I know what we will do."

I looked at Barker. *He didn't know. He doesn't know about Lucinda being dead.* Abelard didn't seem in any state to pretend.

Barker nodded. He tossed the wood down. He took the canteen from me and handed me his flask. "I'll be back with horses, but 'tis a long walk to Virginia Point. So you won't see me until sometime tomorrow."

I nodded.

I prayed the thieves had not seen that Abelard and Alois had survived.

CHAPTER 22

"Barker," I grabbed his arm. It took a couple of tries with the bouncing of the wagon.

Abelard and Alois slept in the back. At least, Abelard lapsed in and out of consciousness, and Alois lay down every time I told him to do so.

I brushed my hair from out of my eyes and thought I saw the edge of land. We'd bounded along for a while, since we couldn't take a horse straight to Galveston, but had to catch the ferry at Virginia Point. I said, "She knew."

"Pardon?"

"Remember that name? We saw her card in Lucinda's things. Madame Sylvie. Well, my friends and I went to a séance. Lucinda appeared, scared the kapok out of me."

"Lass, I'm sure the experience set you and your friends all atwitter, but--"

"Necklace, Lucinda asked about her necklace."

"Aye, that's close to being a tiar--"

"It *is* a tiara." I folded my arms across my chest and felt the dried mud on my skin crack away. "Guy told us how Lafitte's wife had it made into a tiara. What can you make into a tiara? A big fancy necklace."

"Who is this woman?"

Over the journey, I explained to Barker everything I knew of Madame Sylvie from my first meeting in the hall, to the séance. I had spit out every detail before we got Abelard to his hospital and asked Barker, "Do you think she knew about the necklace? Do you think she was trying to find it?"

Barker lifted his hand to knock on Madame Sylvie's door.
We hadn't changed our clothes or washed more than our hands and faces at the train depot. Barker was coated with trail dust, and his hat bore a few dents. Mine might have looked as though it could be a new, crumpled velvet fashion, were it not caked with mud.
The door creaked open on its own.
"It does that." I waved a hand at the door. I marched inside the dark entryway full of curtains.
The darkness and humidity made the room feel as though it closed in on us, but there was something else, a silence as oppressive as the heat. A silence that told me something had changed since the last time I was here.
Barker caught my arm and stepped past me.
I pointed toward the curtain with the main séance room.
He slid open the curtain to the dark room to reveal the table and a woman sitting there. She did not look as if she noticed us or as if she would make any move.
I needed light. I pulled at a curtain to the side to reveal a magic lantern, a set of different-sized bells, a torn white dress on a hook, and a jar of some sort of thick starch that I suspected was ectoplasm. I picked up the thick slides beside the magic lantern projector: a

woman in a filmy dress, a girl in ruffles, a young child, and a stooped man. The slides weren't colored and were out of focus, with mostly white showing.

I'll bet, one those things had snookered me into thinking I had seen Lucinda.

Barker pulled aside another curtain and flooded the small room with sunlight. "She was shot thought the head."

"Shot? Don't murderers tend to use the same means each--"

"Aye, 'twas a different killer. Lucinda's murderer wouldn't have made it out of New Orleans yet. Ours was the only one on the tracks."

"And all the lines are down," I said. I remembered the one that had almost killed me. The city's telephone and telegraph lines would also have snapped like licorice. "The murderer couldn't have ordered this." I set the glass slides beside the magic lantern. "So this is just another murder, unrelated."

"A coincidence? I do not believe in coincidence."

"Then what do you believe happened?" He said "do not" as "dinna," but I knew what he meant.

"Here?" Barker took my arm and led me outside. "I do not know, but I need to talk to my client."

"And I would love to get my girls back," I said. I silently added, *I miss them, and I hope they missed me.*

From the small landing on the staircase, Teddie and Jinxie stared down at me in unmoving silence. The setting sun sent golden stripes across their white dresses.

I had been so glad to get the girls from MJ that I decided to read and take notes on my files at home. I worked fast and now had two girls suffering from the boredom that hits during summer holiday from school.

I stood, jostling a table and sending a porcelain dog to the floor. The figurine was already chipped, and the impact knocked off a front paw.

The girls gasped.

I laughed and trotted up the stairs past them. I grabbed a peanut-shaped angel from a shelf and tossed it down the stairs, where it landed with a satisfying crash.

I steered the girls into my bedroom. I spun around, acquired a target, grabbed the rooster with the broken beak, and tossed it on my bed. "We'll clean everything up. All of this stuff will go to the charity shop." I tossed a set of bug-eyed angels onto the bed as well. "This place will be ours, all ours."

Jinxie laughed. Teddie eyeballed me.

Aunt Cornelia walked past my doorway, doubled back, and looked in with a gasp. "You'll break that!"

"You're right," I said. "Get some boxes for us. Too much to just pile up."

Aunt Cornelia slid her hand over a fat cherub and put it on the nightstand.

I shook my head.

She looked at me with defiance.

I smiled at the girls and said, "I think the two of you need to clear out your rooms."

They started down the hall until Aunt Cornelia cried out, "No!"

"Go on, girls," I said in a soft voice. "Bring out anything you don't want. Remember, it's your room, and you get to decorate it. This is the start."

The girls ran down the hall and closed themselves in Jinxie's room.

I took a couple of aimless steps down the hall after them. I couldn't tell if this was an effort to get away from my temper, which I could feel was about to blow, or the youthful enthusiasm of girls who get to decorate.

"This is Mrs. Gallagher's house," Aunt Cornelia said. "And you can't go giving away her things."

I spun around to face her. "I *am* Mrs. Gallagher." My voice came through clenched teeth. "I'm the only Mrs. Gallagher, and this is my house."

"Well, it's not mine anymore." Aunt Cornelia lumbered down the stairs. "And you can take them to their dance lesson tonight."

"Go ahead and run away," I shouted after her. "Just run away from the truth when you don't want to believe it. Live a life among dead people and ignore the living."

I watched her slam the door.

Behind me, I heard the whines of one girl and sobs of the other.

I spun around to face them, affixing a "Don't fear me" smile on my face.

Jinxie backed up. Teddie put her hands on her hips and said, "She's gone. She's supposed to take us to our dancing lesson at the Garten Verein."

"Fine," I said. "And we'll get ice cream after your dance lesson." I realized I was not above bribing my children and felt no shame.

We hopped off the trolley two blocks from the Garten Verein in a neighborhood of tall houses, all quiet at dusk.

Before us, a familiar man leaned against a lamppost, gave a nod to the lamplighter, and took a draw on his lumpy cigarette.

I struggled to remember him and must have stared since Jinxie said, "That's Aunt Cornelia's friend."

"He talks to her," Teddie said. "She laughs and leans in close." She gave a disapproving frown.

I didn't blame her, since I didn't pay Aunt Cordelia to take my daughters with her for trysts with this man.

He was lanky, and so thin that his black suit and red vest seemed to hang on him. I was sure I knew this man.

He turned to look at me, and I realized I had seen the man before. My memory shuffled and dealt images: a man walking through me in a dream, a man I saw while peeking over the balcony on the night that Barker and I were burglars, and the doorman letting me out the front door onto Post Office. This was Earl, majordomo at Molly's whorehouse.

He smiled at me and took a step toward me.

He might have just wanted to say hello, and his interest in me might be nothing more than friendliness toward a business associate, but I wouldn't take the risk.

I spun around and grabbed at the girls. I ran, pulling Jinxie off her feet and yanking her up so she could get a footing. Teddie ran with me, but lagged. We rounded the corner, and a closed carriage raced around us and stopped before us.

"Run, girls!"

"No," Earl said. "All of you."

I pretended to walk to the carriage, but grabbed the girls and ran again. I only made my way to the curb before someone grabbed me.

"Scream," was the only instruction I could get out to the girls before tight arms grabbed me and held my mouth closed. My nose was also held closed. I stopped flailing so I could conserve what breath was left in me.

CHAPTER 23

The girls pressed against my skirts. I held them as best as I could while looking around.

We were at the top of stone steps, looking down into a brick basement with half-windows above the ground, through which light came from the street. The light rushed in like floodwater to show the broken furniture and crates of preserves littering the area. The air was filled with dust and smelled of damp and mold. I knew where I was; I had seen it in a dream.

I turned around and saw Earl behind me. I made out the figures of a tall man and woman standing in the shadows behind him.

He hitched his head to indicate I should walk downstairs.

"Earl. You don't want to be part of this. Get word. Let someone know we're down here."

He leaned over me with his hand on my arm. "Now, I don't think they'll hurt you, ma'am. You just stay calm."

"They're going to kill us," I whispered to him so the girls wouldn't hear. "Please, tell Mr. Barker where we are."

"Certainly, ma'am." He smiled, and I knew he would do nothing to help us. Whether because of love, lust, or blackmail, he had some sick loyalty to Miss Alice.

I also knew something else: Aunt Cornelia wasn't the only middle-aged woman he had baited. For years, he must have given Sylvie information on the peccadilloes of the elite and learned from her about Lafitte's jewels. Miss Alice must have told him where Abelard was. He was the narrow man on the horse that Abelard had described: the man who had no conscience to keep him from aiming and shooting at a small boy.

I stood and stared at him.

He blinked, or at least I thought he did. It looked like more of a wince.

The woman pushed him aside and shoved my shoulders. Miss Alice, it was Miss Alice.

I tumbled backwards down the stairs, off the side, and to the stone floor.

Thankfully, the girls did not fall. They ran down after me and clustered around me.

Damn! We were trapped in her basement where she'd already killed someone.

"Mother," Beau said from behind his mother on the stairs. "She has children."

"If you'd taken care of things in New Orleans," Miss Alice said to him in the even tones she might have used to discuss the okra in her vegetable garden, "then that wouldn't be a problem."

Beau looked down, and mumbled. "I've tried to stop her. I went to New Orleans to stop her. I just . . . I can't."

Miss Alice huffed before pulling her skirt to the side and striding down the stairs.

She looked near me but did not make eye contact for more than an instant. I realized that she never had:

she kept anyone from looking deeply enough into her eyes to see the darkness within. She caught me staring and raised her hand back before I could duck. She slapped my face with such force that all I saw was a white streak ending in a star, but I opened my eyes and remained conscious. Yes, this woman was strong, strong enough that she could have physically committed the murders. Yes, she had slaughtered hogs and had enough knowledge of anatomy to do the brutal acts.

"You killed that prostitute," I said to Miss Alice. Maisie: she had a name. "You didn't even know her."

"My dear," Miss Alice said in a gentle voice, "I'm not the sort of person to have anything to do with prostitutes."

I hadn't expected her to tell me the truth, but I saw her arrogance was a weakness. "You wanted to cover up killing Lucinda, but it didn't work. People will find out what you did."

"Get this through your stupid head: I had nothing to do with the deaths of those women."

Those women.

The death of the second prostitute in New Orleans never made the newspaper because of the bigger story of the hurricane. Miss Alice had just confessed. She had dressed up in a man's suit twice and killed the two other prostitutes to make Lucinda's death look like the work of a Jack the Ripper.

I swallowed. I realized something else. She killed like that because she enjoyed it. That was why she hadn't allowed Earl to just shoot us in the carriage and dump the bodies in the bay. She wanted to do it. She wanted to carve us up like hogs back on the plantation.

Earl leaned against the doorjamb at the top of the stairs. I knew I could never make it past him, but I might be able to distract them all so that the girls could.

"Earl, you killed Sylvie, didn't you? She loved you and you--"

"Love wasn't what we had," he said. "And I didn't want her making trouble for Miss Alice."

Miss Alice hissed a "shush!" at him.

Jinxie looked up at me. Her large gray eyes showed the lack of expression of one who had seen too much and could not cope. Teddie's dark eyes were cast down at the ground, unable to focus on the world around her.

Would they be able to act when I needed them to?

"Why did Lucinda have to die?" I hugged the girls, pushing them together before me. I bent down to kiss one cheek, then the other.

She let out a deep sigh. "That woman was always a trial. Trust me, no one will miss her. Best that she died so everyone knows she's dead and didn't just disappear again."

I gave a scoffing laugh. I figured that was enough of a challenge to keep her going, but not enough of one for her to let Earl shoot me--at least, not yet.

"My husband probably killed her." Miss Alice said with the hesitance of a woman in the moment of making up a story. "Why, yes, she was afraid of him. I let her know how he wanted to kill her, how he was jealous of her . . . of her influence on his favorite son."

"Favorite son?" I asked. I couldn't see Mr. Wyngate picking the narrow academic as a favorite, but I could now see that Lucinda feared her father-in-law because of the insistent whispers of danger from Miss Alice. She must have spent years manipulating Lucinda until she could no more and then she killed her.

"Do you think I'm lying?"

How foolish that I hadn't realized that. "So you planted the idea in Lucinda that he hated her? Why?"

"Because he--"

"Why would that matter?"

"Because he--"

"Why would she care about what you told her? About him or anyone?" I was shouting at her. I wanted her agitated. I bent down to the girls while Miss Alice was taking in a deep breath to bellow. Between kisses I whispered, "I'll tell you when, but you have to run. Blow through those people. Get out of here. Get to Mr. Barker."

I felt Teddie's throat swell with something she wanted to say, but I whispered again. "That's how you can help me. Help us all." I looked up at Miss Alice and spoke in a loud voice in case the girls asked questions I didn't want her to hear. "Because why?"

"Because he did." She shook with anger, and her words came out in a shout so uncontrolled, it often lapsed into a high-pitched whine. "Because she needed me to tell her the truth, to let her know what to do to help the family."

"You made her blackmail people." I felt my lip turn up in distaste. "You'd do anything to keep the bank afloat."

She bared her teeth to hiss, "It's more than just a bank. It's the family. It's the business. We have to succeed."

"Don't get her ire up," Beau said from behind his mother.

I didn't care. I just wanted to get her angry. I wanted to get her to strike out at me again to keep her occupied. I wanted the girls to have a chance at the door, but I would need help.

"Beau, she loved you."

Miss Alice lifted an eyebrow at me. She was close enough to slap me but didn't.

"Beau," I said in deep tones. "The maid, she loved you. Yes, she told me. I saw her dead in the floodwater down here." I remember the ghost leaning over a cradle, probably the cradle for a child she and Beau had conceived, but never borne. I inched back from Miss Alice.

Beau stepped down the stairs with slow precision.

"Too many people are dead for you to get away, Beau. The maid, she knew. She wants you out of this."

Beau blinked with such frequency, I wondered if he had become consumed by a seizure. "I didn't kill . . . I never, but Mother. . .she won't let--"

"We can go away for a while." Miss Alice turned back to face Beau, but only for a second. She turned back toward me, but her voice held the same sweet tone she used to speak to her son. "Money isn't a problem for us. We just need to get to a ship."

"I don't see how we can, Mother." Beau panted and looked as though he wanted to cry, but dared not before his mother.

"Yes, we can go on a nice trip until things get better." She slid her hand up her chin and over her cheek as she developed words from faraway thoughts. "We'll need a . . .we'll take one of the girls, to make sure Mama here stays out of things."

Her eyes slid over me, then Teddie, and then Jinxie.

Miss Alice patted me on the shoulder. "You'll have to choose, dear."

"What does that mean?"

"A daughter. You'll have to choose one to come with me and leave the other here with you."

"Beau," I said. "Stop her!"

He looked up the stairs to Earl.

The girls would have to go up those stone steps: that was the only way out. *Wait, no. The dumbwaiter.* It was large enough to hold them both.

Miss Alice let a big sigh out through her nose. "Can you be that stupid? You have to choose. Pick a daughter to keep with me and one to stay behind with you."

Could I believe that one of my girls might survive? Could I trust this woman? I shook my head.

A stiff smile spread across Miss Alice's face. "Pick one."

Jinxie's sobs renewed.

"Honey, why are you crying?" Of course I knew part of why she was crying; we were trapped down here by a lunatic and those strangely willing to do her bidding. What I wondered was why "pick one" made her start crying harder.

Jinxie looked up at me. "I'm no good."

"Oh honey, you're wonderful. You and your sister both are." I bent down and kissed them. "And I love you both so much." With gentle hands on Teddie, I turned her to face the dumbwaiter.

"Pick one." Miss Alice slid a hand down the side of her skirt and pulled a long sheathed knife from her pocket. Actually, it was a razor wrapped in a gauze bandage. "You have to pick one."

I whispered with my head between the girls. "Wooden box on the wall. Big enough for both of you. Pull the rope until you are upstairs. Wood box, close door, pull rope."

"Pick one. Pick one. *Pick one!*"

I let go of the girls and backed away from her. The girls stood still.

Miss Alice stared at me with a slight smile that opened and closed with words as she muttered.

"No," I said. "I can't. I won't."

"You have to. You can't save both."

"Let them both go. You can have me. I won't cause you any trouble, not if you let them both--"

"That's not the bargain," Miss Alice said.

I heard a moan from Beau at the top of the stairs. I looked away from the woman with the razor near my throat and to him so I could look him in the eyes. "Beau, you have to do something."

"He knows that," Miss Alice said. "He knows what to do."

The girls huddled at the base of the stairs. I had managed to get everyone's attention away from them.

"Beau," I said in a calm, low, voice--at least, as calm and as low as I could muster when I felt like screaming my lungs out at their highest pitch. "You need to help us. You do that and everything will be fine for you."

"You need to shut up now and choose a child."

I didn't know what Miss Alice was doing since I still had my eyes trained on Beau. He gave furtive returns to my gaze.

"Beau," I said. "Texas doesn't have a law for accessory. You will be tried for murder and hanged. You don't want that. I can't believe your mother would want that. When she calms down and is sane, she won't."

He cringed as if trying to pull himself into a fetal position while standing.

"Choose."

"Mama," Teddie said. "We'll--I'll stay with you."

Jinxie nodded.

"No, girls," I whispered through a ventriloquist-style slit in the side of my mouth. "You need to get help."

I had no idea whether they heard. I did not dare look at them for a reaction.

"You don't have to do what she says anymore, Beau. You need to do what is good for her. Get her help."

With the wail of a wild animal, she lunged for me.

CHAPTER 24

"Run," I screamed. "Run, run, run to the box and get out." I did not watch. I closed my eyes to concentrate on nothing but the sound coming from me. I crumpled down in a crouch with my head bowed over my body to protect my neck from Miss Alice's blade. "Run!"

I heard little shoes scuffle over the dirt floor.

I opened my eyes and saw Miss Alice, blade outstretched, whirl away from me. Earl backed away from the razor, up the stairs.

She must be after the girls. No, she was after Beau. He had come up behind her. She slashed at him and got his chest.

I grabbed her, but I missed, and grabbed again. I caught her dress, but the taffeta slipped from my grasp. I lunged and grabbed again. I caught her waist.

Her arm flailed. She couldn't get back to reach me with the blade, and she couldn't get to the girls. I didn't have enough energy to see what Beau did.

"The bank would have failed without me," she growled. She couldn't keep herself from speaking, and I was glad to keep her going since it diverted energy from that iron vice grip she had holding the blade. "Sextus is an idiot. He never understood. He never realized that I was the one who made money." She tried to flail back with the blade to hit me, but I had a hold on her.

She was too unwieldy for me to knock over, and I feared that blade.

I didn't know what had happened to the girls, but I couldn't think about that now. I had other things to do to help them.

Beau lunged toward his mother. She slashed, but he grabbed her arm.

Earl charged down the stairs and smacked his pistol against Beau's head.

I needed Alice angry. That diverted her energy. What would wind up this matron of society? "You're nothing. You always were, so why would Sextus want your help? Why would anyone? You're a fool."

"Smart enough to fool you. You went chasing after that stupid musician."

My grip on her waist ebbed; her hand with the razor neared.

Musician? Magician. Guy. She led us to him. "You left that note in the rain."

She gave a laugh with no humor, but full of victory.

I kicked her. She wobbled but did not fall. I let go and she fumbled forward. I gave her a push.

A child's voice said words I couldn't make out. I think the voice was Jinxie's.

Focus on the task at hand.

Miss Alice stumbled but still worked to run toward the steps.

I jumped forward and landed on her dress, knocking her to the floor. I looked over the floorboards for the razor. I patted the floor to find her hand.

There! I saw that razor and hand holding it were below her, so I shoved all my weight down onto the woman. I heard--or at least felt--her scream.

A noise--pounding--sounded above.

I dared to look up. I scrambled through an archway. Thick dirt catching me feet and skirt slowed me. Before me, I saw a large cistern with metal pipes leading up and out of the basement. My hands scrambled over the loose rocks beneath the window and above the drainpipe. I thought I might enlarge the opening for the window and get out. I didn't have enough time to do this masonry, but it gave me a goal rather than waiting to die.

Bricks crumbled out of the wall. They scraped my hand, but I kept clawing at the dirt and mortar. Behind them, something offered a flash of light in the dark. I reached in.

The tiara. It was thick gold entwined with diamonds that surrounded rubies the size of small eggs and pebble-sized sapphires. It was beautiful. I pulled it out and almost dropped it to the ground because it was so heavy.

I grabbed it and ducked behind the cistern. I peered out and did not see the girls in the basement. The door to the dumbwaiter was ajar, and I didn't see the platform within.

They must have made it out. Where was Alice?

She rose to her full height. She looked at something beyond.

Earl was fighting someone at the foot of the stairs: Barker.

Miss Alice staggered forward.

I ran behind her and smacked the tiara against the side of her head. She wobbled. I hit her again.

Earl reached into his vest for his gun.

Miss Alice dropped the razor. I kicked it away.

Barker didn't even reach for the gun I knew he had in his pocket; instead he grabbed Earl's arm. He did a little step backward with a straight back and jammed his hand against Earl's chin.

Earl's head lobbed off at a strange angle, and he fell backwards.

"Good," I said. I smashed the tiara against Miss Alice's head and smashed it again until I was sure she was unconscious. Her brain might be damaged, but I didn't care.

Barker caught my elbow and piloted me to the stairs.

"The girls?" My voice came out as a weak croak.

He nodded. "They're fine. They're safe."

"How did you know I was here?" I ran up the stone steps.

"Her," he answered from my side. He pointed down the hallway to where Winnie held the girls in the vestibule. Beside her, Joe the butler stood beside them, nursing a jaw that I'd bet had met Barker's fist.

"I love you, Mama," Teddie said from down the hallway. She and her sister broke free from Winnie's grasp and ran to me.

Jinxie murmured the same into my chest. They held so tight, I feared they might strangle me, and yet I didn't care. I wrapped my arms around them and kissed them. They were my daughters, no matter what I did, no matter who I was, and that was all that concerned me now.

When I stood, I felt Barker's warm lips on my ear. "What are you going to do with your wee bit of jewelry?"

Winnie trotted to us. "You weren't at home, and that surprised me. There was broken china on the floor. I called Mr. Barker, and he told me about Miss Alice." She shuddered with thoughts of gruesome murder.

I disengaged myself from the girls to hand the now-lopsided tiara to her.

Teddie smiled at me, and Jinxie blew me a kiss. The girls looked tiny, framed by the huge, carved doorway to the vestibule of the Wyngate mansion, but so pretty in the lavender and pink party dresses I had sewn for them. Teddie pushed her sister, who broke into a stately walk up the aisle between the few people in wooden chairs. Each girl carried a single rose. The girls acted out their hasty commission as flower girls with pride.

They finished their walk to where Abelard stood with the pastor and his brother, Beau.

The only other guests were Sextus and Eula Rose on the groom's side, MJ and I on the bride's.

The girls had not been given any instructions other than to walk down the aisle and look pretty. Teddie took charge and pushed her sister to stand on the bride's side, and she stood beside Abelard.

Abelard, his arm in a sling over his morning coat, looked toward the vestibule, waiting for Winnie.

Barker strode into the room and sat beside me.

MJ left her seat beside me, gave Barker a peck on the cheek, and she sat again.

Winnie, in a dress of pink-satin swags caught with beaded flowers, started a slow walk down the aisle, but midway across the vast parlor gave a jittery shrug of her bouquet and lifted her skirt with her free hand to trot up the aisle to Abelard's good side and take his arm.

"She's had enough delays," Barker whispered in my ear.

The pastor greeted the audience and led us in a short prayer.

Abelard gave Winnie a smile of pure joy before bowing his head.

As we said, "Amen," Beau leaned down to hold Jinxie's hand and say something to her that made her giggle. His movements were stiff and protected what must have been bandages, stitches, and bruises under his morning coat. He looked up at me with a smile and gave me a nod.

I nodded back.

The pastor spoke of marriage with a wistful smile.

Barker took my hand.

I looked at him, and he winked back. He leaned in toward me to whisper, "The family put Alice in an asylum. She won't be out, ever, from that solitary cell."

"She should hang," I said without fight. I was an attorney and knew convicting a woman was difficult. A known, respected woman from a wealthy family . . . probably impossible.

The couple exchanged vows.

"Winnie wouldn't take the tiara," he said. "She wants it sold quietly. Apparently the bank needs the cash."

"It will just end up in the same trouble."

Eula Rose shot a look back at me.

I gave her a cheerful smile and little wave.

She smiled and waved back.

"Maybe things will change," Barker said.

The bride and groom kissed. Abelard started to lead Winnie down the aisle, but she stopped and said, "Cake in the dining room, everyone."

Teddie ran to me, gave me a big hug around the waist, and asked, "Can we go get cake?"

"Sure," I said. I kissed the top of her head and then Jinxie's before they ran to the dining room.

Barker took my arm to walk with me to the dining room where the girls assisted Winnie with passing out plates of yellow cake. His arm on mine, he kept walking out the side door. Alone with me in the hallway, he smirked and asked, "Any ghosties around?"

I shook my head. "I don't know if there ever was one."

"Then what was it you saw?"

"You'll laugh." I folded my arms across the chest of my striped and flowered dress. "But I'll tell you anyway."

"Please do." Barker's eyes lingered on mine, and he took a step closer to me.

"It was love." I felt a blush grow on my cheeks. "The maid, she loved him. She wanted so much to help him, to make him better and throw off the, well, *evil* of his mother. Her love was strong enough to linger in this thin place even after she was gone." I looked around the hall. "I don't see anything or feel anything from woo-woo land, so I think it was just her love staying to make things get better." I didn't realize I had been moving backwards until I bumped into the wood paneling. "So that's it. I could believe that if something happened to me, the feelings I have for my daughters are strong enough to protect them."

" 'Tis a lovely thought," Barker said. He pulled at my elbow and led me to an alcove where we were alone except for a marble carving of a muscular, winged Apollo and delicate Daphne whose hair had started to turn leafy.

I smiled at him. I was happy, happy with my daughters here, and happy to be in a small enough space to smell his aroma of soap and masculinity. I wasn't even ashamed of my crush. He was a nice man, and he was fortunate to have someone like me intoxicated by him.

He sat beneath the arched window and bade me to do the same by patting the small, white bench beside him.

I sat in the space so small that our knees touched and waited for him to tell me the thoughts that now creased his brow.

"We work well together." He pronounced this as if it were a death sentence. "You are often a logical, sensible woman."

"Thank you."

"Even if the rest of the time you act as though you have been bewitched by pixies."

"Well, that is inventive."

"But you do have a logical mind and can think of things I would miss."

I smiled.

"So, we must make very sure we keep the purity of that relationship."

I folded my arms over the lace dress. I held them so tight, I could feel the green satin lining beneath slip against my under-things. "Just friends, then?"

He examined my face for signs of emotion erupting and gave a nod with what appeared to be a gratified smile.

I smiled back. I stood. "Okay." I turned back to him and, before he could rise, pinned him to the bench with my knee on his thigh. I bent down, smiling at him, and pressed my parted lips to his. I leaned forward, but felt the resistance of his lips give as his mouth responded to mine, deepening the kiss and reaching his hand around me.

His hand slid over my cheek and his arm around my waist, but then both pulled away.

I lifted my face from his, lowered my eyes to bedroom strength, and smiled. I licked the moisture from my lips. "Fine." I turned away from him. "Come. There's cake."

Dash and Barker will be back in the next mystery of the Galveston Hurricane series:

SECRETS OF THE STORM

Galveston, Texas, December 1901

"Why are you frowning, Mr. George?" My hazel eyes followed his gaze to the near ruined house before us, but only my eyes then crept next door to the Victorian house of columned porches, pointing gables, and red-painted clapboard where I lived. The one where guests would arrive any minute for my At Home afternoon. I looked at the jeweled watch pinned to my red velvet dress and straightened the black watered silk mourning band on my sleeve. For Christmas, I opted for a beaded band with embroidered edge.

I needed to be in my front parlor right now. As a woman in business trying to support two daughters, I didn't dare arrive late to my own hostess event, the sort of social faux pas that would make clients stop coming to me for legal advice. Besides, if I said I would be there--and I placed an announcement in the social section of the paper to say I would be--I needed to be there.

I held my hand out for the key, but the building contractor in tan duck coveralls stood with the key--my key--for what was my second house still clutched in his hand. It would be my house in an hour, before the clerks at the courthouse would end their day by recording my payment for back taxes on the lot and irrevocably file it as mine.

"Hello, Miss Dash." Mr. George's brow puckered with the force of his frown as he stood beside me on the brick sidewalk. "Funny name, that."

"Yes," I said. "Short for Dasha, the diminutive of Daria."

He nodded, without seeming interested in my name, but preoccupied by something, something he seemed reluctant to tell me. He stared at the tilting two-story ruin of a house and said nothing. He offered only a few rapid blinks and an agitated gesture that flapped toward the collection of falling columns, detached fretwork, and missing clapboard.

"Is there something wrong with the house?" Something I should know before a pen in the hand of a state clerk made it irrevocably mine in the next hour?

"It's on the square," He said. "All that shiplap floated like a boat."

"Is there anything wrong, I mean, anything more than we can repair?"

I followed his gaze back to the house tilting on the lot beside my house. In this wreck on the land adjacent to mine, I saw promise. I saw the promise of a tower gleaming with polished metal and the hope summer breezes over the veranda.

The loose cheeks of his thin face vibrated in a nod, but then veered off to one side at the last. "No."

A frigid wind swirled gray sleet and took the cold through my velvet dress. "Is there something I need to know? No one's dead in there, are they?"

"No nothing's dead in there." A frown pulled his narrow jowls down. "Nothing that I saw."

I hadn't asked about something being dead in there, I'd asked "someone."

Dead bodies, death stalked the city. Even over a year after the Great Hurricane, people kept finding things no one should ever have to find. I had seen many dead bodies. Everyone in Galveston at the time of the Great Hurricane had seen drowned, and destroyed bodies had laid in the sand along with the bloated bodies of horses and cattle. Some bodies, like that of my husband, had washed out to sea and never been found.

Over 8,000 people had died on the island that day and I feared one of them might still be in this house.

This house that had become flotsam on the storm surge, billowing over the city until a wall of debris stopped it on the empty lot once owned by my mother-in-law. My mother-in-law had died just about where I stood now on the brick sidewalk, when her hair tangled in the branches of a storm-choked tree and roof tiles tore the life from her.

"Mr. George," I said, affixing my sweetest smile to my face. Sometimes, the ash-blonde hair and high cheekbones worked to my advantage. This might be one of those times. "You haven't answered any of my questions, and if I'm to hire you, I need answers." I need them right away.

He shrugged. "I think it's fine." He rubbed a hand of sagging knuckles over his thin face. "You should probably take another look. You know, before-- what did you say?--they record the thing."

"Yes." I spoke fast. I didn't have time to linger over syllables. "Legally, it isn't final until the payment is recorded. I know legal things. I'm an attorney and that's how I knew I could get this place by paying the back taxes. You see . . . " Oh, I was babbling. Something about this man's demeanor made me nervous and I babbled when agitated. "I need to know now if this thing is a white elephant."

His frown turned from the house to me and his head cocked to the side in what a cocker spaniel would show as a lack of comprehension.

My hands jittered through the cold air "I need to know if this a great hole into which I plan to pour money or if it will help my girls and I . . ." I didn't finish the sentence because I didn't want him to know my fears of not being able to support the daughters I had adopted when they were orphaned by the storm.

"Yeah." Mr. George gave a nod that turned into a shudder through his skinny body. "Read about your little thing this afternoon. Hope it goes well for you." He tipped his hat and tossed me the key.

I caught the key, felt it slide through my gloved hands, and clasped tight enough to keep it from slipping free.

"Just take a look inside the place." Mr. George had loped around the corner and away before I could ask any more.

I walked into my picket-fence-bound yard, took an instant to tell myself I belonged in that front room, and shouldn't worry right now about a house I wanted to turn into a rental. I ran to the back of the house, walked in the small building housing the kitchen, and grabbed a knife.

I walked past the gray stick branches of the two dead trees on the dirt lawn. The chill of early winter had finished the slow death of the trees. Yet more casualties from the Great Hurricane, a year and three months ago. I slid a tentative step onto the porch of the house and gave a hard look. The wood steps creaked. The porch swayed beneath my feet until I grabbed the railing. With a groan of nails, the rotted wood came loose in my hand.
I hope there's no one dead in there.
A dead body would take up time I didn't have. No one was there yet at my At Home, but if I were not there before any guests, word of the social failure would be out in the city.

Two stories with a wrapping porch and balcony, it was big, square, and one of the largest that had been caught in the flood waters and deposited away from its origins. Most of the houses lost in the storm had been dashed to boards.

The tall house had peeling paint, woodwork about to fall off, and it was mine. I had paid the taxes on the lot and since no one had claimed the house in over a year or brought a team to haul it away, the house was mine as well.

I tucked my kitchen knife in my belt and walked across the porch, a precarious journey since the house slanted away from a brick post that had managed to stay attached. Propping it up on a new foundation should work. I had brought inspectors and contractors out to see the place and all believed that it was structurally sound and could be repaired to house a family.

I wanted it to house a family. Not my own, since the two daughters I had adopted after the storm were happy with me in our big red home next door. I wanted this house to rent out.

As a secondary corporate counsel--large attorney firms hired me to look over contracts and make legal judgments when they had too much work they could handle in shop--my income was good, but sporadic. A rental place would mean a steady income to provide what my daughters needed.

Careful not to slide my arm over the butcher knife in the belt of my soft red dress, I pulled out a set of large skeleton keys. I remembered one of these had managed to open the door, but I forgot which one. The first was too big to even fit the lock. The second fit, but did nothing. I tried a third, and opened the door.

Howling mercy! I turned away and coughed as mold so strong, it seemed to have formed clouds filled my nose and caught in my throat. Was the mold what made Mr. George so nervous? Probably not, since after the storm, some houses were so filled with mold, the damp, noxious smell filled the street around them.

The vestibule had a green and black line of where deep storm waters had given way to mold. It looked like an artist's unattractive impression of what marble looked like, with the gaps and cracks in the plaster full of thick black thatches. Some bleach and replastering should bring this back. Above, a once magnificent brass light fixture of now bent metal wings with broken bulbs hung from an ornate plaster ceiling medallion. At one side of the vestibule, a staircase of milled heart pine, similar to my own, stretched up to the second story above the twelve-foot ceiling. Many spindles lay on their sides, but I had counted them on my last trip here and found that none were missing. At the base of the stairs, an angel holding a broken light tipped precariously from the massive newel post.

I reached to right the angel, but stopped myself. I didn't have time for this. I had a purpose.

The house creaked. This house was as solid as mine, with the walls made up of two thick layers of wood with bracing between them, but I should expect it to creak with the precarious angle at which it sat.

I made my way through the inches of mud on the floor, crunching through the crust on the top to the sludge beneath. I picked up my skirt and petticoats and tucked the mass of fabric under my corset to keep them out of the dirt. I navigated around the settee and footstool with warped wood and with mold claiming what remained of flowered fabric full of holes. I passed the smashed dining room table that held a single chair, the storm having broken its heavy legs of turned mahogany.

What little furniture I had found in the house-- beyond the settee and footstool in the front parlor and table with chair in the dining room, there had only been a single bed upstairs and a scratched and dented office desk-- provide nothing more than kindling, but there wasn't much of it in the house, anyway. The newel-post angel, elegant light fixtures, and table of substantial wood looked as though the once-elegant house had gone into decay of ripped furniture and missing chairs long before the storm. Maybe the original owners had some financial difficulty or problem that led them to abandon the house even before the storm.

I prayed I would not find the original owners still here, although dead.

Yes, I had inspected the house, but only with a look toward structural repair and not for what odious secrets might lurk within. Anything could be hiding under that smell.

I stepped over a section where mud had been cleared to reveal broken glass on the warped floorboards. I made my way to the far wall of the dining room and slipped my knife from my belt. It clattered against the diamond buckle I wore, a bit of Christmas elegance.

The wall stood out. It was the only one in the house not covered in mold.

Mr. George must have noticed this, since it didn't even have any cracks. I would be foolish to go at it with my knife, but for a smart woman, I had moments of empty-headed foolishness.

I didn't trust the wall. I didn't know why it had no mold, no damage. I slid my fingers over the edge of the fluted window moulding. It sat at least an inch higher than any of the other walls. Something was behind there, I was sure. I hoped there might be an ornate fireplace mantle under the section of wall, but maybe nothing more than a walled-over door.

An expensive tapestry that a previous owner had lost taste for would be nice. Something other than the outer and inner layers of heavy, interlocking shiplap: more heart pine to form solid walls beneath the plaster and canvas.

The door to a back room, probably added in the salad days of this house's existence, shuddered open and smacked into my side.

Tilted house, so doors will do this.

I raised my knife in a way I would have imagined Lizzie Borden to have done with her axe.

"Are you a ghost?" a reedy male voice asked behind me, startling me so, I dropped the knife.

About the Author

Amanda is a compulsive reader who enjoys just about every genre. She started writing to keep her imagination happy when she was between books to read.

When not writing, her husband, college-age daughters, and she are restoring a Victorian house on Galveston. While some people are known by name to waiters at elegant restaurants, they are known to the guys at the salvage yards.

Let her know how you enjoyed the story, the setting, and even ask her what is next for the characters or for her own life: Amanda@goneferalpublishing.com

About the Publisher

Gone Feral Publishing is a few people who glue macaroni on paper and call it "art." Now, they have a publishing company, and a belief that every writer is a reader who got the nerve up to put dreams on paper.

We are a Texas publisher of mystery fiction and elevating nonfiction.

For news, contests, giveaways, and help with putting that dream on paper (and formatting it, and adhering to a standard dramatic construction) Check out our website: www.goneferalpublishing.com

Like Gone Feral Publishing on Facebook.

CPSIA information can be obtained at www.ICGtesting.com
Printed in the USA
LVOW131307080513

332858LV00005B/8/P